Praise for
YOU AGAIN

"Stunning . . . feels eerily relevant, perfect for this time of deep uncertainty and rapidly shifting news. It is dreamlike and immersive, like falling into someone else's alternative reality."

—*New York Times Book Review*, Editor's Choice

"At once a mind-bending puzzle and a profound meditation on love, fate, ambition, and regret."

—*Kirkus Reviews* (starred review)

"So accomplished, so glorious—a complete original from page one. You may as well buy your second copy now."

—Janet Fitch, author of *The Revolution of Marina M.* and *Chimes of a Lost Cathedral*

"*You Again* will have you rethinking everything."

—*Good Morning America*, "25 Novels You'll Want to Read This Summer"

"Immergut's novel pushes at the contours of identity and change, asking how we can recognize ourselves after so many years have passed."

—*The Millions*

"An alluring mystery. . . . Immergut has constructed her tale as an ingenious maze. . . . Think of *You Again* as *A Portrait of the Artist as a Not-so-Young Woman*, on a shelf that would include Claire Messud's *The Woman Upstairs*—but with the addition of a mystery as a compelling chaser."

—*Washington Post*

YOU AGAIN

YOU AGAIN

A Novel

DEBRA JO IMMERGUT

ecco

An Imprint of HarperCollinsPublishers

HarperCollins books may be purchased for educational, business, or sales promotional use. For information, please email the Special Markets Department at SPsales@harpercollins.com.

Ecco® and HarperCollins® are trademarks of HarperCollins Publishers.

A hardcover edition of this book was published in 2020 by Ecco, an imprint of HarperCollins Publishers.

FIRST ECCO PAPERBACK EDITION PUBLISHED 2021

Designed by Michelle Crowe

Library of Congress Cataloging-in-Publication Data
Names: Immergut, Debra Jo, author.
Title: You again: a novel / Debra Jo Immergut.
Description: First edition. | New York, NY: Ecco, [2020]
Identifiers: LCCN 2019050694 (print) | LCCN 2019050695 (ebook) | ISBN 9780062747587 (hardcover) | ISBN 9780062747570 (trade paperback) | ISBN 9780062747600 (ebook)
Subjects: LCSH: Psychological fiction. | GSAFD: Suspense fiction.
Classification: LCC PS3559.M5 Y68 2020 (print) | LCC PS3559.M5 (ebook) | DDC 813/.54--dc23
LC record available at https://lccn.loc.gov/2019050694
LC ebook record available at https://lccn.loc.gov/2019050695

21 22 23 24 25   LSC   10 9 8 7 6 5 4 3 2 1

For Joe, forever

Time is a river which sweeps me along, but I am the river; it is a tiger which destroys me, but I am the tiger; it is a fire which consumes me, but I am the fire.

—Jorge Luis Borges, *Labyrinths*

YOU AGAIN

PART 1

THE RIVER

1/1/1/1

ABBY, JANUARY 7, 2015

I saw myself last night. I drove right by myself. In a taxi, through a winter rain, coming home very late from work, on a shadowed block southwest of the Holland Tunnel. I gazed out the cab window, worn down from my day, and then suddenly she appeared, emerging from a dark doorway in silver platform sandals and a pink velvet coat.

Me. The way I used to be.

I yelped at the cabdriver. Stop! Please stop! He stopped, and I scrambled to pay him, snagging my tote loaded with unfinished paperwork from the office that I'd packed to not finish at home. And my purse holding cell phone and tampons and hair product, and in its deepest corners, a putty of crushed energy bar and compromised ibuprofen gel caps. I gathered up my bags and I leaped. It was raining, a very suspect sea stretched out between the cab and the curb, so I leaped.

The girl—this glimpse of myself—stood back there at the corner, slipping a coin into a pay phone. The mere fact of that pay phone. Extraordinary.

Then I noticed the man. He must have come out of the doorway too. Still holding the receiver in one hand, she—the girl—me, I mean, *me*—turned toward this young man, this tall boy, dark animated hair. He crossed to her, walking with shoulders hunched, face hidden under an umbrella, and leaned over her to allow her its benefits.

I gulped air, gawking. My hands felt numb.

They stood under the umbrella, very close together, talking. I glanced at the dented graffitied doorway, and sure, yes, that had been a nightclub and I had done my time in its pounding, dusky rooms, but hadn't that place closed in the last millennium? Now he turned and saw the cab—my cab—just pulling away from the curb and this guy, this kid, starts to run after it down the block and gives one of those piercing fingers-in-mouth whistles—a practical skill I have always appreciated—and as he runs his umbrella—I can see it's the five-dollar street-corner type—flips inside out in a gust and shimmers under the streetlight like a wet black lily bloom and I look at her and she's looking at him and I know that look. Or I should say, I remember that look.

And then. She walks by me, maybe four feet away on the wide watery sidewalk and doesn't shift her eyes in my direction, not in the slightest. She's looking down, and I understand why: the silver platforms, the cratered old sidewalk, a broken reef of wooden pallets. She's picking her way through it, she's clutching her coat—it's buttonless and just a little tattered, the color of raspberry pudding, and not waterproof, not warm at all.

I recall precisely how it felt to wear that coat, its chill silky lining, the shiver as you shrugged it over a slip dress. I remember how the wind and the water went right through it. On a raw night, that silky lining could make you feel colder than if you were wearing nothing at all.

The coat was purchased at the Salvation Army on Eighth Avenue and Twenty-Second Street. Still there, I believe.

He is holding the taxi door open. His smile is dimpled, in the shadows, his expression wryly pleased. She climbs in—I climb in!—and he abandons his blown-out umbrella in the curb, bends his lanky self into the back seat, and I can glimpse her legs and those shoes before the door shuts.

The rain taps my scalp with tiny wet fingers, and my nose is dripping. Through the cab window I see them kissing already—her hand—my hand—on his hair, and the car pulls away. And she's gone.

I'm gone.

I briefly consider running after her.

I quickly release that idea into the rain. By the curb, the umbrella flutters slightly, with a sheen, like a wing just plucked from a prehistoric flying insect. I pick it up. I sniff it. Don't ask me why. It smells like a wet umbrella. Though it is clearly a bit mangled, I collapse it into my tote. Don't ask me why.

Peer down the empty street.

Not a cab, not a taillight. Only, a few blocks down, a yellow traffic signal strung in midair, blinking stupidly.

I feel shaky and breathless, slightly dizzy and maybe a tiny bit weepy then. I saw her, it was me. Me. It was most definitely none other. I was beautiful and maybe twenty-two and now I'm gone—that was some vision, some message, and I didn't get to understand it. The vision vanished and left me soaked and cabless. My husband would be swirling his vodka and ice in front of his laptop. My sons would be rampaging through first-person shooters in their room, flouting school-night guidelines.

And I'm here on this sidewalk, southwest of the Holland Tunnel, so drenched that my best cashmere cardigan is exuding a hint of its mountain goat origins, and my most expensive work heels, the ones I wear only on days when the boss is in the office, are ruined.

I muster my interior subway map and begin walking, a bit wobbly, toward the nearest stop, three blocks away.

My name is Abigail Wilhelm Willard and I am forty-five years old. No, wrong. I am forty-six years old. Not ancient, I suppose, but old enough to forget momentarily exactly how old I am.

I work as a senior art director at the largest pharmaceutical company in North America. I live with my beloved husband, Dennis, and my sweet teenage sons, Pete and Benjamin, in a narrow Brooklyn two-story house with crusty old moldings and chipped marble mantels and a boiler due to break down this winter.

I used to be an artist, a painter of abstracts, mapping my interior life with outbursts of color—that is true. But that was in another life. This life is about my husband and my children and my work. I am known at my office for my ability to slice through bullshit and lay an idea bare and then quickly act on that idea and make it real.

I am not a flake and I don't see things that aren't there.

My interior life pretty much stays inside.

And I have never been one to dwell on the past.

And yet. Was it not true that lately I'd been falling into an underworld, just before sleep? Plunging into a fog, where I glimpsed half-remembered shadows so unsettling, they jolted me awake again?

I remember that, when I was her, I lived on Twelfth Street in the far west of Greenwich Village. I rented a room in an apartment, a five-flight walk-up, with a balcony.

It was there, when I was her, that my life split like an atom.

The flash still blinds me. I find it hard to look.

For twenty-four years, I have averted my eyes.

From the session notes of Dr. Merle Unzicker, psychotherapist
(CONFIDENTIAL)

A reports a night of wildness with a young man, whom she believes
is named Jamie. All she can recall, she said, was the city seen
upside down, her head hanging backward over the side of his bed as
it shimmied toward the wall.

How do you feel about it, in the light of day, I asked her.

Like this is all I ever want out of life, she said.

ABBY, JANUARY 8, 2015

Whether to tell Dennis about her. What was the name of that tall
running boy?

I stared at the side of my husband's head, his jaw, his familiar
shell-pink ear, its curves etched like grooves in my brain from so
many nights lying next to him, gazing. His shaggy hair, which
every summer still turns deep yellow, as if honoring the memory
of his youth on a California marine base, the wild mustard and
apricot orchards along the air strip, the surf days at Huntington
Beach with his brothers. The five Willard boys had been trans-
planted from Minnesota's frozen lakes to the dry flats south of
LA, and they grew up hearty and athletic, raised by partying
parents on a diet of comic books and Captain Crunch. They all
slept as deep as the dead, Dennis most of all. He was the adored

youngest son, the only one who had turned his sights east, who somehow wrangled a full scholarship to the graduate program at Rhode Island School of Design, the country's loftiest art school, driven by some impulse the rest of them simply couldn't understand.

If he hadn't met me, at that art school, he'd probably have moved back there, to the baked streets of Tustin, I thought now, as I watched his chest rise and fall beside me. He would've married a fellow Californian and lived in a house with a lemon tree.

A finger of urban light trembled on the ceiling above. I was able to dredge up a Jamaican flag. That tall boy had a black-green-gold Jamaican flag over his bed. I never saw him again.

I slipped out from the envelope of warmth—my husband generated enough body heat to melt an ice floe—and padded into the hall to stare into my tote, hung on the banister at the head of the stairs. The umbrella had dripped all over my work papers and turned them halfway to pulp.

Clearly I'd been projecting. Captivated by a moment in some random couple's life, because it so closely coincided with some deeply embedded memory I didn't even know I still had. This was ridiculous. I gave up a cab on a rainy night for a memory I'd forgotten?

It almost made me laugh out loud, as I headed into the bathroom for a pee. The silliness of it. Hallucinating about my lost youth, the road not taken, etc.

I washed my hands. I regarded myself in the mirror. Age forty-six, wan with winter, tinge of red around the nostrils, in a blue nightgown, its cotton thinned from many washings.

That girl. That year. How it reverberates in me still, though the precise outlines of its events remain shrouded in my memory, as if half-seen through a storm of dust.

It could have been funny. Leaping out of a taxi into the freezing January rain to gawk at a young girl who looked like me.

I gazed into the mirror, and it felt not funny.

I would have given her a piece of my mind if we had been able to talk.

A piece of your mind. An odd phrase, isn't it? A mind can't be divided into pieces. Can it?

In my nightgown, in the rain, I threw the umbrella away, stuffing it deep in the trash can near our front steps. I shivered, looking at the metallic threads twisting under the streetlights, the row houses huddled shoulder to shoulder, faces gleaming wet, the inelegant South Brooklyn jumble, brick and vinyl-siding and brownstone, the muffler shop and the vacant lot. At the corner of Fourth Avenue, a sopping mop of English sheepdog squatted while its owner huddled beneath the awning of the new café.

I stood there staring at it all, in my nightgown, in the rain. A wave of nausea swept through me, then receded.

No, I was not going to tell Dennis, my weary surfer of the days and the years, my hardworking partner in life, waging battles of his own to balance dreams and realities, about this so-called vision, or mistaken impression, or buried fragment reemerged on a slippery Tribeca sidewalk. Chalk it up to a very long day at the office, uncomfortable clothing, shitty weather, and not enough protein at lunch.

Forget it, I told myself, as I climbed back into bed, my gown dotted with cold drops.

I rolled over, plumped up my pillow. Set the alarm for fifteen minutes early so I could race to the deli to buy a clamshell of black-and-white cookies for Benjamin's ninth-grade bake sale. Went to sleep.

Tried to, anyhow.

January 9, 2016

From: J.Leverett@deepxmail.com
To: Tristane.Kazemy@montrealneuro.ca,
GarrettShuttlesworth@physics.humboldtstate.edu

Attached is a compressed folder containing diary entries extracted from Abigail Willard's hard drive, plus other pertinent docs and images.

Please be aware: while it was launched under the auspices of my office, I am the sole instigator and overseer of this strictly classified investigation. Reply only to this email address, a secure end-to-end encrypted account.

Regarding the "session notes" from Dr. Merle Unzicker: Psychotherapy records are protected under HIPAA privacy rules; these in particular, but all files here, are highly confidential.

An additional request: I humbly ask you to excuse the personal nature of my involvement with Ms. Willard, as revealed here.

I've recruited each of you because of your specialized expertise. This case has unsettled me, I admit that. My hope is that, through your analysis, the many mysteries about Ms. Willard's role in the bizarre and deadly events of 2015 will be resolved. Then I can put this matter to rest.

ABBY, JANUARY 12, 2015

Riding in a vanilla-scented sedan with Benjamin, my fourteen-year-old prince of the ninth grade, and Pete, sixteen, a junior, notably sulky. Once again, I'd had a restless night; once again, we got a late start to the morning hurdle sprint, the breakfast, the lunch-packing, the scramble for gear and homework. And so this aromatic car was summoned (plastic air-freshener pod stuck to its dash), another twenty dollars torched. At least I could hitch a lift with them down Flatbush Avenue, and enter the subway six stops farther along my route, fewer blocks to walk through this morning's cold fog.

Benjamin drummed his algebra textbook in time to the driver's radio grooves; Pete locked in to his phone.

But as we neared the narrower streets near the school, Benjamin said, "What's going on, Mom?" Red light, blended into the January mist, knots of parents and kids milling on the sidewalk. Pete even looked up from his phone. "Whoa," he whispered.

The street was jammed up with fire trucks and ambulances, so we clambered from the car and walked the rest of the way. Police officers rolled crime scene tape across the school's entry, the wide sandstone arch carved with laurels and shields and other trium-phant Victorian frills. The headmistress, Elizabeth Vong, ushered us and a bunch of others further along—"Side door, please, side entrance." Pete's ginger-bearded rhetoric teacher—Mr. Lavin? Lavine?—shook his head at us and said, "Cleaning staff found a suspicious item in a trash can by the front office . . . they've got to sweep the whole vestibule now."

"What's a vestibule?" said Pete.

"It's a severed foot," said Benjamin, waving his phone. "Ethan just texted me, it's in a Gristede's bag, and it's either a foot or a baby."

"There's no foot in the trash can," scoffed the teacher. "Do not monger rumors. Get to class now, boys, the bell is ringing."

■ ■ ■

"MARIAH GLÜCKSBURG IS TALKING AT MOMA," my cubemate Beth-anne announced as the lunch hour arrived. Leaning toward her desktop screen, she grinned adorably at a mini version of herself there, her round face haloed by the dark nimbus of her hair. She was using the computer's camera to slick on a fresh coat of plum lip color. "Come along?" She stood and slung her purse over her shoulder. Bethanne knew I had gone to school with this art-world luminary. She was just trying to be thoughtful.

I smiled and said I had mock-ups to finish. I left a few minutes after she did, decided to trek the eight or ten blocks northwest to a new noodle shop Bethanne had discovered. She was addicted to sleeping with chefs. "I objectify them," she confided. "It might be kind of a fetish." I took her restaurant recommendations seriously. Wind, by now having banished the fog, pushed and pulled me a bit, noontime shadows sliced down from the tall buildings and fell darkly across the avenue. I turned onto East Forty-Seventh and tried to think about Benjamin's birthday present. What did he say he wanted? A something or other for his gaming console?

And then I stopped.

She was there. I mean, it was me. Again.

She sat on a bench centered behind a wide many-mullioned window.

I had forgotten about the Tradesmen's Library. An eccentric holdover from a century ago, a private lending library that anyone can join for a small fee. The collection was heavy on early American history and forgotten novels by forgotten authors of the 1940s and '50s; the air smelled of must and burnt coffee. It was exactly the kind of place that would have charmed me, that did charm me, when I first moved to New York.

Here it was, still extant, a short walk from my office on a block I never visited anymore.

I had discovered the library when I'd started my first job in the city, right after college. I'd head there during my lunch breaks to sit on that bench in that very window. I would read old books and, since they usually weren't very good books, I'd look up from their pages quite a bit and gaze at the working people passing by in their raincoats, their pumps with the worn heels, their faces with the vertical furrows between their brows, carrying plastic sacks holding their midday salad-bar pickings or last night's uneaten chicken legs brought from home. I'd swear to myself that I would never end up like them, a tired wage slave searching for a cheap lunch or toting a bag of leftovers from some sad far-flung fridge. Ever.

So now I'm seeing this girl, this girl who is me—no doubt about that face, those hands—and I'm entirely aware of the disdain with which this girl is viewing the office workers walking past, one of whom is me.

Everything else in the city seems to drop away. I long to stop and stare—but I can't simply stop and stare. So I keep moving, and soon I am circling the block. Every time I pass the library, I slow to look. She has turned back to the book she is reading—a very fat one. I try to spy the title, but can't.

Sumptuous brown waves, blonder on the ends, gathered in a high loose ponytail. The slight widow's peak.

The skin, January-pale with faint gray crescents under the eyes, betraying late and sleepless nights.

Strong brown brows, thick fringe of lashes on downturned eyes.

Biting on a thumbnail. The remains of a magenta manicure.

One leg folded underneath her, the other tapping the floor in a chunky-soled shoe.

On turn two around the block, I begin to laugh. What insanity is this? I have discovered a twenty-something girl who looks like I used to look in the Bill Clinton era. She has stolen my 1991 clodhoppers! Maybe she found them moldering in the back of a Goodwill store.

Wait until I tell Dennis. He will find this funny.

On the third pass, I soak up all the details so that I can regale him.

On the fourth pass, she glances up and our eyes meet.

Something lurches, in my brain.

Sliding. Tumbling.

For a beat she regards me—maybe with a flicker of interest, or maybe not. Then she simply looks away, the way you do when you catch a stranger staring. She bows her head back to her book.

My heart folds violently.

What I remember about her. About when I was her. And what I cannot remember. What is beyond recall.

Somehow I steer myself back to my desk. I skip lunch.

SESSION NOTES, Dr. M. Unzicker

A's boss says a fresh college grad at the entry level needs to make better use of her midday break. Networking lunches, etc. For her future at her job.

This future doesn't interest her.

She feels she is waiting for something else to happen.

ABBY, JANUARY 20, 2015

Threading through sidewalk bottlenecks to my stop that evening. Clouds collided in the dark gust above Bryant Park. I thought, for the first time in years, of Eleanor Boyle.

She had been my anchor point at twenty-two, when I was that girl. She'd been a year ahead of me at Western New England State, another cash-strapped and ambitious small-town girl who'd opted for the cheap local college while scanning the horizons far beyond it. She landed in New York first. Eleanor swore every other word and she taught me all about clubbing, though we never called it clubbing—maybe the term postdated our actual clubbing days. She wore secondhand silk lingerie, 1930s bed jackets and slips, when we went out, and I'd wear those silver platform sandals, the coat, and underneath an orange jersey dress from the Fiorucci store. Spaghetti straps, red roses printed around the hem.

Confession: I still have that dress. I slept in it, until it almost fell apart. I have never thrown it away.

Now I'd seen the silver shoes, the pink coat, that used to go out on the town with my nightgown.

How many years since Eleanor and I last spoke? Fifteen? No, closer to twenty.

If I called her, perhaps I could ask her: Are you seeing the former you? Is this something that happens to all of us, while passing over the middle tipping point of our lives?

I had to laugh again. This strange latter-day double of me, tossed into my path by a town with a twisted sense of humor.

The subway steps were littered with drifts of spilled packing peanuts, skittering in the windy evening, urban seafoam, city snowdrift.

I couldn't call Eleanor after so much time has passed and talk about such a thing.

These sightings, these oddities just need to be ignored, I told myself, and swiped my way toward an impatiently waiting train.

. . .

BUT THOSE CLUBS, I thought, my hands wrist-deep in soapy warm water later that evening. Rubbing the remains of our pork-chop dinner from the pan. The clubs, the doormen, the clustered hopefuls outside. Those ropes would be unhooked for us, invariably. Eleanor and me. We'd always been so pleased, so surprised. Never bothering to think about why they'd automatically give a nod to such a duo, unescorted, out past midnight on a Tuesday night and dolled up in cheap, cheeky clothing. Not caring that tomorrow we'd be sneakily sleeping at our desks, chin resting on one hand, the other hand idle on the keyboard, perhaps not even showered, perhaps still smelling of adventuring. The perfect club bait. We didn't let that get in our way.

An experience junkie. That's what I used to call myself, when I was her. And it had brought me almost to ruin. This much I know.

Pete walked in behind me, towering, telescoping arms reaching for the cabinet overhead. "I'm shooting paintball with Dmitri Saturday," Pete said. "His brother Milo is taking us, it's somewhere out, Dyker Heights, I think."

"How old is this brother?"

"Old, like twenty-five."

I smiled. "So, did you ever hear what was in the trash can?" I said. "I thought we'd get a robocall from school."

"False alarm, I guess." Riffling around, rustling packages. "I need cookies," he said. "You need to go to the store."

I turned, dripping suds on the linoleum. "You need to ask your dad to go to the store."

Because this was what governed life now. The endlessly scrolling list of our needs. The clockwork peregrinations as we hunted and gathered to satisfy those needs. Where did desires fit in?

Pete stood there investigating the far reaches of the cabinets, where stale crackers often could be found.

"We could bake cookies, maybe this weekend." I dried my fingers on a towel.

"I could get into that," he said, and he turned to me and grinned, his dark eyes lit up.

"I need to buy flour then." I hugged him—and as with every hug these days, his body felt different to me, rangier, ropier, the cushioning of childhood melting away. He returned my hug for a delightful instant, then squirmed, recovering his composure.

And I noticed it then—all down one side of his jeans, a spattering. Black-red dots. A spill or a splatter. "Is that blood?"

"Paint," he said. "I was in the art room today."

"Paint," I said. He was always talking about how he had no interest in art of any kind, and never would. He wanted to study economics. What else would you expect? Child of the struggle.

LONG AFTER MIDNIGHT, I descended to our cave-like basement. One wall was lined with the racks Dennis had built when we'd moved in fifteen years ago, to store my old paintings, which were wrapped in brown paper and filed on their sides—a bit like those old library books, it occurred to me now. I wrestled with the drawer of a dented file cabinet, covered, as everything down here was, with a fine grit sifted from the rooms above. In the drawer, embedded in a schist of yellowing receipts and letters, I found my ancient address book. The spine half-broken, green fabric cover torn and patched with duct tape and a Tower Records sticker.

Eleanor's last phone number was there under *B*.

And look. Scribbled inside the front cover. Mariah Glücksburg's name, a long ago landline, and the address of that little house in the harbor flats.

Scribbled haphazardly, as things happened during my first year in Providence.

In the tumultuous year after I was her—the girl of the musty library and the dusky nightclub. The experience junkie.

And there. On the last page, scrawled in his own hand. Eli Hammond. His building number on Avenue C.

Staring at these pencil marks. A faint map of a lost and somehow perilous region. Somehow dangerous. How?

Maybe I actually could talk to the girl. Maybe I could tell her a thing or two.

Ridiculous.

What would I tell her anyway. Steer her clear of some half-remembered trouble? Or direct her straight toward it?

Because, if you could change the outcome, would you change the outcome?

Weigh all you once lost against all you stand to lose.

An impossible equation. An evil sort of math.

Also, ridiculous. Insane. This was a random girl. A cluster of strangely evocative matter that had sailed across my trajectory. She was not me. Seriously.

In any case, I climbed the stairs and slipped the address book into my bag.

ABBY, JANUARY 24, 2015

Pete shattered a window at a house in Gravesend. A brick landed in the kitchen sink. He hadn't been shooting paintball. He had been committing petty vandalism with this new pal of his, Dmitri. The brick had dinged the aluminum basin and caused the owner's dog to shit the floor.

The call—"May I please speak to the legal guardian of Pete Willard?"—came from the Mill Basin precinct, a squat art-deco shoebox that sat an anxious eighty-dollar ride away from my office through sleet and traffic. I found my son sitting on a bench in a begrimed, crowded hallway. I tried to hold my temper and asked for an explanation.

"It was direct action," he said. "The homeowner is a known fascist."

"A fascist?" I was baffled. "Isn't that a bit last century?" Then I saw he was crying. Just a few slick droplets, down his cheeks, swerving around his nose and over his lip. He wiped at them with his sleeve. I wrapped my arms around him and murmured in his ear. "Please don't worry, sweetheart. It'll be OK. But was it this new friend? Because this isn't like you."

"Yeah it is like me," he said. He shrugged me away. "It's not like you."

This last word landed on me like spit.

Basketball, action films, video games. Yes, he cared about these things. Political philosophy? Not to my knowledge. But what did I know about him, now, this month, this week, this new year. So much newness all the time. Six more inches, forty more pounds in the last eighteen months, and, perhaps it stood to reason, a few more ideas in his head. Still, I wondered about the new friend, Dmitri, who'd joined the class midway through last term—out of the ordinary, at their painstaking, orderly private school. Pete had introduced me to him at pickup, a coal-eyed kid climbing into a snarling black car. "A 2015 Mercedes S550," Pete said as it roared away. "Best parent ride by far."

I tried again to text Dennis. He wasn't answering—but I

knew he had a meeting about a hockey arena project, somewhere upstate—was it Poughkeepsie? I wish I'd listened closer to him, but who catches every detail, every day, of a spouse's work reportage?

Down the hall, a man shouted about a nuisance summons. "I am not a fucking nuisance!" he yelped, flapping his arms.

And while I dug in my purse to find a tissue for my sniffling Pete, the other half of my brain took in the detective observing us, clearly waiting to speak to me. The long-limbed cantilevered stance, with one shoulder against the wall, hands in the pockets of his precisely cut sports coat. A pleasing vertical composition, a tall graceful shape. Dark hair trimmed short to tame a wave, threaded with tarnished silver. A face that seemed shadowed even in the stark fluorescence.

"We'll charge him as a juvenile," this detective was now saying to me, "but be aware that Homeland Security may need to do its due diligence. Take him home now, we're all done, but you'll be hearing from me, Mrs. . . ."

A slow smile, embellished along one side with a single dimple. A smile strategically deployed to reassure me, maybe.

"Willard. Abigail. Homeland Security? For a brick?" I willed my voice not to shake, put my hand on my boy's sharp shoulder, I could see him slumping lower in his chair.

"Welcome to my world, Abigail." He handed me a fat stack of forms. "A win for the terrorists—all these years, they're still killing us on the paperwork front."

"What's next? Do we need a lawyer?"

"Depends. The complainant holds those cards right now. Try not to fret." He reached into his jacket, thick caramel-hued wool, and pulled out a small loop strung with red beads. He sat down next to Pete and slipped the string around my boy's wrist. "Ever seen these? Worry beads. Best way I know to work out the stress," he said. "I learned it from a bad guy I arrested three times. This hooligan stayed frosty through extortion, narco trafficking, and murder-one trials. Never broke a sweat, beat the rap every single time," he said. "He's a happy Brooklynite to this day." He thumped a hand on Pete's shoulder, then rose again and turned to me. "My contact info is on the forms—I'm always checking my email. And that's how I'll keep you in the loop."

Did his hand linger on my elbow just a few seconds longer than needed, escorting us past the yelping nuisance guy in the hallway of Brooklyn Precinct 63?

I wanted to say something about that hand on my elbow, about the gift of those beads. I wanted to demand of him: How different would all this be if we were not white, not from the Slope, if my kid didn't attend that painstaking school?

I said nothing though. I wanted to get us out of there. Maybe I was imagining it, the hand on the elbow. But the benefits we enjoyed, by virtue of who we were: unmistakable.

When we reached the station exit, he held the door open for us. "And look what else, you charmed citizens," he said, as if he'd been reading my mind. "The sun came out for you." It was true, the ugly block was bathed in low orange rays. "It's like you just can't lose."

He turned to Pete. "You want to change the world? Invent an app." My boy nodded silently, face downcast.

The detective smiled at me again. In the strange light, his eyes looked like beaten bronze, and his skin was tawny. He might've been biracial, or a mix of Mediterranean stock, or just about anything. He was clean-shaven with an undertone of dark beard, a slightly crooked nose and a square chin. I wondered who he was, with the vague sense that I would keep wondering.

"I think there's going to be an upside to this little incident," he said. "Now we just watch and wait." He tossed me one more dimple, then disappeared as the door swung shut.

Later, an email from him. None of the gruff world-weariness you'd expect from a New York cop—his written words struck me as courtly somehow. Intimate, even? He reassured me that he'd handle Pete's case carefully. "I want to put your mind at ease. This is a juvenile case and the legal fees will work in our favor. The complainant may drop the charges." And then, "Please call me anytime, happy to meet with you at any point in or out of the station. Here at your service."

And his name and rank. Lieutenant Detective, Criminal Enterprise Squad.

"Criminal enterprise." A broken window, a dinged sink, a prank by teens on a sleepover? Does that qualify as a criminal enterprise?

Criminal enterprise. Homeland security. What did my darling bumble into here.

"In or out of the station."

I reread that bit.

"It's normal boy stuff," said Dennis, when he arrived home at last, late that night, yes it had been Poughkeepsie, and it had been a meeting over martinis, judging by his bleariness. He loosened his tie, unbuttoned his rumpled shirt, and tossed them both on the bed. He always shucked his work clothes as soon as possible, preferring to stroll around the house shirtless and barefoot in a pair of faded low-slung shorts. I had to admire how he pushed back against middle age, working out at a little weight bench in the basement and surfing at Rockaway every weekend from early spring into almost December. He cut corners in some areas, but not there. But ever since I'd met him, in all ways, even in his art, he inclined toward the physical. Now he encircled me with his arms, pulled me to him, the firm, lightly fuzzed warmth of him. "My brothers and I

once tried to explode an empty oil tank at the abandoned hangars."
He laughed. "At least our boy didn't create a Superfund site." He
spoke into my hair. "This is a phase, Abby, you'll see."

ABBY, JANUARY 27, 2015

Life normalized, as it does. Today Esther Muncie peeked, puppet-
like, over the top of my cubicle wall, bleached corkscrewed curls
twitching, frenetic: "Got something for me? Client wants that deck
by five. That means twenty-three needs it by four."

I nudged my monitor in her direction.

"Lavender?" She frowned. "Too gyno."

"What color do you think they'd like in a stomach?"

"Color is your competency, Abby. Not mine." Her little puppet
head disappeared, a shout rolling back toward me. "More options
asap, if you please!"

Color is your competency, Abby.

Gray carpeting on the floor, nubby gray fabric on the wall, gray
molded plastic all around the edges of my domain. But then, up
above, the big square window, a box of sky from this seventeenth-
floor vantage. Looming over my desk, the square pane of glass,
entirely filled with a sharp, glancing blue on this winter morning.

Sometimes I considered this window my painting: I'd ease back
into my chair, raise my face to it, admiring. Different each time
I looked. Pink fish-scale clouds on a turquoise ground. A wispy
white contrail against deep violet. A speckling of charcoal on cement as pigeons dove toward their nests. Snow flurries in urban
dusk: a static of pale orange. I would claim this twelve square feet
as mine, a work produced by a union between the great world and
my longing for it.

At art school, at RISD, they told me that color would give me a career.

Certain moments stay so crystalline in the mind.

For example, the day in Providence when Bremer summoned me to his office. And I sometimes remind myself that art historians place Hans-Dietrich Bremer more than once in Mougins, drunk and disorderly with Picasso, and noted that he had sketched Jacqueline Roque a number of times, alongside Pablo, and also on his own—and that, in Taos in the early seventies, he built an adobe studio that was used for many years by Agnes Martin, whom he called Magsy. The master had summoned me to his office, one day toward the close of my final year. Stacked grapefruit peels, fresh deposits on top of dry and drying, formed a leaning tower on one corner of his desk. He prepared two pouch-tobacco cigarettes with a squeaky little rolling machine. It took a very long time, and I sat there, unable to think of a thing to say. I remember his eyes bright and watery and set deep among many soft and mottled folds as he finally looked up from his task. Lit the cigarettes in his own mouth, then handed one to me with shaking hands. People are always hungry for color, he said, and not many can use it like you do.

I had never smoked a hand-rolled cigarette before. Trying to pick the ticklish threads from my tongue without letting him see.

You, mademoiselle, have a gift for this.

What are your plans, once you leave here?

Are you in love with the young sculptor? Willard his name is?

Will you return to New York with him?

Where you came here from, correct?

Think, though.

Because I have seen what happens to the girls.

They do not always honor their gifts.

He blew plumes through his thick lips.

Color is my competency.

The stomach could be a pale orange, maybe.

ABBY, JANUARY 31, 2015

Black dawn on a Saturday. I flung myself onto the shore of consciousness, desperate for it. Dreams of a plate-glass department store window, splintering and shattering, valuable goods exploding into flames, falling, falling. The realization that I'd triggered this horror, via something hot and unstable and atomic, born of my body.

That phrase—born of my body—was still echoing in my mind as I lay there, awake.

Relinquishing a cozy bed on a dark frigid morning was preferable to this.

Dennis turned over, a heavy log rolling in a deep current of sleep. On his bedside table, his phone, packing tape patching its cracked screen, and the salted-ginger chews, an obscure brand from India that he bought online, many boxes at a time, because they were the only thing that helped when his old craving for cigarettes kicked up.

Dennis is my final man. I met him after I'd been in Providence a few months, still stunned, lost, still emerging from whatever I'd left behind in New York. A handsome hale soldier of art, he seemed, in the Sturm und Drang of the welding studio, decked out in canvas coveralls, covered with grease and paint, an old pair of safety goggles pushed back into his wild blond hair. A cheerful tank commander. I was awed, as were plenty of our classmates, by his brawny constructions, scrap metal cut and bolted into puzzling and brash aquatic forms, and the prestigious scholarship, and the unassuming confidence of this creative savant of southern California, who read no art theory and swept up many student prizes.

When we started talking marriage, I hesitated, because I thought my art would perennially fall in the shadow of his.

That was my fear, when it was clear that our destinies would be linked.

I needn't have worried, though. Not about that, anyhow.

Perhaps I'll get up and sketch. Perhaps I'll draw.

Funny thought to have. It had been a long time. Neither Dennis nor I made much art anymore. In fact, we made none.

A splash of water on my face and then a long hot shower. In the kitchen, I sat at the table with a blank sketchbook open. I warmed my hands around my coffee mug and I thought about her.

Before Dennis, before Providence.

So many of the events are lost, vanished. Most of 1990, 1991.

But certain visuals stay.

Eli Hammond's face.

The building on West Twelfth Street—the five flights of pitted marble steps, the paint-peeling cast-iron banister to help you along the way. At the top, a fire door with a round glass eye in the center.

Now I wondered: What if I stood in that hallway, peering into that peephole? Would she be there on the other side? Would she see me?

Of course not. This would be how I could rid myself of these sightings.

These hauntings.

And so, I find myself there, standing on West Twelfth Street, before dawn on this ice-crusted January morning. A Saturday morning. Just me and the well-padded deliverymen steering their dollies of dairy crates into the grocer on the corner, faces blurred by exhaled clouds. I study the panel of buzzer buttons. No names next to them, only remnants of ancient labels, old bits of tape. But of course I know it's 5B. I hold my breath and I buzz.

Silence. Long silence. Relief seeping in. I could go to that twenty-four-hour coffee shop on Greenwich Avenue—still there? I think so—and have scrambled eggs and wheat—make that rye—toast and still be home before my household begins to stir. The boys will sleep adolescently into early afternoon. Even Dennis, on the weekends, rarely raises his head from the pillow before ten.

And then the door buzzes. Loud. And then the lock opens with a clunk.

Now is the time to run. But instead I enter the foyer, with a grim sense of simply getting past this personal trial. I realize: Whoever had buzzed me in and is currently waiting by the door of 5B at 6:45, now almost 7 a.m. on a Saturday morning, is likely to be testy. I slip my phone out of my pocket, punch it to glance at the launch-screen photo of Dennis, Pete, and Benjamin, in front of last month's Christmas tree. Holding it in my hand as a security measure, I climb up the stairs.

I round the fourth flight and there she is. Peering through a crack in the chained door at the head of the stairs. There I am, just a sliver of young me. Mussed hair, ratty pink pjs, prettily pointed chin. Squinting out of a dark slit at the fluorescent blaze of the hallway.

At me. It is me. Look at that freckle above the eyebrow.

Hello, I whisper.

She pulls the door open just an inch or two more.

I whisper. I'm just . . .

I can't think of a way to explain. What am I just?

Warning you, I say.

She frowns, pursing her lips.

Something gets broken here.

Her eyes widen. Then she shuts the door, a sharp retort. A lock thunks. And then another, and a third.

Many locks on every door, back then.

SESSION NOTES (CONFIDENTIAL)

A could not regain sleep that morning.

She showered, dressed.

At the coffee shop down the block, she ordered scrambled eggs and rye toast. She found a pencil in her bag, turned the place mat over. She began to draw.

Dr. Tristane Kazemy, JANUARY 31, 2016,

Critical Care Surgery Fellow, Neurological Institute and Hospital, Montreal

The blood-brain barrier. *La barrière hémato-encéphalique.* She swerved toward the wide lane up Montroyal, wishing she could choose the steeper way through the woods, but it was too icy this day, this season. In fact, her fingertips were aching, and once again she swore she'd find time this week to stop at the shop on Rue Stanley for real running gloves, something microfiber and heat-retentive.

The light on the snow made her eyes go all spots, but then she had spent the last hour in the dark lab, streaming video. The buffering was stuttered, but the images of Alexandre Carpentier performing his 2008 thermal ablation, crossing through *la barrière hémato-encéphalique* on a sentient patient, had moved her deeply. Quite profound, quite astonishing, to be able to gaze into a man's open, questioning eyes—to speak to him even—and peer at the same time into his skull. The mind and the brain, at the same time. *A la fois.*

She needed a fleece gaiter too. The scarf Maman had knit for her, though so lovely and rose-pink, scratched her face as she bounded up the path. It collected a damp frost where her breath passed through.

Even now, at her desk, the massive files from the case in New

York were downloading, terabytes worth being gulped from the vast cloud. This police official, Leverett, had found—and read!—her doctoral thesis (*Lesser-Known Behavioral Impacts of Congenital Neuropathological Abnormalities*) online. So. Despite the scoffing of Laurin and Buccardi, her seniors at the lab, despite their dismissing her theories as *outré*, she'd sent her best thinking into the universe. And apparently, the universe had taken notice. As if it understood much better than she did the force of her will. As if its attention had been lured by the ferocity of her desires, as if it had been inspired to engage with her narrative. Because the ink was barely dry on her degree, and still the universe had seen fit to send her this stunning opportunity. The uncanny case of a wife and mother of two, a working person with a workaday job, an ordinary person brutally overtaken by the extraordinary. The deep stream of data was cascading this very minute into her hard drive. The thought made her run faster.

2/2/2/2

ABBY, FEBRUARY 4, 2015

On my coffee run, in my afternoon stupor, they jolted me awake. Boots thwapping on the pavement. Shouts in rough unison. Their flags were scraps of red and black, flown on poles that swayed drunkenly above Third Avenue, above their shaved heads and top-knots and hoodies. Three or four dozen people, dressed in black, faces covered bandit-style with bandannas and balaclavas, coalescing out of the air, seemingly, and doing their very best to stop traffic. Trucks and cabs nosed around them, unimpressed. I stood at the corner of Forty-Third Street, waiting to cross to the coffee shop, to pick up my customary Americano with steamed whole milk. This anarchic marching band flowed past me, me and my fellow office workers, we who require potent infusions of caffeine to make it until evening. The air around them crackled. Smack in the middle of Midtown, they were flat-out misbehaving, playing in traffic, barking like a riled-up dog pack. I have to admit, my heart revved as I watched.

Then I spotted Pete's new school friend, Dmitri, his bandanna pulled down around his chin. A short boy, with arched dark brows and a peachy-golden complexion, a fleshy soft face with a round chin, almost pretty. He moved at the center of the marchers, who surrounded him like black plasma. He seemed to be in a position of power, this kid.

He was holding a large hammer in his hand.

As they passed, I called to him. "Not smashing windows, I hope?"

"Just heads," he said, and he laughed. I wondered whether he recognized me as Pete's mom.

Inside the café, the queue meandered from the door to the counter manned by harried baristas. I took my spot at the end, sliding my phone from my pocket, resigning myself to its distractions.

"Working your nine to five, Mrs. Willard?" I turned to see Dmitri joining the line. With him was a compact, powerfully built young woman in black combat boots and coils of fuchsia hair.

"You bet," I said. "And is this your after-school activity?"

He grinned and nodded. "And this is my comrade Twiz. Twiz, meet Mrs. Willard." He still had the hammer in his hand.

"Hey, Mrs. Willard." Her smile was wide, quick, swooping cheekbones and deep brown skin, and her hot-pink locks waved like antennae around her head.

"Abby," I said.

"I didn't realize Pete's mother was a Midtown prole," said Dmitri.

"Prole? As in proletariat?" I couldn't stop myself from chuckling. "Are you two communists?"

"You could say we're refuseniks," he said, glancing at Twiz. "We refuse to take part in a fascist police state that supports killer cops."

"We're trying to communicate that killer cops are part of a bigger pattern," nodded the girl. "The global rise in authoritarian violence." The café's pendant lights reflected in her eyes, which were slightly tilted, adorably doe-ish, and fiery with conviction.

"Belarus is like ground zero for the next wave of fascism," Dmitri said excitedly. "Anders Breivik, the Norwegian mass murderer? You know he learned how to kill in a neo-Nazi training camp in Belarus?"

"I didn't know that," I said.

"And did you know the consulate is right over there?" Twiz pointed to a bland office building across the street. "The president is visiting today. Which is why we're marching. Lukashenko," she added, helpfully. "A soft dictator exporting white fascism. Right there above the Banh Mi place."

"And I'm sure you know the American oligarchy supports the police state, keeping us all in line," said Dmitri. He gazed at me, frowning. "By cashing a corporate paycheck, you're kind of buying in."

"Or kind of buying groceries," I said.

Twiz nodded sympathetically. "The system is rigged against all of us."

I felt myself getting annoyed now. "I admire your passion, both of you. Your willingness to put yourself out there." I turned to Dmitri. "But I wish you'd leave Pete out of this."

"Pete's his own person, Mrs. Willard," said Dmitri, with an abashed shrug.

"Abby," I said, grimly.

"You want to march with us, Abby?" said Twiz. "You have nothing to lose but your chains." She flashed her wide smile again, then she jerked her chin toward the counter behind me, causing her hair to toss like a flowering shrub in a breeze. "Heads up—it's your turn."

I turned to see a barista glaring. "Ma'am," he barked. "I'll ask one more time. What do you want?"

A FAIR QUESTION. Consider the detective, and the email that arrived just as I sat down at my desk again, having refused their invitation to march, sitting back to sip my Americano.

Looks like charges will be dropped, so chief wants me to close this circle. Come in, please, just a few forms to fill out.

Pete is on a trip with his US history class to the Boston Freedom Trail, I replied. And he wrote, let Pete learn his history. He's a minor, you can sign on his behalf.

I'm in Midtown and I work full-time.

I've got a division meeting in Midtown later. I know a place we can meet and get this done. 6 p.m.?

So while Pete trailed a tour guide in a white-powdered wig and Dennis cheered Benjamin at JV basketball, I found the detective in the bar of a steakhouse near Grand Central. He wore another perfectly cut jacket, ash-gray tweed this time. He tipped his head and smiled when he saw me approaching. I felt nerves. Or maybe the tremoring was simply a train rushing by, racing through the tunnels not so far under our feet. A mostly empty highball glass sat in front of him, his hand wrapped languidly around it. He offered to buy me a drink, but I declined and asked the bartender to bring me whatever was on the nearest beer tap. "And how is young Pete holding up?" he said. "Keeping his nose clean?"

"Yes," I said quickly. "No more trouble. He just fell under an influence, I think."

"They're good friends, he and the other one?" In the low light of the bar, his eyes looked darker, but still very keen.

I shrugged. "He just started at Pete's school a few months ago." I took a sip of beer. "It's so tricky when you don't like your kid's friends. If you try to keep them apart . . ."

"It makes the other kid a rock star," he said. "That is tricky."

"You have any of your own?"

He nodded. "Two little girls."

"Just wait. The teen years are too interesting," I said. "But I want you to know, Pete is a good kid. A great kid."

"Seems so," he nodded, downing the rest of his drink. He waved at the bartender and ordered another—bourbon neat. Then he said, "I'll give you some free legal advice, from a member of the New York bar. Take the time to get this record scrubbed."

"OK, yes," I said. "I appreciate your helpfulness." I sipped my beer. "So you're a lawyer too?"

He nodded. "I come from a line of cops and drunks. I thought I might improve on that. Graduated from Syracuse then Fordham Law, got myself a Wall Street gig."

"Oh, that explains the excellent tailoring," I said.

He glanced at me and gave an abrupt laugh, seeming to appreciate the flirty toss. "Hey, the suits were habit forming. I just looked too good to go back."

I smiled. "So how did you end up in the precinct house?"

"I'm walking to work one sunny morning and a plane hits the tower right over my head," he said. "I signed onto the force the next day. Which was probably a fucking idiot move."

"A noble move, in my opinion," I said. "And you're a lieutenant? Sounds important."

He shrugged. "Well, rank up from me and you're chief of detectives, and that's where swank really kicks in, plush digs, plenty of dollars. Not sure if I'm gunning for it or not." He sat back and drained his glass, eyeing me. "I mean, I'm kind of a conflicted human being," he said. "I think I might be cursed with a romantic streak."

He unspooled that slow-rolling dimpled smile, and it made my chest warm a bit, in a way that I enjoyed. It made me feel a bit loosened. "Oh, I know all about that," I said. "I'm what you might call a thwarted creative."

"Well then, we're both fucked," he said. "But tell me something. What exactly thwarts a woman like you?"

I guess I talked too much. My art, and the fact that I'm not making it, is a subject I have discussed with myself for many years, and almost never air. An outpouring was not appropriate for that moment, but I was a bit loosened, after all, and maybe I needed to air it, and there he was, holding me in his keen and handsome attention. I told him about the coming of the babies and the money woes, how these forces chipped away at my time and energy, how my easel now stood draped by a bathrobe in the corner of our bedroom, my tubes of paints in a box under the bed, hardened, unused. How this was nobody's fault but my own. How the road dipped and swerved and how I should have navigated the curves better. Gradually I became aware that the bar had emptied out, the happy-hour clusters disbanded into commuter trains and taxis and subways, and we were still there in the murk, he and I. His hand was resting heavily over mine on the bar. I felt drunk. Four empty glasses in front of me. I stammered something about needing to get home, about the forms. He spread the papers out on the sticky wood. I signed them. When he held the bar door open for me, I stepped out into a very cold, very black night. That surprised me. A few icy flakes blew around. In an unlit passage under construction scaffolding he took my arm, slowed me, and cupped my chin in his hand. In the steam from our excited breath, a small microclimate we created together in this freezing dark sanctum, a long kiss.

Then I pulled back. "I don't do this," I blurted, miserably.

He looked embarrassed. "Me neither. Really. As in, never." He took a long shaky sigh. "What you were saying, it got to me."

And then, this morning, a text: Lunch?

I regarded those letters on the screen for a long time.

She would've said yes. The experience junkie.

I don't think it's a good idea, I replied.

Then let's just keep talking, he wrote.

Yes. Just keep talking. I was entitled to that, wasn't I? A woman who did what was required, every waking minute of her life? Just keep talking.

Long ago, a therapist told me that keeping a diary was a good way to stay on course, emotionally. To gain perspective. And so, since the start of this strange new year, I've decided to start keeping a record. That's what I'm doing right now.

And it does help, typing up these notes—but only up to a point. Because I still seem to be veering off course.

ABBY, FEBRUARY 6, 2015

"The whole family can get down on the floor and windmill. Windmill at home just like you're doing now, that's the way," said Ms. Finch, the school's movement coach, in her gentle north-England accent and gold-buttoned cardigan. Dennis and I locked eyes; I knew his would be filled with swallowed mirth, and they were. I felt a giggle rising in response. Alas, we are not a family that windmills. No. Dennis and I gazed at each other, struggling to remain appropriately solemn, certain that we would not be lying on the living room floor together like this, arms and legs waggling, not even to foster movement fluidity and improved classroom posture in our darling elder son.

"I never knew I could windmill," said Dennis, slowly rotating one leg in the air. "It plays to my strengths." He turned his head and winked at Pete, who returned only a look of angry misery.

As a toddler, Pete, inky-haired moppet of very few words, was diagnosed with a tongue-tangling set of learning disabilities and processing disorders. We've diligently pursued solutions ever since. This is why he and Benjamin are in this swank private school, after all, with its imposing Romanesque buildings, its kind and over-educated faculty, and charming administrators, so sweetly apologetic as they tack fees and charges onto their breathtaking tuition bills. Pete's early trouble signs—the slow acquisition of speech, the stumbling, the biting. All a bit scary for Dennis and me, the shell-shocked new parents. We set our minds to do anything, everything, to make it right for him.

But now we were fifteen years on, prone on a musty Persian rug in the movement coach's office, staring up into her nostrils and her yellowing spider plant. A bit jaded maybe. Windmilling wasn't the answer to brick-throwing, we all knew that.

As we were getting ready to leave, Ms. Finch picked carpet lint off of my son's sweater and said, "Well, the head of school was upbeat at assembly this morning, wasn't she, Peter?" She opened her office door and turned to Dennis and me: "Application season just ended, record number this year." She chuckled. "The way Ms. Vong shut down that police situation. If word had gotten out . . ."

"Word of what?" Dennis said.

"That horror show, the trash can. I'm right here down the hall from the vestibule, so I got a peek at the goings-on."

"Can I go now," said Pete. "I'm missing lunch."

"They whisked it all away," she said. She widened her milkmaid eyes at us, and leaned in, confiding. "A bloody awful mess."

We watched him stride off, shoelaces trailing, and yes, her door was just a few steps from the vestibule, with its scrolled iron coat hooks and polished wainscoting. The trash cans were all gone.

ABBY, FEBRUARY 9, 2015

I arrived at work hungry and my lunch route took me yet again past the old lending library. A few days earlier, I'd even ventured in, even bought a membership. Slicked up, refurbished, but the old books still filled the stacks, still moldering mostly unread. Each aisle I walked along, each corner I peered around, she wasn't there. I borrowed two books by Daphne du Maurier. And now they sat, unopened, on my desk at work. *Rebecca. The House on the Strand.* Perhaps I wouldn't actually read them, but I did enjoy the look of them, the spooky pastel covers.

I checked my phone again. Two days since I'd heard from him, and then just a line— Life is short, I have been thinking of you.

Turned back to my tedious task of the day, tagging a design for production. A new drug for attention deficit disorders. One-eighth-inch margins, 2-point leading. Pantone color 4225 for the background. Alaskan blue.

Peeked at my texts, just to be sure.

Nothing.

Should I go past West Twelfth Street on my way home?

No, I should not.

Maintain a grip, Abigail. Consider how this man is a police officer, consider how he has a spouse and children. Consider how you do too.

Fifteen days have passed without me seeing her. And then, I am going to get my lunch down in the hold of the great barge of Grand Central, and there she is, exiting the Oyster Bar with a short-legged man, bit of a belly, with thick waves of brownish-gray over his collar and a scuffed leather messenger bag over his shoulder.

Michael Hutcherson? My first boss in New York City. How could it be.

He's holding the door for her, she walks past him—the chunky shoes again, the blond-tipped waves, the eyelashes—and his gaze sweeps over her from the rear. And then she smiles back over her shoulder. They head up the ramp, through the tiled passageway toward the street level. I don't think about it: I follow. Outside, at the corner of Madison, the corner of the Grady Advertising building, that towering paycheck factory of silver and blue glass, they stop. I stop a few yards behind them. He leans toward her, glances around a bit. Let me go in first, he says. It's nobody's business, right?

She smiles. Right. I'll wait here for a few minutes. I'll be up in a bit.

Hutcherson pushes through the revolving doors, sun flares on the glass.

The bastard.

That's my voice, I realize. Did I just say that out loud? Did I just speak?

She looks over her shoulder, alarmed. Her eyes meet mine. Was there a flicker? Yes, just a flicker. Did she recognize me from the stairwell on West Twelfth? Or is she seeing who I was? Her.

She turns away and starts moving quickly toward the entry's revolving doors, the flashing noontime glare again, and I'm following her, quickly, close behind, and I say, blurting it, breathless—

"This is strange for me too, but listen. We need to talk—wait—"

She's at the spinning door, hurling herself at it, almost. And I follow fast, in the next quarter-slice, my eyes on her. The door ejects me into the lobby, I reach for her arm and then suddenly—*whomp*—I slam into something hard and I'm down flat, one hip afire with pain.

"Jesus, what's the problem?" A security guard reaches over, pulls me up by my arm. "You OK?"

A waist-high white marble barrier, a desk-slash-fortress wall, extended clear across the echoing entry space. I'd barreled straight into it. "When did they put this thing in?" I asked, rubbing my throbbing hip and straightening my clothes.

"The barricade? Long time ago. Right after 9-11," the guard said. The girl had vanished. She was nowhere. "You gotta have your flash pass to get by here now," the guard said. "You got a flash pass?"

February 10, 2016

From: J.Leverett@deepxmail.com
To: GarrettShuttlesworth@physics.humboldtstate.edu

G, the Abigail Willard case—please put your brain on it asap. I know police work isn't your turf, but a quantum physicist is supposed to explain the fucking inexplicable, right?

Hope you caught our Orangemen pounding Georgetown. A slaughter. A beautiful thing.

ABBY, FEBRUARY 11, 2015

TO DO THIS WEEK:
Research watercolor classes: Pratt. SVA, New School
Tax appt
Pete: vitamins
Ben: dentist

I record my to-do list to show what was at the top. Seeing her, of course. She appeared to be what my Aunt Louise, MSW, would call a harbinger of inner change.

I've decided she's my new imaginary friend, sent to remind me of something. To remind me of what I am meant to be doing, maybe.

I sat in my cubicle, staring at my monitor, at a half-finished insert for an erectile dysfunction drug. I left the penis hanging and searched for the School of Visual Arts website. In seven minutes, I was signed up for art school again. Just a night class, watercolors—but this was a step of some significance. If only for one evening a week, a dedicated return.

ABBY, FEBRUARY 13, 2015

The all-school sing under the vaults of the old chapel. The boys had been dreading it, complaining and asking to skip it. I had been anticipating it with a swollen heart, swollen with memories of them as cherubs, eyes gleaming and fixed on the music teacher, standing at her piano in red wool poncho and matching beret. "All You Need Is Love"—Pete, in kindergarten, piping up with "Everybody now!" Benjamin, running toward me as the second graders fanned out into the pews to present red carnations, dropping the flower in the aisle and then snatching it up again and throwing himself at my lap, eyes shining and his heart, I can still feel it, beating urgently against the top of my thigh like a minnow swimming, as he caught his breath for a few seconds before skipping back to his spot on-stage.

Velvet cheeks, wispy locks, marrow-tender skin. My little creatures.

Now at the sing my boys stood in the back row, barely mouthing the words with faces fixed in a carefully calibrated mix of boredom and sarcasm.

Seeing them, though, there amid their classmates, the boys ranging in heights and angles and skin eruptions, the girls so primped and poised, the children I'd been watching since they were small. The sight of them, a cluster of teen angels surrounded by stained glass and organ pipes, made me tear up, just as in earlier years I'd cried from the sweetness of it all. It was still so sweet, and so bittersweet.

I sniffled through "What the World Needs Now," wishing Dennis had been able to make it. I'd stolen time from work, but he was under the gun.

Then it occurred to me to look for Dmitri. Was the antifascist warrior there? Yes, he was. Tucked in among some girls in the second row, matched by height. He appeared to be singing full-throatedly, I thought I could even pick out his bright treble in the mix.

After the concert, the parents clustered in the theater lobby, eating butter cookies and drinking Dixie cups of apple cider.

"Abigail, right? Benjamin's mom?" A round woman in an orange sweater and outsized eyeglasses seized my hand in hers, warm, cushioned. "Joanie Werner. Serena's mom. With the braids? And the attitude? So, Ben says you used to be an artist."

Used to be an artist.

"Yes, that's right." I smiled at her. "My husband was also. I mean, I guess he continues to be. We both do."

Her eyes widened. "Where do you show, the two of you? Which gallery?"

"Neither of us has representation just now. Dennis is full-time at an engineering firm."

She nodded sympathetically. "And you're in marketing, I think? Here's why I'm pestering you. I got roped into soliciting donations for the spring auction. I'm hoping that you—or your husband or both"—she giggled—"could donate an artwork."

"I don't have anything new."

"Any old one will do." She had turtle-esque eyes and thick black brows that bounced as she unfurled more sentences. The auction committee and the building committee and digital microscopes for the new science lab. A theme for the fundraiser. Monte Carlo or Old San Juan.

I hadn't shown a work in public in almost twenty years. It hardly seemed possible.

Only one of my paintings hung in our home, in the narrow hallway just outside Pete's bedroom. He had titled it Black Bird. I had once upon a time titled it Shade Study #1. It was uncharacteristic. The blackness.

"So I can put you down for a donation? It would be a generous gesture. Such a uniquely generous gesture. For the cause."

"Yes, I'll find something."

"And your husband? Something of his too?"

"I'll have to ask him. I don't know."

"We'll need it by March fifteenth." She rested a hand on my arm and squeezed it. "Thanks so much for all you do, Abby. You are amazing."

Someone started screaming then. A cluster of parents and children backed away from the building's exit doors, moving in unison, fast as a sidewinding snake. "Was that a cat?" she heard someone say.

General alarmed murmurings. The word "decapitated" stuttered over and over. Joanie Werner grabbed the arm of a teacher rushing back into the lobby. The woman was breathless. "Animal cruelty!"

Elizabeth Vong appeared before the doors. "The item has been removed," she called out. "They're taking care of the situation, please stay put!" She looked around brightly at the now silent crowd. "Your scholars gave us a lovely spring sing, didn't they?!"

Pete was nowhere in sight. I spotted Benjamin at the far end of the lobby, huddled on a staircase with some classmates, his hair covering his eyes. A jumble of elongated limbs and abandoned song sheets. A girl's head resting on his shoulder. I approached, but, seeing me, he frowned, and I thought the better of it.

DENNIS HALF-LAUGHED, half-sighed when I told him that night about Joanie Werner's request. "Shit, I've got nothing," he said. He and I stood side by side at the kitchen table, folding laundry, a bottomless task—and, these days, our most reliable mode of creative fulfillment. For example, he liked to construct neat layer cakes of T-shirts, coded by color and logo content: music, sports, miscellaneous. He arrayed them across the table at precise intervals, in the manner of Donald Judd.

"There is that one piece of mine," he said, "in the coat closet."

"You'd sell that?" I hunted for color and pattern matches in the mountain of socks, then bundled them and arranged them in tonality order along the table edge. "I don't think you should."

Dennis chewed on his thumbnail and sighed. "I might get fired this week," he said.

I didn't know how seriously to take this. Yes, he had put a few things on his corporate card that weren't, technically speaking, necessary for his job. That new surround-sound video projection system in our living room, though, yes, sometimes he did need to watch videos for work. But mostly he watched action movies with the boys and surfing movies on his own, late late at night. Yes, there were a few meals at not inexpensive restaurants in which I played the role of, for example, a building inspector from Trenton.

But this was part of life in New York, where you worked too many hours and never got paid enough, so you tried to pad out the sharp corners of life just a bit when and where you could. Isn't that right?

This is how Dennis understood it, anyhow.

"So they fire you. You could get a studio again."

"Yeah. And we pack the boys little cans of cat food for lunch."

"We could squeak by, at least for a little while."

"Squeaking by." He stepped back and scowled at his fabric towers. "Sounds like death."

He stacked the folded garments into a laundry basket and carried the load up the stairs, where they would soon be recirculated by the boys into heaps on the floor.

ABBY, FEBRUARY 20, 2015

"The inner smaller violets are factually alike."

A crisp-mannered teacher named Forest Versteeg led the SVA class, and he began the first evening with a slideshow derived from Josef Albers's observations on the perception of color. In my new sketchbook, I carefully recorded this line, the caption beneath a block of orange, black, and purple rectilinear shapes.

Of course, I had more or less memorized *Interaction of Color* during my studies in Providence. But after an interval of so many years, the images from Albers thrilled me again. My pulse raced to see those stacked and piled swatches, the flat fields of solid tones, so blunt and straightforward on the physical plane, yet so infinitely malleable in the mind. After all, as Versteeg reminded us, no color is the same for any two people. My rods and cones mix a different hue than yours do, my violet is not your violet. And these personal hues are, in turn, overlaid with a personal patina of emotion and memory.

The bars of blue and red, for example, on the cover of the Albers volume. They were visible from my bed, the book splayed spine up on the milk crate I used as a nightstand, the first time Dennis stayed the night with me. I can see his yellow hair, pale and stiffened by sweat like the strands of a dried paintbrush, as he lay, exhausted, asleep. I can taste the pebbly old raisins I chewed on while he slept, all I could find in my student kitchen.

The first class ended with an hour of painting, value and color studies. I worked in a range of greens. Versteeg's neatly cuffed jeans whispered rhythmically as he strolled behind us, watching us in our silent work. He paused for a long time behind me, each time he crossed to my side of the room.

Finally, the hour ended. A bustle by the sink as class members rinsed brushes and pallets and dried them with flannel rags.

"So . . . Abigail Willard?"

I turned away from the crowd at the sink to find him standing just behind me again. Steel-framed glasses, pale stubbled cheeks. I nodded. "Abby."

"I was a gallery assistant at Broder and Wilcox. On an internship from the High School of Fine Arts. I remember the opening night of your solo show, so impressive—you must've been what, early twenties?"

I could feel my face reddening, a helpless sensation. Humiliating.

"Twenty-five or so."

"I'm not sure what I can teach you, Abby," he said, solemn. "Our roles should most likely be reversed."

I tried to counteract with a broad smile and assured him I was desperately in need of review. I said starting back at the beginning felt so refreshing.

"It's certainly your right," he said.

I could feel other students listening with curiosity. Their bustle had gone hush.

"I used to search for your work online," he said. "I always wanted to buy a piece for myself."

He wondered why I'd vanished, he said. Why, he wondered, did I stop showing my work? What happened?

This should be astoundingly flattering, this whole thing. So how come I wished to melt, wicked witch–like, into the floor, leaving only my little brushes behind?

"Life happened," I said, with what I hoped was a light chuckle. "See you next time." I fled.

ABBY, FEBRUARY 23, 2015

As it happened, the former Broder and Wilcox gallery was now a gourmet grocery, just across from the sporting goods store where I took Benjamin to buy new cleats, the spring sports season approaching and his feet, as ever, lengthening. The big window was slapped with paper signs advertising Tuscan olive oil and cheese from the Pyrenees.

I sent my son ahead. Try things on, I said. I lingered in front of the grocery.

A February night in 1994. Almost three years had passed since I'd left New York for grad school, since the time of Eli. The debris of it still shifting, settling, inside me. But somehow, I'd landed back in the city, with Dennis, our twin MFA diplomas drifting somewhere in our messy sublet on Flatbush. And then, this show at Broder and Wilcox. Jillian Broder's gallery was not messy, it was not on Flatbush. It was a blinding white box with wood floors on Broome Street, prime SoHo, cast-iron columns painted white, and a spotless acre of window overlooking the street. That night, a soft dry snow started falling just as the plastic cups were being stacked on a card table and the jugs of wine were being unscrewed. Within minutes, powdered sugar frosted every branch of every tree on the street, revealing their shapes, giving them glamour, so they looked like a line of skinny wild-haired girls. The snow gently covered the dirty cars with clean blankets. I remember feeling grandeur, momentousness, as I stood before that expansive and towering window, waiting for the first guests to show, looking out at the snow. The purple shadows fell down from the buildings across the way and I remember exactly what I thought: I was thinking, so this is a beginning, this is a kind of birth too, and it's every bit as miraculous and world-altering as the kind when a squinting little newborn comes slipping out of its mother's body. A new life is being born in this gallery tonight, and god it's embarrassing now but it really felt that way to me. Like the moment the gallery's double glass doors swung open and the first strange pair of eyes in a stranger's face rested on my work, the cosmos would register my arrival. Maybe the snowflakes might pause mid-fall so that I could go outside and walk between them, view them from all sides, and know that, yes, I'll always know that this moment happened, and that everything else sprang from it.

One work sold. A small still life of grapefruit, painted in the classroom of Hans-Dietrich Bremer. I never even learned who bought it. But that's what you hope for, when you set brush to a new canvas, that it will at some point sail away, this vessel of your soul, into the wider world. The other paintings from the show are wrapped and buried in those racks in the basement.

"I'm starving, Ma." I went into the grocery and bought Benjamin a tiny five-dollar bag of chips. Then I went across the street and bought him the shoes.

And as I sat on the subway headed for home, jostling shoulder-to-shoulder with my younger son, who was lost in some television show on his phone, I told myself: you made the correct choices, you did what was required. There's a nobility, surely, in unrealized dreams. Are the blossoms on that weeping cherry tree in our backyard any less beautiful because they don't bear fruit? Dreams that don't come true are not any less dreamed.

I was exhausted, with a pounding headache, by the time I got home. Benjamin kick-boxed around the backyard to test his new cleats. I threw up in the toilet and lay down for a nap.

ABBY, FEBRUARY 25, 2015

For Forest Versteeg's class, I decided, I needed new boar's-hair brushes and tubes of M. Graham watercolor paint, the kind with a little honey blended in for extra unctuousness. Cadmium red, of course. Naples yellow. Prussian blue and raw sienna—these two mixed together, I remembered, create a deep, cool-hued green-blue-black, the color of a pond in dense shade.

I walked into New York Central Art Supply on Third Avenue, and the ancient floors under my feet creaked in some dormant sector of my brain. I would know that sound anywhere. I would know it from my grave. And then the smell wrapped around me like a hug. Acrid and penetratingly clean. The sharpness of the pigments, the dry dusty scent of pine wood and canvas.

I declined a clerk's offer of help, preferring to examine the racks of brushes at my own pace, pulling them from their labeled slots, running their exquisitely soft tips on the back of my hand. I chose a wide flat one and a skinny round one and was turning to choose a plastic palette for mixing paints—I knew just the kind I wanted, with the row of dimples along one edge.

And there she is. End of the aisle. Pulling down a box of charcoal pencils from a high shelf.

Hello, I bleat, surprising myself.

She looks up from the box—she'd been reading the label on the back. She nods uncertainly. Black diamond-patterned tights, flat white sneakers. A pale-pink denim jacket.

Do you know who I am?

A tiny frown. She shakes her head.

You. This sounds insane. I moved a step toward her. She is sidling back, away. I mean, you later.

Okay. She hugs the long flat box to her chest.

My name is Abigail Willard.

Her eyes grow all wide and wary, eyelashes loaded up with mascara, lids precisely edged with liner. I spent a lot of energy on makeup back then. The long sessions in front of the mirror. Pleased at what I saw.

And your name is?

She says very slowly, hesitantly, People call me A.

A for Abigail. Right? I understand that I may sound demanding, or scary, but I continue. Am I right?

She stares at me.

Listen to me, I say.

She stares. Her eyes replicate Pete's, the brilliant lit-from-within brown slivered with black. Unnerving.

You will take steps and make choices, I say, my voice cracking now. They could be the wrong ones. They could be.

You're out of your mind, she murmurs, backing away. She drops the box, which unlids itself in midair, the black pencils raining in a clatter, dark hashmarks all across the floor. She's gone. I'm slowly picking them up, and she's gone.

I don't recall how I got back to my desk. I sat through the 2:30 marketing meeting as if deaf and dumb.

SESSION NOTES

A left the shop without completing her purchase.

She says it's not surprising that you'd encounter disturbed people at an artists' supply store.

The strange woman might be some kind of omen, she says. Perhaps having to do with poor choices. Says she should end the affair with her boss, though she now realizes this could pose difficulties.

ABBY, FEBRUARY 26, 2015

At a baleful hour on this midwinter night, a mom named Katherine Erdmann called to say that Pete was passed out in her sunroom. "He's so big, I can't budge him. And Jeffrey is on business in Sao Paolo."

Annoyingly, she pronounced this place name with a perfect Portuguese inflection, though it was three in the morning and Katherine Erdmann was not Portuguese.

She opened the door, in a long zip-up robe, squinting. I'd never seen her without her glasses. They made her look much smarter. "I think they were drinking. I'm not sure what they were doing. Eliza is crying in the bathroom and the rest of the kids have gone home."

Pete's cheek was pressed up against an enormous ceramic pot, the stems and leaves of a sizable peace lily bent over him as if to tend to him. Spittle gathered in the corners of his mouth, and he snored softly.

"Look at our darling sprout," said Dennis. "Christ."

"I was out at my book club. *Go Tell It on the Mountain*." Katherine looked at me and whispered, "James Baldwin."

"I know, I know." I reached down and waggled his foot. He whimpered.

"Who brought the booze?" said Dennis.

"Oh, I'm sure it was that Dmitri," Katherine said with a shake of her head.

Again. Dmitri Petimezas. Troubling urchin. I'd asked around about him at school. No one knew exactly who his parents were, they never showed up for anything. I'd spotted him lately, a few times, on the front steps in the morning, dressed in an expensive puffer coat, always the latest basketball shoes. I even searched online. His Instagram profile photo caught his pretty face laughing, covered in paintball splatters. In the few posts, he posed in various European cities.

"Dmitri was questioned by the cops that morning, that whole incident last month, the vestibule thing." She frowned at them. "But then so was Pete."

My stomach plunged, Dennis and I exchanged grimaces. "How do you know he was questioned?" I demanded. "I didn't hear that."

She shrugged. "I'm lucky. Eliza tells me everything."

"Pete, can you get up?" Dennis grabbed one of his arms. It flopped like a rubber tube.

Bushwhacking through the peace lily. I got behind him and tried to lift his head and shoulders. Dennis grabbed a foot in each hand. On his dirty white sneakers, handwritten letters, in red marker:

ANTIFA. RAGE BRIGADE. We budged him about six inches, he stirred. "I don't like tequila," he moaned.

ABBY, FEBRUARY 27, 2015

It was a long night of ruminating, sitting by my delinquent child's bed, making sure he didn't choke on his own spew. Eyelids radish-red. Strands of hair snaking wetly across his forehead. Maybe a little drool at the lips, reminding me of baby days, until a tequila-infused belch jolted me into the now again. Plenty of time to think and rethink. Visit and revisit.

Pete, questioned by the police. Again, the police and my boy.

Antifa? What on earth.

And speaking of police. The detective and I were texting every day now. In the space of a month, it had become rampant flirtation. He joked about showing me his favorite Caribbean beaches. "I have family there, the islands. I know the sweet spots they don't share with the likes of you." Sometimes the conversation strayed into serious confessions of our frustrations around marriage, kids. Harmless, or not?

The sightings. Five times in two months. That seemed harmful. Terrifying.

The foundations of my life seemed to be sliding, hairline fractures appearing.

My long trail of ruminations led to Eli Hammond.

Eli and that girl.

He'd pull a paperback—*Down and Out in Paris and London* or *The Sheltering Sky*—from the back pocket of his jeans—remember how people walked around with soft, worn books in their back pockets, volumes sized and bound to be kept close in just that way, ready to be thumbed and wielded like totems?

Romania, Gaza, Somalia. We need to go. See it through our own eyes. Don't you want to see it? he asked.

His eyes were the color of a clear sky sinking into darkness. When he talked this way, when I was lying there gazing into them, I wanted to see it all.

Instead, he left me behind. The returning memory of his eyes made tears come to mine, as I sat there over my sleeping son.

She was not merely a reminder, this girl. I was beginning to see: she was some kind of destroyer.

Finally, I left Pete's bedside to dress for work. My face felt frozen with exhaustion as I sat on the train, arching over the canal and the rooftops and the scrap-metal yard. You don't have to recalculate the losses and the gains, refigure the cost of everything in your life, I told myself. All you have to do is get through this day.

ABBY, FEBRUARY 28, 2015

"Is that a cricket bat?"

"Yeah," Dennis said. "That's a cricket bat."

I played the videos over and over, sitting up late on the sofa with Dennis: black-hooded marchers, clamoring signs and slogans in many languages, DEATH TO COMPLACENCY, NAZIS RAUS, ALIANZA ANTIFASCISTA. Brutish weapons in their gloved hands, sledgehammers and wooden cudgels. Footage of shattered shop windows, burning trucks, the soundtrack of foreign sirens, wailing, strident. These antifa, these global antifascist brawlers, who fought in the streets and sometimes committed violent and dangerous acts in the name of freedom and justice. Our sixteen-year-old dabbling in this? Could we forbid it? Ground him? After dinner, we had cornered him in his room to talk about the drinking at the Erdmann house, and Pete had assured us he was finished with that. "I'm not really interested in that kind of partying," he'd said. "You don't have to worry about it."

But surely there was reason to worry about this other, unnerving new interest. "Let's just stay on top of it," said Dennis now, as I clicked on *Antifa Square Off with Riot Police in Hamburg*, a nighttime action, orange flames flaring, whistles, chanting, police impassive behind plexiglass shields. The footage ended abruptly when a protester blocked the camera with a black-gloved hand. Dennis shut the laptop's cover and turned to me. "We just keep close tabs, make sure homework gets done, no more incidents. I mean, you can't mandate a person's beliefs, right? Look, it's antifascism. At least he's not, like, pro fascism."

Yes, I agreed that would be worse.

"And at least he has a passion?" he said. "Isn't that what the school's always saying—encourage your kids to develop a passion?"

"I doubt this was what they had in mind," I said. Dennis offered a tired smile, kissed the top of my head, and went up to bed. I opened the screen again, stared at figures scrolling by, a pixelated frieze, wavering in and out of focus. One video after another, over and over. Finally I fell asleep there, the laptop dying alongside me.

In the morning, I dragged myself up to our room, bare feet shuffling up the stairs, and Dennis and I dressed, tugging our clothes from the grip of the ornery little closet, as if all were normal, just another workday.

As if all of this were normal. Normal, that some kind of international strain of rage had infected our child.

Normal, to be indulging in a strange semi-dalliance with the law officer assigned to a case against this firstborn son.

Normal, to see yourself, as you were then. Talk to yourself even.

Normal, to be teetering with every step you take, on your path to the office, to the supermarket and the bank and the school, skirting the abyss between true and false, past and present, dream and reality.

Normal, to be passing Bryant Park, rushing through gathering dusk on your evening commute and see yourself there, on the steps, sitting, smoking a cigarette. Right under the lion. In your pencil skirt and a pair of puffy white sneakers.

Grabbing a cigarette before getting on the train.

Freeze in mid-stride, practically fall over.

You see the brand of smokes. Marlboro Reds. You'd picked up this habit, the first week you met Eli, stealing his Marlboro Reds.

You hesitate. You notice the almost-plump hands, the bitten fingernails. The tender wrist stacked with thin metal bangles.

Then, a nausea hits you again, a fear that you'll vomit right there at the corner of Forty-Second and Fifth, with the rush-hour mobs swirling around you.

The feeling passes. The girl rests her cigarette on a ledge, now she reaches into her messenger bag and pulls out a wand of lip gloss.

And then you remember this moment, this day. Yes, you see the file box next to her, overstuffed with ragged houseplants and a mess of papers. She has just quit her job at Grady Advertising. She has decided that office life is not for her. Not for her, sitting in a cubicle all day.

She is free.

She has quit the job to pursue her desire to be a serious painter.

This is what she tells herself. But you also recall: you'd just met him. The first flash of intensity. So fresh, so powerful. It was hard to get out of his bed.

She applies the lip gloss, tosses it back into her bag, and straightens up. The lion, above, watches you with stony skepticism.

I need to talk to you.

You realize you haven't said this out loud. So you rush up to her, say it again. I need to talk to you.

She pins you with her gaze now. You again, she says.

All around the two of you the rush continues, as if there has not been a massacre of time and space, right here in their midst; they don't seem to register that laws of the universe are bending as they dodge around with stress and love and anger on their faces.

Their faces are infinitely different. Only two are the same. Yours and hers.

Let's go somewhere and sit down, you say. If we could just figure this out.

We? There is no we. I'm not going anywhere with you. She stabs the cigarette out on the plinth beneath the lion's paw. His pupilless eyes, regarding this, and everything so wrong that is happening here.

I'll give you my card, you can see our name.

You fumble in your bag, searching, open your wallet, dig around hoping to find a stray business card. No one uses business cards anymore, but the corporation still insists you have one.

And yes you locate one single card, corners dog-eared. You hand it to her; she reads it with a furrowed brow. Novapharm? That's where you work?

It's a good job, you say. A good paycheck.

She looks up at you. I'm done with paycheck jobs, she says. Never again.

It works, you say. This life works.

But do you love it? Do you love this life?

Her eyes, set wide, opened wide, questioning. You have to look away from them, to try to formulate a response.

You'll see, it's not like you think.

The card flutters to the ground. She has dropped it.

Maybe because it's your only card it seems important that second to rescue it, but it's just past five on Fifth Avenue and the sidewalk is jammed, and brogans and pumps are stepping on it now, it is skidding across the pavement. Finally you retrieve it. It's your only one.

You straighten and return to her, but she has gathered up her box and purse and is slipping into the stream of people, slipping away.

But did you read the name, you hear your voice shout. Our name. I am trying to help you. Save you!

You realize you have no idea why you've said this. Save her from what?

As she disappears, your eye comes to rest on a pack of teenagers just down the block from the library. A kid with a shock of blond hair—your shock-headed second son—locked in a kiss with a girl. Green parka, gray corduroys—that must be him.

Voice out loud again. Benjamin! Or was he a figment of the imagination too? The kids seem to hear it, the call of a watching parent. They scatter like pigeons, disappearing into the park.

Dr. Tristane Kazemy, FEBRUARY 29, 2016

It is leap day. A movement exists now, a campaign, a meme perhaps, she'd seen it all over her feeds, to encourage one to take risks and adventures on this date. It happens only once every four years.

A *l'année bissextile*. Once every four years, and so the thinking goes, why not take a leap?

Le Neuro opened at 7:15 a.m., and she was already there, waiting. Only a fellow, not a full staffer yet, so no key, not yet. In this wintry dark, the campus was deserted, bleak as tundra. She stood outside the entrance stamping her feet, waiting for the first keyholder to arrive.

The trees had turned metallic in the cold, trunks like steel columns, twigs like bent wire.

It's 7:25 now, and she had to admit it, besides feeling deeply cold, she felt deeply angry. Perhaps this Willard case, when she broke it open, would force the attention of her bosses Laurin and Buccardi. Perhaps this incredible dossier, the bulging virtual folders of scans and transcriptions and analysis—perhaps it also contained the raw materials of her future. Certainly, it could be a career-making case; certainly, at last, it would bring the promotion that Buccardi kept saying she deserved. And with it, a copy of the entry key to Le Neuro.

She wasn't the type to cry sexism. Still, Laurin. Always the Monday-morning murmurs about snowbound *liaisons a Mont Blanc*. A crisp "mademoiselle" tossed in her direction could tilt the weekly departmental like a veering ship. Laurin was most definitely a factor.

All of this must be forgotten in the lab though. By eight she had been allowed inside and already had immersed herself once more in the dossier. She gazed at the neurological scans, the contents of one woman's head, luminescent blue-black and white, across two monitors. Today is leap day, she told her brain. You must leap.

3/3/3/3

I am forty-six, and Mariah Glücksburg is forty-six. I know this because her birthday is the same as mine. I recall a double party in her drafty old house down in the flats of Providence, near the water, an old rowboat in the backyard where, during the party, two people lay entwined, sleeping off the effects of mushrooms. Dennis was there—it was where we first talked, in fact. He knew Mariah, he had met her in a Latin American poli sci course; they were the type of art students who would take such classes for fun, back then. And of course he had been drawn to her, because she was ravishing. Thick dark hair, halfway down her back and sumptuously waving bangs around big turquoise eyes, petite, curvy, fetching in her paint-smeared overalls and many rings and ear piercings. Bewitching, really, we all were drawn to her, and she shared my birthday. December 20. Final projects were done, buses and trains would be caught out of town the next day, so what better time for a big wild birthday party in Mariah's little wooden house by the bay.

Mariah had gone to Swiss boarding schools and Cambridge and had interned with Cy Twombly in Rome; her father was some kind of diplomat, and her grandfather was some kind of Greek royal, someone not on the side of the angels in World War II. That hint of sinister history just amplified her mystique, somehow. Obviously, she knew more than any of us about how to mix drinks, how to roll a joint, how to flirt with professors and lure them to attend your birthday parties. Even Bremer came by, in a windbreaker, with a cane, and sat for a while at the kitchen table, a jaunty smoke between his fingers, gingerly eating chips and dip and smiling in mild bemusement as his students attempted to charm him.

And yes, it was the night Dennis and I began. I'd seen him at that birthday party, in the kitchen churning with celebrants, pressed close to Mariah in the corner, mixing cocktails for the other guests, bumping hips, laughing and drinking from the same bottle. But later it was he and I who tumbled from the party into the cold street. I balanced on the back of his bike through wintry predawn Providence, and by the time we got to my basement apartment up on the hill he was winded and sweaty, I was half frozen, and remember how hot his skin was when I touched him with my painful fingertips. In the one-room hovel steam seemed to come off his body as he shed his coat, shirt, shoes, pants and I warmed myself in it, clinging to him.

A moment I can recall so clearly. It was when I began to emerge from the haze.

And so tonight, twenty-two years and two months and twelve days later, headed for my night class, I waited for an elevator and the doors opened. Mariah Glücksburg. Still stunning, more so maybe, a bit more sculpted and drawn with age, and a comely streak of gray in her hair, still a cascade of shiny black curls, and tight stovepipe jeans tucked into expensive boots and a gorgeous red leather coat. We regarded each other for a moment. Did she recognize me, after all this time? At this point, I was not sure who I even looked like at all.

But she grinned. "Well, it's you," she said. "The amazing Abigail."

"Mariah," I said. "How unreal."

"You're here to teach a class?" She stepped off the elevator, gave me a two-cheeked Euro air-kiss, buttoned her leather coat, so rich and soft-looking I was tempted to lean over and bury my face in it. "I just finished a guest lecture in Luis Iglesias's seminar, god the students in this place, I mean, I believe in continuing education, but these people just make me sad. So what are you teaching—let me guess, it must be oil painting, right?"

I smiled faintly, "I'm taking a class, in fact. I'm a student."

"No." She put a hand on my arm. "But surely you don't need to be doing this?"

My face felt rubbery so perhaps it came out more like a grimace. "I read about your new work, MoMA, I am so happy for you," I said.

She squeezed my arm, let her hand drop. "Yeah, it was astounding, that. I mean, worse was the solo show at the Tate. A lot of hubbub. I'm still recuperating." She pulled out her phone. "Give me your number, I'll ring you. I'm racing."

ABBY, MARCH 5, 2015

The Hull Foundation's headquarters sit on a quiet block near the United Nations. The foundation is a shadowy organization. My general impression, uninformed, is that it carries out benevolent deeds in the world's poorest places, but then I have a trace memory of ties to arms manufacturers and Arctic drilling.

At its heart is a jungle, a glass-enclosed public atrium. I brought my baby boys here, in strollers, to see the tall palm trees; sit in the lush humid silence on a midwinter's day; use the large, spotless bathrooms finished in biscuit-hued stone.

Forest Versteeg has urged us to paint every day. The atrium has always been a fine place to sit during a lunch hour. On this Thursday, I entered through the south side entrance, my tote bag over my shoulder, containing brushes, paint, palette, paper, and a foil-encased turkey wrap tucked under my arm. As I tugged open the reluctant glass door, the air rushed to embrace me, lavish and soft, so memory-laden.

My favorite spot faced the small square pool. Tossed pennies freckling its floor, in one corner a small spout eternally convulsing. Toddler Pete dropping coins, watching them spiral to the tiled bottom, Benjamin nuzzling into his carriage, dreaming his infant dreams. My preferred bench was secreted, invisible from most of the walkways, enclosed in a maze of palmettos, date palms, and giant anthuriums. These latter, with their stiff blood-red blooms throughout the year, might offer a tasty opportunity to dab a bit of crimson into the green.

The spot is usually empty.

But this day it is not.

A small pad rests on one knee. She curls over it. Head bowed, hair hiding her face, but of course I know who it is. I can see her brush on the paper. I can see the paint on the paper. It is loose and lovely, quite good, really.

Wordlessly, I sit on the adjoining bench. She doesn't look up. I set my turkey wrap down, pull my small collection of gear from my bag, open the little plastic container of water, wet a #6 round brush.

Our eyes meet. Abigail, she says.

That's right.

She looks at the palette I've just removed from the tote. You're painting?

I nod. I am.

She shifts her eyes to the palmettos she's describing with a blackened viridian. I watch her brushstrokes for a long while.

I've forgotten how to be loose, I say. Like that. Like you do there.

I don't know what I'm doing, she says.

The air is so green-smelling and thick, it's dizzying. I squeeze a few drops of paint onto the palette. I'm not sure I can work in her presence.

Why are you following me? she says.

I am here to paint, I say. I will try entering the unimaginable slantwise this time, to sit calmly within it, so maybe I can steal a longer look.

She lifts her face. It makes no sense, she says. I don't like it. She begins squeezing water from her brush into a baby-food jar (scavenged, I knew, from trash barrels at the little playground on Bleecker where the nannies tended their charges). Tossing her things into her messenger bag, black canvas with orange buckles and straps (purchased at that army surplus shop that once occupied an entire block on Canal).

You're leaving?

This makes me very uncomfortable. She stands, holding her work flat, balanced on spread fingers in front of her, blowing on it. Are you really an artist? A working artist?

I'm . . . working. Yes. And you?

She turns and slips her bag's strap over her shoulder, the wet paper teetering on her splayed hand. I'm thinking of applying to graduate school. With her free hand, she slips a brochure from the outside pocket of her bag and passes it to me. On the cover, a classroom shot. Hans-Dietrich Bremer, in a shabby cardigan, standing over a table full of students. I'm working on the portfolio, she says.

Though it's not due till . . . Flip that thing over, she says. When's it due?

I check the back cover. November 29, I say. I look up at her. Well, you've got time, I say. Then I have to laugh. You've got lots of time, I say.

She is staring at me but oddly past me too, a glance one might give a lit lamp in a dark room.

I hand her the brochure. Listen, I say, that boss. You could file for harassment. You should file for harassment. You're out of a job because of him.

She knits her brows, looking perplexed. He wasn't harassing me, it was just . . . Her voice trails off. That's not why I left my job, she says. I left my job because I'm going to be a painter. She walks away, her drying study still wobbling atop her outstretched fingertips. Then looks again, back over her shoulder. This makes me very uncomfortable, she says.

ABBY, MARCH 6, 2015

The following day. After work, instead of barreling on to Brooklyn, I found myself exiting the subway in the Village. I climbed from underground to wander West Twelfth Street again, a cold spring dusk filtering down the sky like silt. Trying to finally penetrate this weirdness. Figure it out. Should I get my head examined or sell my sensational tale on the internet. Should I try to steer her in some different direction. Or fix her to the path.

Along the low blocks, the once-shabby row houses are decked with glossy doors and careful plantings. The shops crammed with used records and secondhand junk have been replaced by spare and deserted boutiques. But even back then, when the streets were trash-strewn and gunpoint muggings were commonplace along the darker stretches of Washington and Greenwich Streets, underneath the tracks where the occasional freight car still rumbled, even then, though, the neighborhood had been wildly desirable. It was seen as a New York City triumph, to score a room on far West Twelfth.

It had happened only via faithful observation of a quasi-secret ritual. The initiated—the natives, or those who had an older sibling already ensconced—knew where and when to go. Each and every Tuesday morning, seven a.m. The *Village Voice*'s lobby on the Bowery, a small street-level cubby of dirty linoleum and gold-veined mirrors. Be there by 6:50, because the surly, huge-bellied man appeared with his damp-ink, finger-smearing bundle precisely on the hour. He glared at the mob for a moment. Fished slowly around in the pocket of his work pants, extracted a little pocketknife, bent uneasily to slice the plastic ties. The ties sprung away from the stack of tabloids with a crisp snap, the surly man took a wide step backward, and then the swarming began. Shameless shoving and elbowing. If you were agile, you might be able to secure your copy then nab one of the three pay phones right there in the lobby.

Share in WVill near Hudson, private room, futon included, no smokers, no pets, $275. I plugged my coins into the slot and started dialing.

It was Eleanor Boyle who'd tipped me off to the Tuesday morning *Village Voice* ritual. She finished Western New England U a year ahead of me; observing this ritual, she'd procured a mildewy basement room at the corner of Bethune and Washington Streets.

Peeking out her bedroom window at foot height, she could see the late-night businesspeople kicking at each other with their glittered man-sized stilettos.

My landing in the city had not been soft. I'd entered the week before this, two days after my graduation from Western New England U, where I'd taken every class in the anemic art department and earned a BFA without miring myself or my money-strapped parents in debt. I entered via the hot hellmouth of Port Authority. A fat, wobbly-wheeled suitcase teetering behind me on a little leash, a shopping bag of vinyl albums under one arm. In my purse, a four-hundred-dollar check from my grandmother Rosalie.

I swiftly discovered that I couldn't cash this check at a bank unless I had an account, and that I couldn't open an account without a fixed address or a job. At the fast-food chicken joint on Eighth Avenue, my distress must have radiated. Or perhaps they just wanted me to clear out, with my obese American Tourister and my rapidly disintegrating bag of music. A girl in a smiling-chicken paper hat led me out onto the sidewalk, pointed up the avenue: CHECKS CASHED. "They take their cut but you get the rest into your pocket." And so, following her advice and Eleanor's, I slotted myself into a closet-like fifth-floor room two blocks away from her place, 268 West Twelfth Street.

My roommate, Gregory, held the lease and the bigger bedroom. I didn't see much of him. He worked noon to eight at a no-appointment-needed salon in Midtown and was out after that. At four a.m. I'd hear him crossing just outside my door, his spurred motorcycle boots scraping the wood floor as he paused at the fridge to swig out of my jug of skim milk (always marked with my name and DO NOT DRINK MY MILK) before turning in.

It was a place to sleep and hang my little dresses. Eleanor came over, sat in one of the two metal folding chairs that comprised the living room furniture, looked around, and pronounced it a proper New York dump.

But there was a balcony. Narrow, just space enough for two people. And a warped wooden bench and an ash bucket filled with

YOU AGAIN | 69

dirty rainwater. Peeling plaster over concrete traced with cracks, and a rusted drain in one corner.

Still, a small place to perch high in the air, just under the open space of the sky. Below lay the interior of the block, where wealthier Villagers tended gardens. A young man in very short shorts was sunbathing on a tiny patch of grass, spread-eagle, zinnias bursting like cartoon fireworks all around him.

Eleanor and I ogled him, sharing one of her clove cigarettes. She was wiry and brazen, her Irish-red hair in a wavy bob, her long legs showcased in zebra-striped tights. She was already, after a year there, nonchalant about life in the city, even blasé, in a way that seemed enviable to me. She auditioned fruitlessly for acting gigs, worked temp jobs on the trading floors, and frequently dallied with the rowdy, smug boys who apprenticed in such places. Her impressions of their seduction lines and in-bed sounds made us squirm with laughter as we lay on the scratchy Bolivian blanket I'd bought to cover my bedroom's stained carpet.

"You need to figure out what to wear to your job interview," she said.

"I've got my cousin Carol's suit." I showed her the tan jacket and skirt hanging on the back of the bedroom door. Beige, the color of bread crust.

She looked unimpressed. "I'm taking you to that seven-dollar manicure place. You can't get a job in this city without a professional manicure. It's like a fucking New York law."

When I think how I turned up for that interview. My fingertips glowing magenta, the broad-shouldered blazer, the skirt fitted with a hidden safety pin at the waist, and my hair pulled up and piled away from my face. And a conviction about life, unexpressed and unexamined, but as present and real as my own body, that all avenues were open to me.

I marched into that office, sat down with Michael Hutcherson, nabbed that entry-level graphic design job. Twelve thousand per year, production department, a light-starved back-corner desk in the sky-scraping rookery of Grady Advertising. Three months later, he invited me out for a drink to discuss my prospects. Four drinks later, we were making out in a cab. How old had he been then? I did the math. Forty-six at the time.

The age at which I now found myself.

Yes, found myself. Because, again, here I stood, loitering on West Twelfth Street, regarding the same three stone steps that climb to the same entry door etched with the same numbers: 268. Thinking about pressing that buzzer again.

Instead, my phone trembled in my coat pocket. A text from Dennis: Where are you?

Such an excellent question, my love.

I scanned the streets, just to see if I might catch her returning home. But no. I drifted toward the man-made chasm two blocks away, where the staircase for the Brooklyn-bound descended.

March 13, 2016

From: GarrettShuttlesworth@physics.humboldtstate.edu
To: J.Leverett@deepxmail.com

Swamped, but spent time over midterm break on the Willard matter. I've scribbled a few formulas that excite me quite a bit.

Conflicted woman, this Abigail, based on what's in the file. And you clearly found her a person of interest, JL. How are things at home?

ABBY, MARCH 17, 2015

"Oh crap, I guess we should have windmilled," Dennis said over the phone, when I told him that headmistress Elizabeth Vong had summoned us for an emergency conference.

As an infant, Pete didn't babble. Pete didn't babble, he didn't burble, he didn't produce the adorable spit-bubbly strings of "baba-bab" and "dadadadada" that erupted from the other tykes we knew. When his peers started saying "bowwow!" at every dog that passed, Pete would smile silently, his dark eyes lit up, but he wouldn't contribute a "bowwow" of his own, no matter how many times I read *Go Dog Go*, pointed at each dog, and said "bowwow." Expressive dysphasia was diagnosed at five.

Now, at sixteen, he usually alternated between surly and silent, and homework rarely happened without a scramble for lost handouts. His teachers asked him to complete extra vocabulary worksheets—he was now a high school junior with standardized tests dead ahead. "I don't give a shit what 'exigent' means," he'd mutter.

Ms. Vong, in a pair of red-framed glasses and bold asymmetrical jewelry, tilted her head empathetically as we walked in, looking up from a folder opened on her desk. "Good day, Dennis, and good day, Abigail!"

Settled in chairs opposite. Dennis rested his hand on mine, then gave me a quizzical glance—mine was trembling. I pulled it away.

"Pete has come a long way with us, I have been so gratified with his progress." She sighed, in an apologetic fashion. "So, what brings us here today." She passed her fingers over the open folder again, as if reading Braille. "Being so bright, as Pete is, but lacking that facility to express yourself. Struggling with the dysphasia. And"—she glanced down at the open file—"dyslexia as well?" She shook her head gently, smiled at each of us carefully, in turn. "Must be very frustrating for him, even more now at this transitional age."

Clearly, it would be worse than we feared.

"Perhaps that is why he has written graffiti in the boys' room espousing violent revolution," she said. She looked down at her folder and read, "The fires of the Antifa will blaze forever." "Dax Lives." "Avenge Killah P." She looked up at us.

"Kill a pee?" said Dennis.

"Killah." She glared. "Like a killer. Followed by the letter 'P.'"

"At least he has a passion," said Dennis.

"He's such a gentle boy," I said. "He's never been violent."

"Perhaps not," she said. "But that brings me to the next issue. We believe he's been involved with these gruesome situations in the trash cans too." She fiddled with her trapezoidal earrings. "I'm afraid we have no definitive proof, but on the day of the spring sing, he was seen icing his hand with a frozen fruit bar. And he has been influencing other students. Well, one other student. And I can't have this spread any further."

"The other student, who's that?" said Dennis.

"Dmitri Petimezas." She drew out this name, as if its many hard consonants tasted delicious in her mouth, but her face betrayed nothing.

"He's the instigator," said Dennis. "I'm sure of it."

She shook her head, just slightly. "He confessed that Pete created the graffiti. And your son admitted it." She picked up the phone and pressed a button. "Lucy, send Pete Willard in, please." She hung up. "We've had him reading in Ms. Finch's room, just down the hall."

Dennis took my hand.

Pete shuffled in, avoiding our eyes, a finger stuck in the pages of *The Grapes of Wrath*.

"We will work with you," Vong said. "But first, I must impose a suspension. A week to cool off. Given the volatility of it all. I'm sure you understand."

LATER. ON MY PHONE IN THE DARK KITCHEN, I pecked out a long text about it, poured out my worries. Pete has been suspended; he's espousing revolution. And, as usual, a little spike in my pulse as I saw his name come up, a response. He is an intelligent boy; he will figure things out. Who doesn't have challenges in this world? Do you know, I have dyslexia myself, Abby, undiagnosed until my thirties. Apply yourself, my teachers would say. That was me at Pete's age.

I would really like to see you, he added. Just say when and where.

Then a postscript: And tell Pete to be careful. It's kid stuff now, but you never know who's surveilling.

ABBY, MARCH 19, 2015

For three weeks, Benjamin had been insistent: I did not see him on Fifth Avenue kissing a girl. "That wasn't me," he protested. "I was at track practice." Last night, he had dropped a basketball down the stairs; at the bottom, it leaped up and cracked the window next to the front door.

He said this while shoveling handfuls from a bag of finely shredded mozzarella cheese into his mouth. Little bits snagged on his sweatshirt or tumbled to the floor.

"I was saving that to make pizza."

"I like Santo's better. Can we order instead?" Benjamin looked a lot like Dennis, as I first saw him. The irresistible sunny looks.

The large green-hazel eyes, impressive width of shoulder. Wheat-colored hair with a vibrant wave to it. Skin that easily soaked up a tan.

Pete looked like me. Finely boned, pale and prone to sunburn, wide-set dark umber eyes. It was two days into his suspension. I climbed the stairs to his room, where he'd been battened down, not leaving except for meals.

In the narrow hallway, I passed the shelves of books and the black bird painting, and the sketches of Dennis and me, when we'd done our turn at modeling for Mariah Glücksburg. Likely our most valuable possessions at this point.

When we'd arrived home after the visit with Vong, we'd cornered Pete. He admitted he'd become involved with something called The Brigade. "It's about solidarity and social change, and I've just been to a couple of meetings. It's nothing for you to worry about. It's not your business."

"Solidarity with who?" I said. "We are your parents. Everything that is your business is our business, as long as you live in this house."

"That's simply not true," Pete had said.

It cost us two and a half vacation days each, Dennis and I, to stay home with our teenage miscreant. I guess we may not get out to Tustin this year, Dennis had said sadly.

Now I knocked and opened Pete's door.

"What," he glowered. He sat in bed, his laptop balanced atop his knees, headphones on. With a sharp, raised shoulder, he nudged one side of the headphone askew.

"We're ordering Santo's for dinner. Pepperoni?"

"Can I go to paintball with Dmitri and his brother Milo again this weekend?"

"Hell no," I snapped. "Not happening." I glowered at him.

"What's the deal with these people. That Dmitri is a menace," I said. "And the brother—what's his story?"

"I think he sells, like, imported things," Pete shrugged. "I don't know."

"Imported things?" I shook my head. "Like cocaine?"

He rolled his eyes then stared down at his screen. "Pepperoni," he said gruffly. Then added, "Please." Pete always said please and thank you—this was a point of pride for him.

Thirty-two minutes later, we unboxed a square pizza that stretched halfway across the dining table, a pocked battlefield of tomato sauce and oozing cheese, cratered with pepperoni. Choosing their first slices, the boys leaned over it like strategizing generals. Benjamin said his English homework was to write down a true story. "I want to do the crash of the B-2 Bomber."

"It was an F-4 Phantom," corrected Dennis. He chewed his slice thoughtfully. "Thirty-eight foot wingspan, silver fuselage. The size of that wreckage in the field behind the school, tremendous. And the horse. That lonely horse. Every afternoon, I fed him my leftover lunch. I'll never understand why he didn't run. He just stood there. I watched the whole thing, we all did, because it was recess. We heard the engine sputtering. And did I ever tell you this? Mrs. Perry, that was my third-grade teacher, she said, pray for him, that poor animal is burning, she said, as we stood there and watched it."

"The pilot got away?" Benjamin asked.

"He ejected," said Pete, with an air of authority.

"Yes, but of course we didn't know that at the time. And we didn't care. We only cared about the horse." Dennis always sighed at this point in the oft-told tale, and said, "The sound of the crash was something. Like the final ten seconds of the world." In my mind, this was the origin story of every artwork he'd ever made.

I needed to talk with him about the incident with Benjamin on

Fifth Avenue, about what we should do about Pete, his political experiments, the trouble at school. I needed to talk to him about the sightings, and yes, the correspondence with the detective, give it all some air, let go of secrecy. But perhaps I'd do it tomorrow instead. For tonight, it was fine, I decided, just to be with him and with our two best creations. Beloved humans, chairs creaking under their weight, locked down by gravity, grounded in space and time. Of course, yes, they're the ghosts of tomorrow. They will be supplanted by newer and older versions of themselves. But at this moment they are just exactly and only here, and they are my real and my now.

ABBY, MARCH 26, 2015

Seven days pass, with antifa videos tromping through my late nights, and during the day, I tried to focus on the particulars—packing Benjamin's favorite cream cheese and jelly sandwiches in his lunch, fetching dry cleaning for Dennis, showing up for work on time and paying attention at meetings. I tried to respond coolly to all communications from the detective. Any way you looked at it, I told myself, it was unwise.

I had some success in corralling my errant mind. But I failed to banish her. She has quit her job. Her life stretches before her. Staring out the window during one of those meetings to which I've pledged my full attention, I longed to see her again. Glimpse her, if just for a final time. Certainly, this odd happenstance would end soon. It wasn't going to last. How could it? And I recalled one of her most frequent haunts.

And on this particular Thursday evening, she is there, haunting it. The Corner Bistro, a place for generations of young strivers, offering cheap burgers and beers and a crushed, cozy proximity with one's tribe. Sitting on a stool wedged between the battered wood bar and the front window. The day's last light outlines her profile in gold. The Stones are playing: I am just living to be lying by your side. She is sketching in a notebook. I take a stool next to her. She glances up at me, then turns to the paper again. She is drawing a hand. A male hand. When I see it, I feel my own hands turn to ice.

I know that hand, I say.

She shrugs. Could be anyone's.

No. That is someone's, I say.

She nods slightly and breaks into a small smile. And are you in love?

I have love in my life.

Her pencil, moving in the white space.

And are you painting? she says.

I'm trying.

You need to, she says. She meets my gaze at last. Because to create beauty and meaning, to make something that has never existed before . . . I'm sure that is worth more than anything.

The Stones have stopped and Coltrane scolds us with his horn.

It seems like people lose that so easily. I don't want you to lose it. Her voice quavers.

He's not good for you, I say. Maybe trying to send the conversation in a different direction.

She turns the page in her sketchbook, lips curving into another small smile. He's my poison of choice. Best drug ever.

The drugs are where the trouble begins, I say. Why not save yourself the heartache. I hate to feel the maternal impulse bleeding in here, but I do. I hear it in these blurted words. I feel it in my gut as I recall searching under the bed for a lost earring, a silver hoop, searching for it in dim dawn light and finding a shoebox of paraphernalia instead. Smoke-darkened glass, a lighter, bits of foil and paper and two glinting needles rolling around the bottom. I didn't know the specifics—I was afraid to ask. I put it out of my mind and focused instead on the intoxications he supplied to me, the matchless high of his regard.

The way things happened is how it must be, I remind myself. To bring me here. The course is set. The path is determined.

I couldn't possibly live without him, she says, as if she's just seen my thoughts on a passing billboard. She stands and extracts a wallet from her bag, drops a few dollars onto the table.

My treat, I say, pushing the bills toward her.

She shrugs and pockets the money, rips her sketch from her notebook and leaves it on the table. You seem stuck, she says. I think you need to make a change. Get your head straight. Maybe call this person. I used to see her, but I'm done.

She slings her bag over her shoulder. You need to get your head straight, she says.

She leaves, but there is the paper on the bar. The hands of Eli. On the flip side, she has written a name and a number.

SESSION NOTES

No-show, again. Apparent termination without notice.

Dr. Tristane Kazemy, MARCH 30, 2016

The scans, again. The brain looked clean, normal. But one must bear in mind that meningioma can remain undetectable for years. A node, a tiny cyst or calcification, tucked discreetly in a sulcus, pressing against an important structure, can disrupt. The tiny hidden pea, she sometimes thought of it, recalling the illustration, the lovely maiden in red braids prone atop the tower of mattresses, in Maman's tattered translation of Hans Christian Andersen, bought almost sixty years ago in a bookstall in Tabriz.

No one could see the pea. Yet its presence deprived the princess of happiness.

She spent time each week simply gazing, in between teaching, diagnostic rounds, departmental meetings. The MRIs, the CATs, the 3D angiography. Finally, she showed the scans to Buccardi. He'd peered at them briefly and said they appeared clean. "But perhaps show them to Laurin," he said. "You know he has the eye. Besides, how much longer can you keep swiping the screen every time he walks by?" He winked. "Sooner or later, he will want to mix in."

"I just want to fully inhabit this first."

Buccardi nodded. "I understand, Tristane. This is your get."

She knew that Buccardi and Laurin, her superiors, had conferred about how she'd been spending her hours. She was, it was true, stealing the lab's time for this off-the-record situation. And how did she come by this case, and who was paying for this time she spent? She saw them, spooning sugar into their petite cups, the sidelong glances as she approached. Laurin was proud of the lab's new espresso machine. She made it clear that she would stay loyal to her Earl Grey.

4/4/4/4

ABBY, APRIL 6, 2015

Spring came wafting into town one night while we were all asleep. Trees bristled with buds one morning, and then the next, it seemed, were blossoming with slutty abandon. Rushing to work and home again, I tried to catch their fragrance as I dashed by.

This evening, I detoured to walk through the gardens in front of Rockefeller Center. All the years I've lived in New York, I have never missed seeing the tulips in bloom there. Flowers are a mundane obsession for an artist. But they lure me.

Above the buildings, the sun's last rays strobed on fast-moving clouds. People leaned over the rows of red and yellow and white blooms, bowing and waving as the tulips did the same.

I found a bench, sat next to my big work-stuffed bag. I unzipped my boot slightly and rubbed my cramped calf. Would I be able to get a seat on the subway home? Red frilled tulips shivered. My gaze wandered over them then came to rest on a couple leaning on the rail surrounding the flower beds. The woman, the unruly honey-hued hair.

The unmistakable pointy chin above the fake fur collar of her coat. The man faces away—but of course, I know who it is. She leans against him, and her hand is under his scuffed suede jacket, going up and down his back. I can see it moving under the fabric, a buried rhythm, like the bass line of a complex piece of music.

The couple turns and stares up at the buildings, seeming to discuss something they see up there. Behind them, a row of white tulips flicker in the breeze, foam on a fast-falling stream.

She looks so happy. I have forgotten the feeling that inspired that look. Deep, fresh infatuation. Straight from the wrapper, fresh from the source. Her smile astounds me. How long has it been since I smiled that way, so that my soul haloed around me, practically visible?

Then, though it is hard, so searingly hard, my eyes focus on him. So it is not scary enough that I should be haunted by myself. Now him too.

But I want to look. I want to see. My eyes, my hardworking-mom-and-wife eyes, feast on the boy in a way that, in a more evolved part of my brain, horrifies. Because this kid is what—twenty-three or -four?

But I look at him, half a head taller than her, long dark lashes, dark brows, straight brown hair flipping over his ears, strong cheekbones, strong nose, something watchful, hopeful, and slightly blurred in that face, a face out of a Manet painting, something classical and eternal about it. I gaze at him, and the buried river overflows its banks. I allow myself to remember, bits of him rising up through my mind like bones resurfacing in the flood, his clouded smile, the camera in a beat-up leather sheath, the apartment outfitted with a wooden wire-spool table and folding patio chairs and a shelf filled with pulpy old noir novels and philosophy books. My oddest Christmas ever, spent in the drafty, sprawling East Village apartment of his parents and his childhood, overlooking a snow-swept Tompkins Square, sitting around a spread of deli containers with his father, the alcoholic high school history teacher, and his mother, a masseuse who kept an array of electric sex toys on the kitchen counter next to the coffee maker. She threw tarot for us and told me my fate was bound up with her son's, you will draw your last breaths together, she said.

When I met him, he was working two jobs, as a waiter at a Marriott in Midtown and doing paste-up at a disreputable classifieds newspaper. The night we met, he told me he'd been carrying three plates of cream cake across the ballroom when Rabbi Meir Kahane was shot a few feet in front of him. He kept a bloodied polyester napkin tucked in a plastic bag in his closet. He showed it to me the third time I slept over. After we'd been fucking for around a month, he admitted that he'd been dabbling in various street drugs, had been for years, but always under control, he said, and he never shared needles, and he was in the process of kicking. He had plans, he said. Witnessing that assassination had awakened a desire in him, a thirst to be close to bloodshed and action, and to photograph it. He had that old camera, inherited from his Ukrainian grandfather, a Red Army photographer who used it to document the Battle of the Dnieper. He was aiming to become a Robert Capa. He would venture to war-torn places. And you too, he said, to be an artist you have to see everything, he said. In the meantime, he'd bought a police scanner and snapped photos around the city, pedestrian deaths, murder scenes, occasionally selling a shot to one of the tabloids. He used the darkroom at his paste-up job and earned extra cash for film by picking up an occasional bartending shift. Down at the bar where we first met.

No. I won't let myself go to that particular memory now. I stop myself. I tear my gaze away, struggle to rezip my boot. But he is holding her now, he leans back against a concrete planter. Now he's pulling her to him, one leg between hers as they stand in this clench, and his hand is in her hair. I am impaled by the sight. The pronounced veins on the back of his hands. The twisted rope brace-let around his wrist. His hair sliding over her face as they kiss. And the way her body presses into his.

I just need to run. I grab my bag and eject myself from the bench, rushing past them without looking, my boots clicking away beneath me. Toes too narrow, heels too high.

And then I stop. I turn. The girl and the boy still stand in their embrace, more fervent now than before. I don't know what to do next. And then I do. I walk up to face them. Excuse me, I say. Their heads jerk up.

I don't understand why this is happening, I say.

You again, she says.

I turned to him. And you too.

A ring of paler blue around the irises. I'd forgotten.

You don't understand, I say. I am *seeing* myself here. The timbre in my voice is rising, though I'm trying to hold myself together.

She clutches his arm. Let's go, she says.

I'm ready when you are, he says. He stares at me, distressed.

I stare back. It is too much, seeing him here, standing in front of me again, after everything.

After the break. Because now, out of the murk, the void in my brain that swallowed our history, his and mine, comes a thought:

Eli Hammond no longer exists.

And then an image: his body, far below me, under the settling storm of dust.

Lying dead, in the garden, flung down in all his beauty.

The next thing I remember, I was five stops past home on the F train. My entire psyche was flooded with panic. No, more than that. With panic and terror. My head pounding with it, pulsating even—I felt as if my skull were expanding and contracting rapidly under its thin cover of skin and hair. It must be noticeable, must be ballooning in and out like the throat of toads I used to see, back in Massachusetts, in the damp summer evenings when they'd hop up from the little brook at the edge of the lawn and hunt bugs under the porch lights.

No one around me seemed to notice my head. The subway car was crowded, but they were all lost in their own lives. When the doors opened, I stood, steadied myself, crossed the platform, and caught a train the other way, toward home.

ABBY, APRIL 9, 2015

Mariah Glücksburg lives across from the Armory on Sixty-Seventh Street, in a carriage house with a rooftop studio enclosed in glass and a garage on the ground floor, in which she kept a gleaming black SUV and a vintage Vanagon that she used for summer painting excursions all around the country, sometimes driving herself all the way to the tip of the Yukon to find a certain yellow in the sky.

By the elevator at SVA, she'd punched in my cell number, and this morning, my phone flashed her address and an invitation for cocktails. Dennis wasn't included. "Tell her I say hello," he texted as I left my office to head uptown, and somehow I read the text as dismayed.

The night was cool, the house was warm. She showed me into a large lofty-ceilinged space, kitchen, living room with a black marble fireplace, miles of low white-suede sofas and immense windows opening onto an enclosed garden. "I'm stripping down," she said, taking off her blouse, down to a simple navy camisole underneath.

Her arms were alabaster, honed. "Indoor heat is so drying to your skin," she said, scooping ice into two glasses, then pouring whiskey over the rocks. "Women our age, they get so avid, so kind of tightened up. But you, Abby. You seem different. You've held up well."

She set the glass in front of me, dark gold liquid in sweating cut crystal. Heirloom crystal, I supposed, from the fallen Greek royals. A life-sized painted portrait hung over the mantel, a heavy-browed military man with medals and ribbons on a sash, a tiny poodle on his arm, a revolver on a columned pedestal. Next to that was a small portrait of a teenage girl in a pink frock. It could have been Mariah, with the dark upswept curls and the cheekbones. She followed my gaze.

"Both were painted by the studio assistant of John Singer Sargent, when the artist was a very old man in Vevey," she said. "Not bad. That's great-great-grandpop, and the little one is my great-aunt Thea." She frowned. "She was known for sleeping with major Nazis." She swirled her glass and flopped onto the sofa across from me, crossing her ankles on the vast coffee table, atop a stack of art books. "I prefer baseball players," she said with a smile. "And you?"

"Well . . . Dennis and I are still together."

"Ah," she nodded. "That stuck." I saw some subliminal flicker in her eyes. Maybe something had happened, then, between those two. I had never been certain. I chose not to say anything at this particular moment. Choosing to tuck that information away.

She sipped deeply, continuing to eye me. "You always gave off sort of a damaged-beauty vibe, a bit of a tragic heroine, when I'd see you around," she said. "Back then."

I laughed. "Hardly. I did arrive in a muddle, I guess. I had a rough time in this city, just before I came up to Providence."

Could I tell Mariah about the young man who somehow died in the garden then rose again at Rock Center? About the year of Eli, just before I met her? No, I most definitely could not. "I wouldn't be that age again for anything in the world," I said.

"Agreed," said Mariah. "I was a fucked-up little thing."

"You?" I laughed. "You were a blazing inferno."

She invited me then up to her studio, a soaring space with clerestory windows on three sides, through which one could see the swanky neighboring apartment buildings bowing over, almost in supplication to her work. The walls were covered with works in progress, mostly in shades of ivory, cream, white, layered and meticulous with brushwork that appeared tiled or woven, and floor-to-ceiling flat shelves were filled with paintings, which she listlessly pulled out, here and there, to show me. She had a period of stripes, a period of swoops, a period of circles. I'd seen many of these works before, in the *Times*, in *ARTnews*, when I'd been able to bring myself to look at *ARTnews*.

Then she turned to me. "And you're back at it. I'd love to see your new work," she said.

"Oh, not any time soon," I said. "I'm really not ready."

"Doll, you were born ready," she said. She threw herself down on a lushly cushioned chaise and gazed at me. "You were always a better painter than me."

I drained my sweating glass and said nothing.

"You knew that, right?" she said. "If you didn't, Abby, you were the only one."

ABBY, APRIL 14, 2015

What it feels like: my heart is a box with rusty hinges. Some change is forcing it to open, millimeter by recalcitrant millimeter. The hinges scream, painfully.

I don't know enough about you, he texted.

What do you want to know?

What were you like as a girl, where'd you go to school. How come your kid is a commie.

Pete is not a communist.

Ha, I know. But come on, give me some history on Abigail Willard. I want to know more.

I'm sitting in my cubicle. I would like to flee my home, my family, my life, to paint, to wander, to experience this new man. I allow myself to imagine us tangled in warm, well-worn sheets, letting the city run outside, allowing the morning to drift into afternoon.

Just as she gets to do.

How much more? I text.

April 16, 2016

From: J.Leverett@deepxmail.com
To: GarrettShuttlesworth@physics.humboldtstate.edu

I can free up funds for data modeling. Not that I have a clue what that is. But for this case, whatever it takes. I officially apologize for calling you geekwad the whole time we roomed together freshman year. You read poetry, you talked about antimatter and entropy. I was a dumb shit.

ABBY, APRIL 19, 2015

Standing at my easel, I feel like an open bucket, a rain barrel. I like to imagine the top of my head open, and the colors pouring in from some higher plane, some great source. Not God, not the sky. Instead, it's the bright storm of energy that clangs and sloshes over and around every existing thing, energy and light and the juice that powers us. In my best moments, I can almost feel it burgeoning, primed to release its bounty, to make life richer, and deepen into art.

The trick though is remembering to stay open to it. Our heads close off, in this twenty-first-century world. Every time you peer into a screen, direct your eyes there, the roof on your head slides shut. When you feel downtrodden, your whole being slides downward, and the lid closes. When stressed, anxious, angry, energy is pulled down, the door closes.

And who among us, the working stiffs, the frazzled parents, isn't always contending with at least one or two of these down-dragging states, at almost all times?

The better painter, Mariah said.

If this were true . . . could it be true? Bremer, warning that I needed to honor my gift, to safeguard it. Why hadn't I.

I had done instead what adults everywhere on the planet strove to do, dedicated themselves to securing a safe perch in a hostile world, and there was no dishonor in it.

But painting was my language, and I had fallen quiet all these years. That's what Eli had said, he said, you don't talk as much as some but you spill your feelings here, in this work. I can still feel his hand touching the surface of my painting, coming away wet, and how it made me so excited to see my oils on his fingers, though he'd marred the work, I didn't care, I took his hand and pressed it to my black T-shirt and wore his mark, in pale blue and violet, for the rest of the year.

I knew now. I remembered. Eli didn't break my heart by leaving. He broke it by dying. I tried to make sense of this notion, which shattered—all over again—the underpinnings of my present life. I failed to make sense of it.

And it was all so long ago.

My memory of it was just gone.

Like he was gone. Long gone.

How could it be?

On this Sunday April morning I stood at my easel. I tried to will the roof open. The household was warmed by the sleepy breathing of my family, a mellow early sunlight was seeping into the rooms, and Dennis was spread out in the bed behind me, dreaming with a faint frown. I picked up the palette, yellow into gold, inviting something soft, something like buttery milk. I began to lay down a ground.

ABBY, APRIL 20, 2015

An Evening on the Riviera arrived in spitting rain. The rain frizzed blow-outs, blurred mascara, disheveled the well-groomed. Joanie Werner stood under the arch at the top of the school's front steps, her curls gone wild, the silver sequins on her tunic dress scattering the light from the streetlamps. She waved at us.

"My artists!" she cried. "Wait till you see! Your work looks museum-worthy in there." She threw an arm around Dennis and kissed his cheek. He looked at me, baffled—he'd never met her before. Then she kissed me, rum on her breath.

She turned from us and gazed down the rainswept block. "Have you seen Stan the Weatherman? He's calling our live auction. I'm his designated handler and he's twenty minutes late."

We left her to her vigil and hung our wet coats up on the rack by the door to the gym. Dennis looked dourly handsome in a dark blazer and black jeans. I had nixed the bolo tie.

"You don't like me to have flair," he'd complained.

"Not in your personal dress, no."

He'd flung the bolo tie and one of its pronged longhorns left a minor gouge in the wall. We'd been arguing all day over one thing or another—who had vacuumed last and when, why our gas bill was so high, and who had forgotten to take Benjamin to the dentist. The nerves, I had to assume. Nerves about the auction—because it was the first time either of us had shown a work in public in years.

Cardboard palm trees and signs read NICE and SAINT-TROPEZ and CANNES; the bartender wore a striped T-shirt and a jaunty yachting cap. We both ordered vodka and tonic and took long first sips.

A man I recognized vaguely as the dad of one of Pete's classmates approached and handed us each a numbered paddle. "For the silent auction," he said. "Spend freely and often!"

"Actually, don't," Dennis whispered as we moved away.

He was shaky, more shaky than ever, about his job. He had heard from his boss's assistant that expense accounts were being reviewed.

Gift cards from local boutiques, coupons for hot stone massage and waxing. Dennis wandered off to check out a pair of mountain bikes parked in a corner. I idly browsed the jewelry table, arrayed with pendulous necklaces made by some of the craftier moms. A hand-knit scarf, seed-stitched, in peacock blue. I made a twenty-five-dollar bid on that, to get my number on something, just to be able to say I made an effort to shell out.

Then. My painting—the black bird, on an easel in the corner.

And next to it, Dennis's steel sculpture from the coat closet, a stack of flat, raw-edged circles, four feet high, complex and surprising from many angles. It had been in the closet since Pete was about five and had almost pulled it over on top of himself.

No one was around, so I glanced at the sheets of paper, laid out on a nearby table, where prospective buyers were meant to scribble their bids. The uninterrupted whiteness was blinding, blizzard-esque, arctic. No one had bid for the black painting, and no one had bid on the circles.

Nearby, on a small easel, sat the only other artwork for sale. A little acrylic of a sailboat. It had at least fifteen bids, the highest $2,350.

I picked up the pencil laid atop the bidding sheet for *Circles in Repose*—that was what the closeted sculpture was called. It had earned Dennis the most prestigious grad-student award at RISD, the Huntington Prize, granting him a cushy job teaching under-graduate studio art and a stipend of ten thousand dollars. He'd won it at the end of our first year in Providence, right around the time we'd realized we might be in love. It had seemed a door opening to a far-flung vista of happy years, a winding ribbon of road that led to fulfilled expectations.

I glanced over at the bar, where I'd last spotted Dennis. He was nowhere in sight. I wrote down my paddle number, along with a bid: $2,400. Just to get the ball rolling. Just to give it some momentum.

Then I hit the bar myself, bought another vodka and tonic. I greeted a few people I knew, asked about their kids and their jobs and so on. I made another circuit of the gym, but couldn't see Dennis anywhere. Finally, I headed out toward the coatrack and restrooms, and then I saw him standing in a back hall, where the door stood open to a loading dock. A dad with a long gray ponytail passed him a joint. It was the first time I'd seen him smoke in years.

"This is Larry," he said. "Kind enough to share his medication."

Larry saluted me with a finger. "To this type of event, I always bring a little something. Keeps me calm." He offered the joint to me with a little bow.

I smiled and shook my head. "It makes me paranoid."

"She used to love it," Dennis said to Larry with a sigh.

"Didn't they all," Larry said. He took a long drag.

The weatherman's voice boomed down the hall. The live auction had begun. The three of us watched the rain and listened to people spend their money—three thousand here, sixteen hundred there. A membership to a golf club on Long Island. A trip to Nova Scotia. Lunches with famous authors and backstage tours of Broadway shows.

Finally it was time to go. We bid Larry goodbye and Dennis helped me on with my coat.

Joanie Werner was huddled with some of the other parents of the auction committee, tabulating bids from the silent portion of the event. She looked up as we walked past. "Your painting sold for twenty-one hundred bucks!" she said. "And your sculpture, Dennis, sold at twenty-four hundred! So exciting!"

A genial dad seated at the next table asked for our bidding paddles to be returned and compared their numbers against the bidding sheets. "OK . . . my man, so looks like you won a painting. *Untitled* by Abigail Willard," he said to Dennis. "And let's check your number, madam . . . well, hey, you won a sculpture. *Circle in Repose*." He smiled up at us. "Congratulations! That's a nice haul. So will you folks be paying by cash or check this evening?"

ABBY, APRIL 23, 2015

Three days have passed. Time enough for us, Dennis and me, to process the idea that we paid almost five thousand dollars for our own work. The black bird went back on its nail, and I insisted his tilted circles should find a spot in a corner of the living room, but then yesterday, Benjamin knocked it over, leaving a splintery white gouge in the wood floor and severely bruising his big toe. It was stashed in the hallway closet again. And we have settled upon the idea, Dennis and I, that perhaps our work was too good for its setting, there among the paper palm fronds and poker chips of the ersatz Riviera.

Then today, Pete was crying, in the backyard, sitting wedged in a child-sized plastic chair, one of a pair we'd bought so many years ago, now muzzy with city grime on their backs and undersides. His long legs stretched into a blackened plastic kiddie pool, cracked on the bottom, bright colors and cartoony bunny faces managing to be both besmirched with black moldy stuff and faded by the sun.

One time he pooped in that pool, sitting as a little naked fat baby in the sunshine. He smiled, he pooped. I scooped the little floating biscuits out with a cup.

When angry, anxious, despairing, Pete loses his speech again. I can almost see it bleeding out of him in these moments, as blood drains from a frightened face.

When it happens, Dennis will try to touch Pete. Approach him, try to envelop him in a bear hug, or, if our boy won't allow that, then simply a hand on his arm, his back, his burst of dark hair. Breathe, he'll say, just breathe. It's OK, it's all going to be OK.

And this always, when I see it, ignites even more turmoil in my brain, in my chest, because I both believe and do not believe it's going to be okay. I love and hate my husband for his reassurances, for his demeanor of steadiness. It feels to me like the bedrock of our family's life, and its fault line, the shiftiest quake zone in the most volcanic region on earth. This because, so often, I simply don't buy it—the comforting vision he's selling—and I know that often he doesn't either.

And how do I react, when Pete becomes stymied and speech-strangled? I feel the hot steel cord tightening around me, the cord that is still umbilical, the searing live wire. I become his cracked mirror, refracting his despair, mixing it with my fear for him and my love.

I try not to show him my distress. I try to pull myself together and be a grown-up, of course.

What do you want to tell me, my darling? How is it we have so many secrets from each other? Things you don't tell me, and I have things I don't tell you. I used to deal daily with your poop and we had no secrets, no space between us.

I took his hand into mine. A warm and alive object that had once rested in my hand so often, it seemed an extension of my body. My son, do you remember walking around the city hand in hand, day after day, along shop aisles and subway platforms, across every street crossing, every square of every sidewalk, miles and miles hand in hand?

He pulled it away. He squeezed his eyes closed and rubbed them, taking a long shaky breath. Reddened splotches down the sides of his nose, a few small angry pimples on his chin. He gave his head a little shake, as if to toss the tears away.

I didn't want him to catch me watching him, so I stared down at his feet. His sneaker still bore that legend: ANTIFA RAGE

BRIGADE. And now another, I hadn't noticed: DAX VIVE. This, I recalled, was one of the scribblings in the bathroom at school, per Vong.

Maybe this would help him find his words again, to talk about this. As he settled a bit, I leaned over and ran my finger over the inked white canvas. "Who is Dax?"

"Some kid killed by fascists, ten years ago. In Italy. Dax Cesare. He's famous there."

"Why this concern about fascists? Is that from your AP Modern Euro class?"

He snorted. "*No.*" He looked at me directly, rims of his eyes still a bit swollen and pinky-red. "This is a coming storm. You just don't want to see it. You want to bury yourself in your cozy life."

I let the words sink in. But I do feel danger, every minute, I wanted to say. My cozy life is closer to calamity than you would ever dream, my dear one.

You don't say that to your struggling child.

"Believe it or not," I said, "I still have ambitions and desires. Things I want to create. Even moms have dreams."

His lips bent into a smirk, but I could see him considering this, a little furrow in his forehead.

"It becomes hard to hold on to it," I said.

"A giant part of the problem is late-stage capitalism," he said.

At least he has found a passion. "So how did you truly get into this, sweetheart," I said gently. "Was it that Dmitri?"

"No. No. No. It was not that Dmitri." He stood abruptly. He paced a bit, his jaw muscles clenching. He made some soft swallowing sounds, as he sometimes did when his tongue got locked. Then he turned to me. "Open your eyes, Ma. This is me. Now. This is who I am now. It's real. It's happening. Really real and really happening." He turned and stalked into the house.

ABBY, APRIL 24, 2015

Really real and really happening.

In the hotel room in the late afternoon, I heard sirens through the thick curtains. They grew louder as I sat in the desk chair, smoothing my hair in the mirror there. Allowing myself to study the reflection. Allowing myself to rest for a bit with what I saw. A seasoned woman in a black sweater, about to fuck someone new for the first time in twenty-two years. Feeling the enormity of it, and at the same time thinking this does not matter. This woman, she is a temporary assembly of atoms, here so short a time, she belongs to no one and nothing.

Why did I text him? A slow day at the office, a bad morning at home. Those weren't the reasons, of course. There were no reasons.

I sat resting my palms on the cool of the glass-topped desk. The wailing vehicles passed beneath the window and then sounded farther and farther off. As they traveled away, I let them tow everything with them but the things in this room.

Then he knocked on the door and it began in the little entry, my back pressed up against the light switches.

He wrapped one arm around my waist, his hand found a space where my sweater rose up, his hand found the skin over my hip, his mouth was on mine. I ran my fingertips over his face, soft and rough, and his ruthlessly trimmed hair, a bit bristly, nothing shaggy or beachy about him, this man seemed incredibly tart and clean. I breathed him in deeply, kissing his neck, lime and ice and metal.

He stepped back then, picked up my hand and kissed it with a smile. "Not to rush," he said.

I sat down on the bed and bent to slip off my shoes. "Good to see you, again, Detective," I said. I felt bravado. Whether it was false or not, I just decided to go with it.

"Glad you got in touch," he said. His teeth were even and pearly and small. He unbuttoned his shirt, approaching, until sleek cinnamon-hued skin filled my field of vision, and though I felt doubt and fear tickling at the fringe of my consciousness, I willed myself to stay in the moment, brushed my hands down over all his exhilarating strangeness and let all thinking cease as I lay back, my grip asking him to follow me down, falling and falling and falling.

He was still asleep, when I left him there, five in the evening, for the subway home.

Crossing the lobby it struck me again: how far off center I'd strayed. How very askew. Not only doing what I'd just done, but choosing this hotel in which to do it. The Marriott on Lexington and Forty-Ninth. The gunshots, the rabbi's blood pooling on the ballroom parquet, I remembered now how Eli looked when he told me about it, gesturing with those wiry restless arms, his eyes glittering.

Back then, I didn't understand its significance. I'm not sure Eli did either. He was just excited by his proximity to the crime.

But historians who analyze such things now say that Meir Kahane's killing planted the seed of hate that reached full fiery flower on September 11, 2001.

By 2001, Eli had been gone almost ten years.

And now, as I hurried across the hotel lobby, a bit breathless, mouth and heart and pussy a bit swelled up and a bit raw, head lowered though it was unlikely I'd run into anyone I knew, I thought, even the year 2001 was spiraling away into distant history.

I stepped out of the hotel into a downpour. Across Forty-Ninth Street, I thought I saw a girl in a raspberry-colored coat, lingering, loitering, as if waiting for somebody, an umbrella hiding her face.

ABBY, APRIL 27, 2015

A phone buzzes differently when the news is very bad.

"Pete has confessed," said Headmistress Vong. "And there is a detective waiting to see you."

It wasn't who I feared it would be. Instead, a round-shouldered and wide man in a beige windbreaker was standing next to Pete when I entered Elizabeth Vong's office. He introduced himself as Lieutenant German Pizziali. He had crossed black eyes. Dennis rushed in right after me, disheveled, face a bit sweaty after running from the subway, and he hurried to Pete and took his hands and said, "Are you OK, sweetie." Our boy looked scared out of his wits.

"Confessed to what? Is this a criminal proceeding, has he had legal representation?" Dennis demanded. I felt a wave of immense gratitude for him.

"Yes," I chimed in. "What kind of due process do you have here? And anyhow what's the charge?"

"Don't say another word," Dennis said to Pete, placing his hand on our boy's head.

"The trash can incident. The investigation has finally been completed," announced Vong, enthroned behind her desk.

"We had a backlog, only two guys on staff, our juvenile-crimes lady is out on baby leave," explained Pizziali.

"Pigeons. Decapitated," said the headmistress.

"Pigeons?" I looked at Pete, who avoided my gaze.

"Headless," the detective said, "pigeons without heads."

"Is it illegal to decapitate pigeons in this city?" Dennis demanded.

"Pigeons are conscious beings," said Vong.

Pizziali shrugged. "Flying rats, I always say."

"And we believe it is connected to the bathroom graffiti. Because there was a bit in the bathroom . . ." Vong looked down at the open file, scanning. "Off with their heads."

ABBY, APRIL 28, 2015

I am sorry to hear about this latest with Pete. But I will reach out to Pizziali, I know the guy. Leave it in my hands. I was glad to hear from you, even if the circumstances are not the best. I wanted to get in touch, but you said not to, so I've been waiting. Thinking of you, probably too much.

I'm reading this text, past midnight, when the doorbell rings.

Beside me, Dennis doesn't stir.

A knock now, insistent.

I peek through the window alongside the door. A figure, dark against the dark, glint of metallic shoes.

Fresh from clubbing, perhaps.

My heart clenches, stops, I feel a wooze coming on. Her? Here?

When I open the door, we stare at each other. Hard to say who looks more frightened.

Have you gotten your head straight? she says.

I am dumbstruck to see her, to realize that she has found me, instead of the other way around.

No, she says. I can see that you haven't.

And then, at once, a thought comes to me: bundle her in your arms, bring her inside, show her—show yourself?—your life. The good in it. Despite the recent turbulence.

I swing the door wide and gesture her forward.

She raises her brows in surprise, but steps inside.

I usher her along the hallway, into the kitchen, where we will be farther away from the sleepers upstairs. She is absorbing the house, in all its cluttered corners, keys and mail on a table, the sofa strewn with rumpled pillows, man-sized shoes left with their tongues lolling on the rug. She turns slowly around, examining every inch, it seems, with unblinking eyes.

Then she whispers, who is that?

I whip my head around. A slow-moving shape turns the corner at the foot of the stairs. One of the boys, Benjamin, maybe? Wandering sleepily for a glass of milk, as he has been known to do, in the middle of the night.

In a bit of a panic, I lunge for the basement door, urge her down the stairs. Thankfully, she moves fast, gripping the wobbly banister and feeling her way. I follow, shutting the door softly behind us. As I reach the foot of the stairs, I can hear the fridge opening now, a cabinet, a glass being set down on the countertop.

A tiny bit of light leaks into the gloom from a back casement window, and my eyes adjust. She is staring at the shelves of my wrapped paintings. She reaches out and runs her hand over one rectangular spine. Fine grit slides down the paper to the cement floor. She looks at me. Abigail, she whispers.

I say nothing.

Is this your work?

I say nothing. She continues to brush dust from the paper-covered flats. It is your work, she says. Do I see a glaze of tears on her face, or is it in my eyes? Above us, I hear the footsteps of my son, back along the hallway, up the stairs.

You need to go now, I say.

The street is deserted, the night sky moonless and cloudless, just a few pinprick stars mutely watching. I am appalled at myself for inviting her in, I will her to disappear. She trips over our buckled front walk, steadies herself. Then she turns to face me, to face the house. She looks up at the roofline, down to the low stoop, scanning the whole of our little domicile. She looks at me.

Burn it down, she says.

She turns and takes a few steps into the darkness and then she vanishes. I sink to the hallway floor. I wake at five in the morning, still lying there.

Dr. Tristane Kazemy, APRIL 30, 2016

This past weekend, she'd bored a date, an investment analyst named Samir, with her musings about the meningioma, about how she couldn't see it but perhaps she could almost sense its presence, lurking in those images.

"Or maybe there's just nothing there," he said. He would rather discuss the poire pochée or the lavender sorbet that they were sharing in alternating spoonfuls.

She couldn't talk anymore about food. Food was the only thing anyone in Montreal wanted to talk about anymore.

Samir turned out to be a skilled kisser, able to activate a current, and she would have liked to take him to bed. It had been a while. But the North American Neurological Association conference was in session. Her superiors had flown off to the designated resort in San Diego, and they had not invited her along this time. They tried to frame her being left behind as some kind of advancement—she would "direct coverage of the lab." "This could be a kind of test flight," Laurin had said with a smile in the weekly floor meeting, "for our doctoresse."

No matter, she thought. Let them hit golf balls and sun themselves. She had a plan. She agreed only to meet Samir now and then for a sip of red wine at Bar le Pins, after which she would return to the much more compelling brain of Abigail Willard in the lab.

5/5/5/5

ABBY, MAY 1, 2015

In midair, there is no reversing a fall.

"I will ask you again. What's your complaint," Dr. Singh said, rapping his stylus impatiently on the tablet device balanced on his knee.

How long had he been sitting there on his little wheeled stool? I hadn't noticed him enter the examination room. "Yes—sorry. Fainting, headaches. Occasional vomiting. Dizziness. My neck is knotted, my shoulders feel achy."

Hallucinations. Adultery. I didn't say those out loud.

But at least I was here, docilely paper-gowned and barefoot, in the bustling Flatbush Avenue office of Dr. Avi Singh, our family practitioner. He had squeezed me in, when I'd finally called after waking in our front hall. I'd explained the symptoms that had plagued me since—yes, longer than I realized—since early this year, January perhaps. I should've seen him months ago but procrastinating on self-care is the bad habit of the busy working mom. Finally, the goateed MD checked me up and down, backward and forward, and could find nothing wrong. He peered again and again into my eyes with his little flashlight. He stood frowning at me for a long while, then at last he said, "I'll order a CT scan. Strictly precautionary. I predict it will be clean. And I also predict that the symptoms will resolve if you reduce your stress. You are under significant stress, correct?" He glared at me. Yes, I admitted, I was under significant stress.

He nodded, satisfied. "All the mommies are under a lot of stress." He jotted on a notepad, tore the page off, and handed it to me. "For your neck and shoulder pain, stretching and massage. This spa down the block does a very good shiatsu."

Flatbush seemed unusually crowded. Kids just released from school, the beginnings of the commuter rush. On the packed sidewalk, I had several narrow misses with skateboarders. One boarder whizzed by with a flag flapping from a pole, red and black and with a logo I couldn't quite make out. As I climbed the slope toward Grand Army Plaza, I heard shouting, chanting. A firecracker popping. A group of teenagers shoved past me, headed toward the noise.

As soon as I stepped into the Singh-endorsed spa, the hubbub was replaced by plinking harp music, babbling from a little electric fountain in a ceramic pot, the thick drowsy smell of many houseplants. "Welcome—walk-in?" said a sylph-like woman, appearing from behind a beaded curtain, winding long red hair into a knob atop her head. She took my bag and coat, poured a cup of green tea from an ornate urn, advised me on a thirty-minute deep-tissue therapy. "I'll go tell Frida you're here, she's one of our most beloved practitioners."

I returned to the street window, gazing out as I sipped my tea. Feeling a bit glum. Spotting a few more black-clad demonstrators, mixed in among the commuters and shoppers. One held a handwritten sign overhead: INTERNATIONAL WORKERS' DAY. Then another: SMASH FASCISM.

I recognized that block printing—the same flared, loopy letters had appeared on the many handwritten cards Pete had given me over the years.

And yes, there at the bottom of the waving signpost was my boy, in the pack, a slouchy beanie pulled over his brow and a red bandanna wrapping his skim-milk face, but unmistakably my boy, next to a petite girl. The snaking pink hair, the cheekbones of burnished mahogany—I recognized her from the coffee shop, I'd met her a few months ago. Twiz, her name was? They were chanting in a group, like a team readying to take the field. The sound of their shouting was far away from this hushed sanctum, I couldn't make out the words, but Pete raised his fist, and then he turned, and over the head of the dreadlocked girl, exchanged fist bumps with another kid. Yes, that was indeed Dmitri Petimezas.

They spurted into the center of the wide vehicle-choked avenue. Blocking rush-hour traffic? My Pete, planted before the chrome grille of an eighteen-wheel truck. He looked so puny, the truck reared up above him, a behemoth of steel, belching smoke. I was awash with terror, but also, deeper down, a subcurrent of awe. Should I rush out and grab him?

The truck's horn bellowed. The marchers raised their fists higher and pumped their signs. Just then the truck's cab door flew open, and then the driver burst out, a hulking man barreling toward the demonstrators, cheeks red and mouth twisted in fury, his arms swinging.

Warm lemon-infused green tea, a douse right in the face, was enough to stun the man, make him stumble a few steps backward, so that small Twiz and I could push him down to the ground. He was unhurt but looked very confused. I heard roars of approval, more demonstrators clustered around him. I backed away and found myself eye to eye with my son. "Mom?" he said, but I could hardly hear him. The commotion roared on around us.

I threw my arms around him and whispered in his ear. "Death to complacency," I said. "And don't be late for dinner."

I squeezed him tightly then left him there with his comrades, who flowed back toward the sidewalk, marching, up the slope toward the plaza and the park. I headed in the other direction, toward home. No need for shiatsu now. I felt unknotted and airy enough to float away.

ABBY, MAY 8, 2015

Benjamin found a six-toed cat prowling around the trash cans. It was as skinny as a cardboard cutout of a cat, almost, and approximately the same color, a flat dun brown. "He meows like, 'Wowza,'" Ben said, and he declared that this scrap of fuzz would be named Wowza and would live in the backyard in a super cat palace Ben would build by hand using planks and bits of old carpet. "He can be our baby," said Gianna.

Benjamin, my light heart, my high-arcing wavelength, the treble note in our family, his easy grace as he bounded down the stairs three at a time, rapping under his breath. And Gianna, his very first girlfriend, who sometimes stayed for dinner. When I arrived home this evening, the happy couple were chopping veggies for the salads that were more or less the only thing she would eat, dressed with a coconut oil she carried in a small bottle in her purse. She had certainly been spending more and more time at the house. Per Gianna, she would otherwise be home alone, eating pickings from a deli buffet. Her single parent was an asexual workaholic, she informed me matter-of-factly. "She works on Wall Street," Gianna said, while turning a pile of baby carrots into fat circlets. "Big bucks, long hours, and she tells me she can be around or she can leave me a big pile of money for my trust fund, and I said, trust fund, please."

Over at the stove, Dennis sautéed chicken in a pan. I wondered that he'd arrived home before me. He shot me a look I couldn't really interpret—but it was unmistakably out of the ordinary. "Ben, would you mind turning this chicken. I've got to talk to Mom." Dennis handed him the tongs, then guided me upstairs to our bedroom and shut the door.

I hadn't seen the detective since our afternoon tryst. I hadn't allowed myself. We had gone quiet again, for two weeks now. I had managed to evade guilt for a while, but now it followed me, a poisoned cloud, wafting around me. I could barely breathe. Surely Dennis could see it.

"It's over," he said.

My blood stopped in my veins. "Dennis."

"I'm fired." He sank onto the bed.

Half my brain understood instantly what he was talking about—it wasn't what I'd feared—but the other half refused to process his words. I responded with a dumb shake of my head.

"Abby, they called security. These fucking linebackers in polyester suits showed up with empty boxes, and they watched everything I packed."

He rested his elbows on his knees and rubbed his face with his hands. I moved to comfort him, an automatic thing, my arm around his shoulders, murmuring that it would be okay. But in my head I heard breakers, waves of dread crashing.

"Hey, we'll figure it out," I said, stroking his back.

He looked up at me. "You know, I'm thinking of maybe going back to the studio for a while. Instead of looking for another job right away. We could scrape by on your check, and the job market stinks now anyway."

"You said that sounded like death—scraping by. Didn't you say that?" I walked over to the window. "But if that's what you want to do. I can understand that. Totally."

"I know we'll figure it out." He sidled up behind me, and now he rubbed my shoulders for a while. Then he kissed me with real warmth and then returned downstairs to finish up his chicken.

At dinner, the conversation bubbled around me. I thought about the money we paid out at that auction—three-fourths of our pitiable savings account. Our rainy-day money. Now our rainy day had arrived. That cash would be sorely missed.

That night, late, sleepless, I returned to the bedroom window. A film of shivery moonlight coated the rainwater-filled kiddie pool in the backyard below. A disc of light wavering like the threshold to another dimension. I could almost imagine diving out the window, plunging through this lustrous wormhole. I'd be back there with her. At the beginning of it all.

Once again, the thought arrived: What outcome would I change, if I could change any outcome at all?

Turning from the window, my glance drifted over Dennis, now just an abstract form, a creation of shadow and light. His face was turned away from me, his head fallen into the darkness behind the ridgeline of a pillow. He didn't stir. He hardly seemed to breathe.

I pulled my robe from its hook behind the door and slipped it on. I peeked in on the boys. Benjamin slept with one arm resting over his heart, as if saying a pledge of allegiance to the god of his dreams. Pete's room was flooded with the strange moonglow. The wind must be picking up again outside. The shadows cast by the tree in our neighbor's yard washed back and forth over the bed and my sleeping child, like black sea grass. Above him, the window overlooked the street.

And there is A. Again in the shining shoes. A short black dress.

Standing across the street, mostly in the shadow of a leafy ginkgo, her face a pale white smudge, a small twin of the moon. I can't see her eyes, but I feel them on me.

I back away, tripping over something, a plastic bottle that falls and spills. A sharp strong odor—rubbing alcohol?—fills the room. Pete sits up.

"What the hell, Mom?" he stutters.

I gather some bathroom towels, and together we mop it up. He swears the bottle of isopropyl alcohol is for a chemistry project. He even shows me the handout from Mr. Littrell on chromatography— "The separation of a mixture by passing it in a solution or suspension or as a vapor." I keep checking the window. I see only the swaying silhouettes of the trees.

When the mess is swabbed up, the house settles again. But I am still awake. Downstairs, I dig into my big work tote. There, in the nethermost regions where I'd buried it in an attempt to forget its incitements, a crumpled piece of coarse-tooth paper. A ragged torn edge, the fine sketch of his hands. And in my terribly familiar half-cursive scrawl: *Dr. Merle, 212 692 7545.*

ABBY, MAY 11, 2015

"I am being haunted by myself." There, I'd said it out loud.

"Tell me more, Abigail."

Classical music trilled from an old clock radio. Wasn't that tune faintly familiar?

"I am seeing myself all over town," I said.

Piano, flute, violin, each emoting in turn, diligently. Clearly the music was meant to screen out the comings and goings at Pam's Kickin' Kuts, which shared this second-floor space above a cell phone store on upper Broadway. Still, I could hear the distant roar of blow-dryers and the thump of dance beats. Dr. Merle Unzicker had come down in the world, a bit, it seemed. Hadn't she, once upon a time, practiced in an airy prewar apartment high above the Hudson, with a row of arched windows and a big ficus tree?

Yes, she had. Now she was here above the cell phone store with a plastic fern and a dish of dusty peppermints.

"Do you remember me?" I asked her when I'd phoned for a first consultation. "I came to you, at twenty-one or -two. New in the city? A bit lost, a little wild?"

"Dear, I'm sorry. I will try to find the file. I will request a search for it at the Iron Mountain." Her voice was raspy, with an accent of borough New York, the kind you don't hear so often anymore.

"Where is that?"

"Oh, it's in Jersey. A secure file storage outfit in Hohokus." She was clearly happy to have an excuse to linger over the vowels of Hohokus. And who could blame her?

Dr. Merle Unzicker entered my life the first time via Eleanor Boyle. When Eli started visiting crack houses to photograph them, and I suspected he'd been trying the drug himself, I'd turned first to my longtime friend. "Of course, a guy like Eli is going to do awful shit, Abby," she said. "One has to factor that in." She sounded wiser than you'd expect for a person wearing emerald-green spandex shorts, glitter-striped knee socks, and high-heeled Mary Janes. We were waiting to enter a club in the dark industrial zone at the western end of Fourteenth. Just across the street sat a rolling bin of bones and fat, piled for rendering. A butcher, appearing from behind an aluminum door, tossed a slimy white mass on top. He stood there for a bit, smoking, studying us, then winked and gestured an offer of a cigarette. The meatpackers were excellent banterers, if you were willing to stop and chat. But Eleanor and I had reached the head of the line, the citizens of the night winding down the block behind us. We hadn't gone out together in a while, due to my entanglement with Eli, and Eleanor had moved on too, racking up several interesting sexual conquests and discovering this new club, dungeon-like and vaguely Middle Eastern in theme, hookah pipes and tasseled tents.

Eleanor waved away the butcher's attentions, then turned to me and said, "I have a shrink for you." Her roommate, an exotic dancer-slash-performance artist, swore by one Dr. Merle. "A miracle worker, according to Zoe," she said. "A specialist in existential ambivalence, and that is what I'm seeing here . . . you know that Eli is a fucked-up freak, but you are paralyzed, insecure, plagued by poor self-esteem, and this is just so typical of our age and gender," Eleanor said knowledgeably. She had been a psych major when we were at Western New England U, until she switched to drama.

"Fuck you, I am not ambivalent," I said. "I'm absolutely in the driver's seat with Eli. He always asks me what I want to do, he lets me take the lead."

"Oh, he *lets* you take the lead, does he?" She grinned.

The gatekeeper at the door was a tiny man in a top hat. He looked us over. "Nice socks," he said to Eleanor.

"Thanks, baby," she said. He lifted the rope and waved us through.

So here I was, returned to Dr. Merle the miracle worker. The classical music warbled on and I tried to fill her in. Since she didn't seem to remember me anyhow, I talked about Dennis, how I loved him, Pete with his challenges, Benjamin and his omnipresent girlfriend. And then, finally, about the detective.

Dr. Merle listened, nodding, wheezing a bit with every breath. Her body, curled into a wheelchair, was so small and slumped, more rag doll than woman. A needlepoint footstool propped up her feet, clad in pumps so tiny they did indeed look like doll shoes. Her eyes were bright and alert, peering out of her splotched, creased face as if through a layer of desiccated fallen leaves. I couldn't recall much about what she'd looked like a quarter century or so ago. No wheelchair, certainly. More hair, perhaps? Now her silver fluff was scant, just a gossamer suggestion of hair, really. Beneath it, lavender veins squiggled across her skull.

Divulging my transgression felt cleansing. Dr. Merle said, "You are endangering your marriage, of course. But it may be a sign of evolution. You must proceed with great caution and care," she said. "Stay your present course, if you can. The silence." She tapped her watch. "Time is up for today." She frowned as I stood. "As for this haunting," she said. "We must of course examine this."

"Oh that." I regretted telling her. It was too insane even for a shrink. "That's just kind of a joke I play on myself."

"I see," she said. "Good day then."

Walking past the whirring hair salon and down the stairs to the street, I wasn't certain I'd be coming back. I'd named my troubles, confessed them out loud, and this unburdening was probably all that I had needed. I did not suffer from existential ambivalence. I didn't want therapy. I didn't want to turn back the clock either, not to Eli Hammond, not to the drowned pleasures of my youth. On my train ride home, my thoughts turned instead to Pete and his comrades, to their crude campaign to disrupt the future.

Dr. Tristane Kazemy, MAY 12, 2016

Spring is always so skittish in Montreal. Some of the trees still wore dirty skirts of snow. In a fit of optimism, she put away her gloves and Maman's wooly knits. She could feel the ground gradually softening beneath her feet as she crossed the lawns of campus.

Similarly, she thought, she could feel the Willard case yielding, slowly yielding under her scrutiny. After studying hundreds of images, from hundreds of different angles and depths, and finding them clean, she kept returning to this one. It showed a shadow. A void really, detectable only by scrutinizing the subtlest displacement in the tissue surrounding it. An anomaly. At last.

Though she'd sworn to utmost discretion, she risked showing the image to Buccardi. He frowned and nodded. Could be. You have shown it to Laurin?

No. She had not spoken to Laurin since just after his California junket. "Our doctoresse has run the lab startlingly well," he announced, at the first departmental meeting upon his return. "We here at Le Neuro are very lucky to have this woman, so brilliant, so productive." He smiled across the crowded conference room to where she stood, near the door. "And well formed. Forgive me, I am a mere mortal, and so I must say that this lovely dress truly makes the most of you, Mademoiselle Kazemy."

So no, she would not share her findings with Laurin. The case that had come to mean more to her than anything in the lab, more than anything in her life. Certainly more than Samir. She told him about the shadow. "Does this mean you can finally move on from this, then? Mystery solved?"

No, she told him. Mystery deepened.

ABBY, MAY 14, 2015

At a faux-French café around the corner from school, Forest Versteeg sat on a wicker bar stool. He sipped an iced drink through a straw, his phone drawing him in, his pristine white slip-on sneakers angled on the footrest. Waiting to order, I mulled both the apricot tart and whether to approach him.

I didn't remember him from the Broder and Wilcox gallery. But it had been the most overheated exhibition space in the city at the time, with legions of young interns and gallery assistants. This was pre-Chelsea, when SoHo was just tipping over into the East Village, and Broder and Wilcox occupied the perfect central position on Broome Street.

My color-saturated abstracts, soft at the edges, surely seemed too serious, too heartfelt, amid the showmanship and snark of that era's art world. Painting had begun its fall out of favor. Installations, video, performance art attracted all the heat. But Jillian Broder decided to take a chance on me. "Three months out of RISD," she cooed, looking at my slides. "Maybe you'll bring emotion back." Oh, her long silvery hair, so shimmery and almost white, like fishing line or polyethylene thread, spread over the back of her exquisitely cut suit jacket. Fanning over the sharp tailoring. I touched it one time, very gently, behind her back, just to see if it was real.

Versteeg didn't look up from his phone until I said, "So is Jillian Broder still around, do you know?"

He looked up and yes, seemed happy to see me. He scooted over to free up enough space, I set down my bag on the counter and sat beside him. "In fact I see her often," he said. "My husband and I spend a week every summer at her place in Western Mass. Northampton, do you know it? It's lovely there, so green, so lush— and so gay." He grinned, revealing incisors as sharp and white as his perfect white shoes. Then he noticed the spiral-bound watercolor pad sticking out of my bag. He pointed to it. "May I?"

I nodded, then watched, strangely numb, as he paged through it. Color studies à la Albers, overlapped blocks of azure and green and violet in increasing and decreasing intensity. A few pencil sketches. He paused on an image of Pete, slouched at the kitchen table over a textbook. I had surreptitiously drawn it after dinner the previous night, as I tried to talk to him about this Brigade group and the incident on Flatbush.

"Don't worry about it, Mom. It's just something I'm doing."

"I just hoped we could talk about it."

"Does everyone have to talk about everything?"

"No. I suppose not. . . . But at some point let's talk about it."

"At some point."

Forest pointed to Pete's balled fist. "Brilliant," he said. "So much dark energy there." He closed the sketchbook and handed it back to me. "Why are you taking these classes anyhow? I'm like embarrassed to be teaching you."

"Lifelong learning is a thing. I am desperately in need of a refresher course, at the very least. And you're a good teacher."

"Well, I love it. But I'd rather be painting, of course. This pays the bills."

"Tell me about it," I laughed. "That show at Broder and Wilcox? Exactly one painting sold."

"I suppose I didn't remember that," he said, quietly. "I just remember your astounding work. I was so awed by you. Maybe that's why I've always remembered that show as a sellout."

I gave him a little smile. "Just one sale. A still life, Bremer's grapefruits. The man ate a lot of grapefruits."

"I still cannot believe you studied with H. D. Bremer. Incredible." Forest swirled the ice in his glass and chewed it, contemplating me again. "I want to help you reinvent yourself, Abby. I like that you have these children and a husband, and you're still out there trying."

I wondered if I could skew this as a compliment.

"I could introduce you to my gallerist Matthew Legge-Lewis. He's like the new Jillian. Just as genius, just as ruthless. Also, my husband." He picked up his backpack and slung it over his shoulder, stood from his stool. "I've got to get the room ready. See you in class?"

ABBY, MAY 19, 2015

Breaking the afternoon silence like a plow turning soil, a blunt-nosed sports car rumbled down our block, passing me as I struggled home carrying a jumbo bag of cat food and a rotisserie chicken. It rolled to a stop in front of our house. Pete bounded from the front door and was climbing in as I approached. "And you're going where?" I called out. The car was a late-model Mustang, the yellow of hot dog mustard and I could feel the engine's growl in my gut.

"Milo is taking us to the Rally for Reading," he yelled back, over the din.

Dmitri popped out of the car's passenger side. "It's a door-to-door fundraiser in Queens, Abby," he shouted. "For Twiz, she's opening a tutoring center at the Brigade. Positive action!"

The driver had buzz-cut black hair, a squared-off beard. He nodded at me, eyes hidden behind aviator shades. "Nice day, Mrs.," he called.

Milo. He co-owned a business in Queens ("Olives, aluminum, funeral statuary," Dmitri had explained once when he was over, "kind of import-export") and made the interborough crossing every day from the Petimezas manse in Mill Basin.

Now he gave me the thumbs-up. "I will give them a ride home. Not too late."

"Don't you have a bio test tomorrow?" I said.

Dmitri chirped, "We'll quiz each other on the way!"

"Test isn't till Monday," shouted Pete. "And Dmitri's sleeping over!" The car's engine revved and they were off before I could respond. I watched the car's taillights sink away down the slope. My son had just roared off with a menacing stranger. Why hadn't I thrown myself in the way, or at least thrown my jumbo bag of Meow Mix in the way?

Maybe because I have become a menacing stranger, too.

The house sat empty. Benjamin was off with Gianna, and Dennis was at work in his studio. Yes, he had rented a studio somewhere in Bushwick. I had yet to see it. Freed from his job, he'd descended quickly and deeply into the maelstrom of his art-making. Sometimes he'd stay until one or two a.m., showering late at night—his work had always left him with a sheen of sweat and burned metal. Once in a while he stayed all night, catching a bit of sleep on the cot in his studio. "It's taken me so long to get back to it, Abby," he texted me. "I hope you won't mind if I just stick with it."

One night when he stayed away late, I wandered again down into the basement, to the racks of paintings. We'd moved them here when I'd shut down my last studio, the space I'd rented at the back of a textile factory in Chinatown, after RISD. When I'd lost the lease, two years after the Broder and Wilcox show, Dennis had helped me cut sheets of glassine and brown shipping paper, snapping lengths of packing tape. He helped me load the paintings into a borrowed van. With frigid water, all that ever came from the sink taps, I'd scrubbed the paint remnants from the porcelain basin and tossed my old tin-can paintbrush holders in the trash. That was the last time I'd had a work space to call my own.

Now I pulled a wrapped rectangle from the shelf and tore back a corner of the paper. Pale-green celadon and a stroke of orange. The vibrancy packed into a few square inches. My hands were shaking as I ripped the rest of the covering away.

And then I was back there, an afternoon in August, a stretch of bay, a boathouse mostly unused. A rusting rack of old canoes listing under an oak tree. Dennis had driven me down to paint because my old Honda refused to turn over. We'd fucked with considerable success that night of Mariah's birthday, but since then, I had been avoiding him. I was still crawling from the wreckage of Eli Hammond, I guess. Not looking for attachments.

But this day, by the water, things changed. Unpacking my paints and easel, late-day heat, insect buzz, and lapping water. He pulled the canvas, wrapped in muslin, out of the trunk. He asked if he could have a look. When I nodded, he eased the cloth away.

He studied it for a long while. I set up, I pretended not to be watching. "Your colors," he finally said.

"Too much?"

He set it on my easel with relaxed ceremony. I'd worked hard on the willows, and I saw now I had captured some of their verdant complexity. It was good work. "I wish I could see the world like this every minute," he said. Then he turned and put both hands on my shoulders and pulled my mouth to his. In milliseconds, it seemed, we were down on the ground.

"Someone might see," I murmured, when we were clinging together, clothing shed. "No one here," he whispered.

"I think I'm too messed up for anyone."

"Nah." He propped himself on an elbow. His green-gold eyes meandered along my body. I could feel them on me, as strange and strangely pleasant on my naked skin as the sun's rays and the breeze were. "Not for me."

The painting sat above us on the easel, I gazed at it, and it gave me a green gaze back. Maybe that gaze held some foreknowledge?

In a year's time, this square of painted canvas would hang in Jillian Broder's place on Broome. It would be much commented on—"Luminous brushwork and a confident description of nature's quieter moments," said *ARTnews*.

In five years' time it would be sealed away under glassine and tape.

In twenty years' time, the emerald would shimmer at me under a bare bulb in our basement at 2:13 in the morning.

I smoothed the torn paper over the canvas again and propped it on a shelf by the stairs. Maybe, I thought, I'd bring it along to Forest Versteeg's place this summer. The invitation for a weekend in the country had been extended.

I climbed two flights, washed my face in the bathroom. I was feeling woozy again, the nausea. I lay down again between the sheets of the empty bed that smelled of my marriage, the mingling of two bodies over many many years, and I fell fast asleep.

Dennis woke me at dawn. "Holy fuck," he screamed from downstairs. He bounded up to our room, an envelope tumbling onto the floor as he held up a single letter torn open. "The Viennarte show," he said. "Me."

ABBY, MAY 28, 2015

CT scan rooms are arctically cold. My arms goose-pimpled in the paper gown as I lay on the table waiting to begin. Dennis stood over me. He was still vibrating with the news, this stupefying invitation—how was it possible?—to the exclusive annual show in Vienna, where astronomical money was spent, and art careers were launched and relaunched. He sought my hand and squeezed it. "You're hurting me," I said.

Dr. Singh had sent me to an imaging specialist named Dr. Arminbutt. The boys found it hilarious. Dr. Arminbutt was scanning my brain. A first look inside. They shooed Dennis out, shot some contrast fluid in my arm, offered me a sedative, which I accepted gratefully. Then the table moved, and like a needle into a buttonhole, I was threaded into the white plastic scanner ring, which would map my brain sliver by sliver. I don't think I fell asleep, but I fell. I mean, I saw myself falling.

There in the thrumming ring. Falling.

The balcony, breaking. The railing, collapsing.

A falling boy. With him, a falling girl.

The old cracked balcony that buckled under our weight. Boy and girl in a clinch, locked in an embrace, leaning against the rail. We were intertwined when we fell.

We tumbled together.

He fell, and I fell too. Now I remember. How could I have forgotten?

I fell too.

I survived. He did not.

I am rolled out of the ring. We will send the report to your primary, said the doctor with the comical name.

May 27, 2016

From: GarrettShuttlesworth@physics.humboldtstate.edu
To: J.Leverett@deepxmail.com

The best way to explain what I'm beginning to think: Imagine your life as a stack of photos. All the pictures in the stack exist all at once, but you may view them only one at a time. Maybe Abigail Willard's stack includes a few multiple exposures—sequences captured with some degree of transparency, one atop the other. Multiple spacetime moments visible all at once.

But visible solely to her. That's the why. Why her.

ABBY, MAY 31, 2015

I write this in a hotel room, the harsh glittering mosaic of Brooklyn out the window, and I feel as if I could peer through the night and see the smoking ruins. The day is a horrendous jumble in my mind, a mess I can't untangle just yet. But it began like this: with Dmitri Petimezas, who'd slept on an air mattress alongside Pete's bed, eating a giant portion of cornflakes out of a mixing bowl, watching CNN. Dmitri's hair was flicked in odd angles. Pete ate cornflakes from a mixing bowl too. Their clothes were wet. I asked them what they'd been doing. They said they'd been out for a walk and got caught in a passing rainstorm, and in fact it had been raining on and off. There was a strange smell in the air, something like lemon-scented cleaner and chlorine, a faint whiff of indoor pool, almost. A smell I had never before smelled in my kitchen.

An hour later I caught Gianna sneaking down the stairs, my new ankle boots in one hand, and Benjamin's underwear in the other. "I was just going to borrow the boots," she whimpered, handing them to me. I held out my hand for the underwear. "These are mine," she said, clutching them to her chest with a gesture I'm pretty sure I'd seen her do with a Styrofoam baguette when she was playing the street waif Cosette in the school's production of *Les Mis*. "Does your mom know you spent the night here?"

She nodded. Then shrugged. "Well, my mom knows I was sleeping at a friend's house," she said. "She may have not been clear on whose house, but she probably doesn't care, because she likes all my friends," she said.

"Where's Benjamin?" I said.

"Oh, he's still asleep, I think?" As she headed out the door, she called back, "And I told him that scented candles might be romantic but they are full of toxins and cause indoor air pollution!"

Just then Dennis came stumbling down the stairs, running a comb through his hair, his nice sports jacket in one hand and the other bandaged from a nick he'd given himself with the circular saw. He wore a pristine white shirt with a sharp collar and a tie I'd never seen before, slashed with green stripes that matched his eyes. He kissed me distractedly. I remembered that he was meeting with the Viennarte curators that morning, that he had asked me to drive him there, and here I was still in my robe and bare feet. I promised him I'd be ready in four and a half minutes, tore up to our room, yanked on a pair of shorts and a T-shirt, and rifled around looking for my purse and sunglasses amid the debris of Dennis and me. Then I saw, on the floor near a pile of his tossed-off clothing, a single key, with the letter M written on it in permanent marker. I put that in my pocket, and then the car keys too.

I waited behind the wheel as he met with the curators at a severely plush restaurant in Midtown. I sat in the car, his chauffeur, double-parked, in my flip-flops and shorts, and I took the key with the M scribbled on it, and then without knowing why, I was driving up Lexington. I turned onto Sixty-Seventh and careened to a stop in front of the carriage house and damn if that key didn't open the door. The house was empty, as I knew it would be—because Memorial Day had passed, May was ending with a soaring heat wave, and I knew Mariah must've decamped to her Sag Harbor house. As I entered, her work seemed to watch me, so strong and eloquent in its slashes and stripes and silence.

A pounding reverberated from the base of my throat all the way through to my shoulder blades. To steady myself, I perched on one of the long suede sofas. Several different smells curled around me like discordant music. Tire rubber: that must have been from the collection of mountain bikes hung on hooks in the hallway that led to the living room. I couldn't imagine Mariah on a bicycle, so perhaps they belonged to her man, as she called him. The frames were enameled in hard bright aquas and yellows and tangerines, and inscribed with Italian names—Volarini, Scalfata, and so on. I imagined this man, narrow-waisted, biker's legs.

So tire rubber, yes, but also a trace of paint and solvents, and fruit—the open kitchen was just to the right and I could see a bowl of summer stone fruit, decaying aromatically, gracefully, a sensual marker of the passage of days—and then, underneath, there was an unmistakable aroma of Dennis. And then I saw: right there on the coffee table, atop a lavish program from the Tate show, with a Mariah painting on the cover, a sultry deep red spiral, a whirling gyre one could plummet through forever. And at the center of the vortex sat a package of his distinctive Indian chews. I pick it up and inhale. This smell is Dennis, gingery, toasty, slightly sweet.

And then the day begins to refract. Various scenarios present themselves, as I look back on this slice of hours, this segment of a life that most of the world would agree to call the final day of May in the year 2015. Which scenario happened, which did not. At the moment, I really could not say. I can only present a series of bullet points.

- Here is me, Abigail Willard, rising from the sumptuous white suede, padding in my soiled flip-flops over the white carpet as thick as marshmallow. And I enter the kitchen with its bowl of lusciously decomposing fruit and few signs of cooking, and yet I see a gargantuan aluminum chef's stove and a stack of crisply folded linen dish towels, and I stand there and I stare at these things with my brain feeling as if it is sliding down my throat to my gut and my hands begin to shake. I flick one of the gas burners on and off. A blue flower of flame leaps into being. Roars like a thing alive. Gutters out.

- And then here I am again, back in the car, sitting outside the lunching place of the arbiters, the curators who have been granted the right to decide the fates of those somehow driven to spill their souls onto the walls and floors of empty white rooms. I am sitting in the car in my shorts, my thighs stuck with sweat to the vinyl seat of our cheap and battered car. I pick out a text on my phone: Meet me? Tomorrow, maybe? I want to see you again. I push send just as Dennis emerges from the restaurant. I say not a word, he says not a word but seems to be in some transported state, I can see it in his faraway gaze, he smiles at me absently and finally says, well that went well, and as I drive him home, forging a slow path against the obstinance of early-rush-hour, I am stuck on the fact that the sentence starts and ends with well.

- Here is the family Willard, walking home from Szechuan Palace, four people and one bag of leftovers, the boys of gleaming messy hair and bold brows and large athletic footwear, the blond-graying man with his softening but still fit body and torn T-shirt from a Laguna Beach date-shake stand, and here is the mother, widening but still retaining some loveliness of shape in her striped sundress and sandals but something lost and deeply distracted in her eyes, each of which is set deep above a pillowy blood-darkened half-moon of skin, badge of months of poor sleep and decades of toil and devotion.

- And she is distracted, the mother, because she thinks she sees the girl, A, herself, disappearing around the corner down the block, her honey-tipped curls a-bounce and a-sway and a slender ankle in a red sandal, just kicking up slightly as she darts out of sight around the corner of the avenue, the avenue at the end of the block about eight or nine houses beyond where the Willard house sits. The mother thinks she sees this but is unsure because it has been a day already full of befuddlement.

- And now they are in front of their house and the top story is veiled by cloud, a black cloud that looks like it was made by smudging charcoal crayon with the meaty side of a human hand curled into a fist. A stroke of orange in the black.

- One of the boys says, I think the house is on fire.

- Just after these words, the trucks come bellowing. The engines dwarf everything on the street, cars, neighbors, the humble row houses of brick and vinyl. Gleaming and towering and brawny, awash in spinning light, they roll to a stop still screaming. The entire world—or at least the entire block— seems to rear back and hold its breath in awe.

PART 2

THE TIGER

6/6/6/6

ABBY, JUNE 2, 2015

Everyone knows the bar. It turns the corner of East Seventh and Avenue B. This bar has been turning this corner since sometime before 1900. Tudor-esque arched doors and crusty many-paned windows that, when you're inside them, make it feel like it's always raining outside. The grimy air enfolds you, the music is always whatever is most downbeat that year, the walls are shingled with yellowed flyers from bands and clubs of years gone by, layered and rough as scales.

And here I am, it is early 1991 and I am seated on a stool where the long stretch of varnished wood just begins to coax itself into a curve, the horseshoe that allows the bar's patrons to stare at each other across the ramparts of liquor bottles. I'm waiting for Michael Hutcherson, my boss at Grady Advertising, who is already an hour late. The bartender has set another slippery glass of vodka and tonic in front of me, and I'm sipping it through a mixer straw. Michael Hutcherson and I are over, I decide by the time I've sipped halfway to the bottom. But how will I break it off with him and not lose my job? Michael Hutcherson is my boss. My situation seems impossible, and I feel impossibly stupid for getting into it.

Then I notice: four stools down. A green bottle of beer and a soft pack of Marlboro Reds on the bar in front of him. A rangy white boy with hair the coppery-brown of whiskey in a glass. He's talking to the bartender about Iraq. "One hundred and thirty kids incinerated in one push of a button," he says. "The missile was made by Texas Instruments, by the way." He gestures with his bottle toward the cash register behind the bar. "Oh shit," the bartender says with a frown. That company's logo is written in gold letters above the machine's screen.

So I'm thinking about the tragically fucked-up nature of the world now, and then the guy realizes I've been listening, that his words have hit me. He rubs a hand over his sharp clean-shaven chin. His T-shirt reads UN CHIEN ANDALOU.

The bartender says, "Eli, this girl's looking for a drinking partner, I think. Better step up before somebody else does."

The guy gazes at me and says, "She seems like she's waiting for someone."

I take a sip from my straw. "I was," I say.

So fast one can fluctuate from state to state. Horror to hope. Weird humans.

That night, in the 7B bar, Eli Hammond and I drank like we were vying for a trophy. While we did, he told me about witnessing the Meir Kahane murder, which had happened three months before. "Gunfire that close makes a big impression," he said. How his ears rang from the volume of the blast, with the gunman so close, the guy ran right over the shattered plates of cake Eli had dropped, tracking blood and frosting as he fled. "I was so buzzed. I don't think I slept for three days afterward."

The next noon I found myself nude in bed, a pair of men's underwear balled up by my foot, a faded and frayed pair of Fruit of the Looms. I felt a hammering across my forehead. He was gone. And the phone did not ring, and I did not have his number.

Remember that you could go hours and days wondering. The phone simply would not ring. The phone hung there in your dingy bedroom in your underfurnished apartment, utterly inert, a plastic wart on the wall, and it simply didn't ring. Finally you had to stop waiting and emerge from your room and live your life.

Two weeks passed after that meeting in the bar at Seventh and B, and one day during my lunch break, feeling restless and lonely and hating Grady Advertising and Michael Hutcherson, I determined that I again needed to see the Jackson Pollocks on Fifty-Third Street. I liked to soak myself in the dribbled palette of fifties pinks and olives and blacks and silvers. I liked to muse on the cracks in the enamel he used, paints meant to be applied to cars and houses, and though his paintings were not so old, they were already splitting and flaking with time. There was one, called *One*, that had a Cadillac pink that truly slayed me. It still does.

Afterward I'd often go to the museum cafeteria, and sometimes I would sketch there, or read a book. This time, tables were mostly occupied, spring break, the town full of tourists. One free spot in the corner.

At the next table, a young man in a faded red T-shirt and jeans, golden skin revealed at their slashed knees. He wore a Walkman, they were relatively new, and it still seemed strange to see people sealed off in a private sound bubble, not sharing the aural world occupied by the rest of us. His eyes were closed. I sat in the chair opposite him and slid my sketchbook from my bag. The planes of his face, angular, the sideburns and the emphatic chin, the whiskey-sheen hair, in disarray, just brushing past his ears. The boy obviously did not own a comb. Of course I began to sketch him.

"I should have called," he said. Suddenly his eyes were open. Evening blue. Reflections of the room's pendant lights, like quavering stars.

I blushed and put down my pencil. "I'm sorry, I hope you don't mind. I just . . ."

"Abby, right?"

"Right."

"I wanted to call," he said. "I had a girlfriend. Then. I don't now."

A half hour later we were in his bed and this time I remembered everything. I still do. I remember this though so much else is gone.

He lived in that tenement building on Avenue C, deliciously decrepit, shared with a few of his equally alluring friends. Sneakers and bootleg videos and ragged comic books lying open everywhere. I think we must have spent twenty-four hours that day, in his allotted chamber, just big enough to fit his bed, fucking to exhaustion, then recharging ourselves by listening to the music winding up the fire escape and swirling through the window, sinuous snakes of sound. We pounded our bare feet against the wall to the beat of the cumbia flickering up from below.

He'd dropped out of Columbia film school after losing his scholarship due to chronic class-skipping. ("It's a long way uptown," he sighed, a little ruefully.) His interest, after the Kahane assassination, was drifting toward photojournalism anyhow. And he had those cameras of his grandfather's, the ones that had seen battle on the Eastern Front. So to afford film and rent, he took on more shifts pouring ice water and wine in the Marriott ballroom, black blazer with his engraved name badge. And every Monday and Tuesday he worked an overnight shift at the free newspaper, pasting up classifieds for massage parlors and pyramid schemes and miracle cures. And ducking into the darkroom to develop his film when no one else was around.

Three weeks after we met, I quit my job. And so, when he wasn't working, we were together, at his apartment or mine, where we had more privacy, since my roommate Gregory was rarely around. I would sit in Eli's lap on the wobbly old bench on the balcony. We smoked his cigarettes and flicked the butts into the rain-filled ash bucket. Recounting for each other essential episodes in our personal histories, laughing about the stupid things we'd done, as if the stupidity of youth was already behind us, which of course it was not, our hands exploring each other under our clothes, the warm realms of air and skin, the dense insistence of his cock, proclaiming itself. We often invited it out into the night air, it was dark enough there, high up above the little gardens that filled the block's core, and it felt secluded, even if perhaps it wasn't. His was the most beautiful I'd ever seen or will see, the strangeness of that, still, that a cock could be beautiful. It was. We'd fuck against the railing or on the damp crumbling cement, not particularly comfortable but we were well beyond caring about that. It seemed significant, what we were doing. So important that we wanted any bird or cloud or star passing over this canyon to witness it, two humans pursuing pleasure, maybe even—as we might have felt it—transcendence, defying every mundane thing in this world up to and including mortality.

This is the memory that unfolded in my mind as I sat in that very same bar twenty-two years later. The place still beer-stinking, still tattered, a baseball game still slowly and silently unspooling on the TV hung in the gloom. Waiting to meet the detective.

My home life had buckled under a hail of flame and ash. I wanted to seek refuge in a dark place. And maybe also defy mortality. I'm at that age now, after all. I knew it was a terrible and foolish impulse, to reach out to him.

He had texted back: You know that place at 7th and B? We could meet there, maybe?

Yes. Yes, of course I knew the place.

Everyone does.

THE LITTLE BABY ALBUMS I'd so diligently filled out had been transformed into stiff sheaves, more like wood than paper, by the time the flames passed through and the hoses had drenched the rooms and the flood had dried.

"The house is sixty-eight percent inhabitable," the deputy fire marshal had told us, the day after. The four of us stood with him in the small front yard, bleary-eyed from a sleepless night at a Times Square tourist hotel. Neighborhood kids horsed around on the sidewalk behind us, gleeful at this unusual excitement on the block. The fire marshal, a square-shaped man, smoothed his luxuriant mustache as he surveyed the scene. "You could live in there, but you better hope it won't rain." He gestured toward the sky with a jerk of his head. "And it's kinda looking like rain."

How could we make such a decision, where we would live, whether we sleep in the rain? Dennis and I couldn't even locate our own house, we were so dumbfounded still—coming from the hotel via subway, we actually wandered too far down the block, missing number 312 completely, and it was Pete who said, "Where the hell are you going?" The black gaping monster mouth across the second-floor facade, bits of charred wood and plaster dribbling out of it like crumbs of its last meal. The shriveled leaves hanging in a black fringe on the Rose of Sharon bush that had been on the verge, just yesterday, of bursting into purple blossom. As we gazed at the mess, Dennis just kept saying "I don't fucking believe it," and I really couldn't say anything at all. My voice box seemed to be one more thing left twisted by the blaze.

The boys were the ones who first started picking through the rubble. They found the baby books. Also the black bird painting, water-damaged, gradations of darkness muddled into a mess. Ruined, really, though Dennis insisted that he would take it directly to the best restorer in the city. His *Circles in Repose* sculpture suffered just a few scorch marks, which he claimed added gravitas and might be just the thing that would finally vault the piece to greatness. "I'm going to show it to the Vienna curators," he said to me. "Straight out of the smoking ruins."

"You think?"

"Turn disasters into happy accidents," he said. "It's the only way."

I stared at him. I wanted and needed his comfort and solidity. But in my pocket I still had the key marked with the *M*. I hadn't yet said a word about it.

The fire marshal found the staircase structurally sound. The master bedroom had been mostly spared, though water damage happened there too, of course, as the great hoses rained down. The boys' rooms were a blackened zone, with the gaping front wall. In Ben's closet, I salvaged a tiny pair of yellow rain boots.

Meanwhile, Dennis and the marshal yanked open the heat-warped basement door, descended to check on the boiler and water systems. They came up smudged and coughing, Dennis carrying something under his arm. A brown rectangle. He sank to the floor, kneeling with his head hung over the wrapped painting. "It was the water heater," said the fire marshal. "A blast of steam and flame down through the pipes, just blasted everything within range." He clapped his hands on his pants.

"All the paintings," said Dennis miserably, "except this one, it wasn't with the others." A torn paper corner, exposing brilliant green, glistening, tissue in a wound.

All the paintings. The boys continued to sort through the wreckage. I wandered back upstairs, to the blackened hole. I sat on the floor, staring through the hole at the clouds. Then I noticed a charred paper half under the bed, with fat lettering: OUR TIME IS NOW. And an unfamiliar Brooklyn address, and a date and time. Under it, handwriting, Pete's loopy scrawl. It read: "We will not only fight, but come out better for having struggled with and for one another. Perhaps we will not only make a life from within the ruins, but create a new world."

THE RUINS. The words swivel through my mind every waking moment, even as I am back at work, sitting at my desk, trying to focus. The smoking ruins. A week later, they still haven't made any determination about how and where the conflagration began.

Maybe I'd lit the spark, somehow, that afternoon. Mariah's gas burner. Dennis's lunch with the ordained powers. Was she on the board of Viennarte, had I read that somewhere?

Much of the afternoon was not recoverable in my mind.

Driving Dennis home from his lunch meeting, my legs hot on the vinyl seat, speechless with fury in our broken-down Isuzu, weak air-conditioning, and my husband in a daze, still half-blinded by the spotlight cast upon him.

Me, standing under a cool shower, trying to get the car sweat off me.

Some pointless argument between the boys, which ended in Pete shoving Benjamin into the banister upstairs.

And Gianna talking about candles.

And Pete and Dimitri Petimezas and the boys' wet clothes and the chlorine smell.

And the truck driver flattened on Flatbush Avenue.

And the text I sent that said meet me.

And the blue flower of flame.

And the ginger chews.

And the red spiral.

My head throbbing, something trying to escape, some bulging thought too big for my skull.

A, finding scraps of burned foil and smoky glass in a shoebox under a bed on Avenue C.

A, falling with her arms wrapped around the boy, falling into a void where memory ceased.

A, a shadow against shadows, seen through a bedroom window that no longer exists.

A, flicking out of sight down the block, a flash of red, a bird vanishing into forest.

And, just before that, opening a fortune cookie at Szechuan Palace. Empty, without fortune.

That means you can write your own, said Benjamin.

Or you're going to die tomorrow, said Pete.

Looking into his eyes, so like mine, like hers, sitting in that dingy familiar clattering eatery with the half-consumed platter of kung pao chicken spread before us.

Now what kind of thing is that to say, scolded Dennis. I will give Mom my fortune. He handed me the slip of paper.

A GREAT CHANGE IS COMING YOUR WAY.

FOR MY RENDEZVOUS WITH THE DETECTIVE, I sat on the very same stool at the bar at Seventh and B, just on the cusp of the curve, that I had chosen the night I first met Eli Hammond. Don't ask me why. A group of suit-and-tie boys clustered at the other end of the bar, erupting in howls of laughter every now and then. A few women, moms on a night out perhaps, drank martinis across the bartender's pit. Everyone looked clean, pressed. Yes, the place was still crusty and gloomy, but the ragged patrons of former days had been somehow spirited away, and so the bar's crust and gloom had the faux quality of a historical re-creation.

When he arrived, he leaned over to brush a kiss on my cheek, discreet, in this public place, but unmistakably imbued with heat. He too looked clean and pressed. He sat beside me, his eyes on mine. Mirrors in a dark room. Shining but revealing little. Three weeks had passed since I'd suggested we meet, but then that was the day of the fire. And then everything after. It had begun to seem like a bad idea again. But here we were. Was the old stool wobbling under me? I certainly felt woozy.

We both ordered beers, nothing too strong, I think we both understood it was best to keep our wits about us. I told him a few things about the conflagration, about living in the hotel, about the burned baby books.

"And my friend Pete, how is he faring through all of this? Steering clear of trouble, I hope?"

I smiled and nodded. "Just, you know, busy with school." I gulped down the remainder of my beer.

"Chief of detectives announced his retirement today." He swigged his beer. "Major reshuffling ahead."

"You're going for the job, I hope."

He shrugged. "I need to break a big case. Your pal, Pizziali, he's up against me."

"That guy?" I laughed. "I wouldn't think he'd be much competition."

"He's not, but he is. He's a determined little fucker, and he is hot on this antifa so-called brigade, wants to tag it up as domestic terror." He shook his head at me. "I think it's garbage, Abby, don't you?"

"Yes," I said. "Stupid kids' stuff, really."

We fell into a long silence.

"So . . . how are your girls?" I asked.

"Nina is obsessed with the *Titanic*. It's a bit morbid, she's encyclopedic on who died, ages, and nationalities. Marlie, she's still into princesses, so, you know, everything is pink and sparkly in her world."

He didn't mind talking about his kids, but clearly, he didn't want to be talking about his kids.

I didn't want to talk about my kids either. Or my house. Or my troubles.

I wanted to be like her again.

I reached under the shadow of the bar and took his hand. Looked again into his eyes. "I wonder what we should do," I said.

"What feels good to you?" he said, voice low.

Around the blurry edges of my vision, the other people in the bar had evaporated, the bar had unfolded to emptiness, we were alone, a pair of voyagers.

"You do," I said. The aliveness was extreme. Like living every day of my life all at once. Bone, skin, veins vibrating with it.

"I'd like to just stay right here, in this moment, in this place," I said.

"Then that's how it will be," he said. "Always."

He lifted my hand and kissed it. Then he pulled his phone from his pocket. "Should I find us a hotel nearby? Or we could cab it to the Marriott."

ABBY, JUNE 11, 2015

Mariah's show at MoMA, almost at the end of its run. As I walked to find lunch, threading through sun-dazed throngs along Fifth

Avenue, I realized I wanted to go. I wanted to see her work hanging there in the spacious hush. I stepped into the museum, its air-conditioning and quiet enveloping me, sudden as a plunge into a perfectly cool pool.

When I saw her work, I tasted salt. Tears. Three rooms hung with large paintings, optimistic, powerful, defiant, shouting a dare to the universe. I dare you to ignore me, they said. It is impossible. I cried because I loved them so. They made me want to dare. I was so grateful for them. And for her, truly. She was a master, and we had been young together, and I admired her so. And, apparently, she had fucked my husband.

The complex snarl of emotions overtook me. Quite blindly, I drifted from these galleries, rode the escalators down, and then I found myself on the floor of the Pollocks. I turned from the corridor into the room of *One*, the large mural-sized work, as big as the side of a tractor trailer, athrob with splattered energy.

Like something out of quantum physics, matter birthing.

Standing in front of the painting, too close: a young woman in a pale denim jacket.

Studying it, her whole body yearning toward it, her face inches away.

Really, too close. I glance around. Where are the guards? None in sight.

I take a step or two closer. But then I freeze.

She reaches her hand toward the painting.

No motion sensors? Were there motion sensors, back then?

Holding my breath. I watch as she traces a crack with her fingers.

And then a small flake flutters to the floor.

She has defaced the Pollock.

She bends to pick it up.

She turns to leave, staring at the chip of paint in her hand. As she comes near, I can see it's about the size and color of an eyelid.

I block her as she's hurrying from the room.

Did you actually do that, I say. I am enraged. She is a defacer. Destroyer.

She registers shock as she recognizes me. She presses her hand to her side. That chip of paint, hidden in her fist.

It's a little good-luck charm, she says, trying to maneuver past me.

I grab her arm.

You are so lucky, I say. So very lucky. He dies. You don't.

Look, she says. I know you want to help me. I don't want to hurt you. It's just. Her eyes go wide and dark. I'm not you. You are just a person looking at art on the wall. I will be on the wall.

I release her. Absorbing the blow. And then she's gone, of course. The painting is still there. As ever, pulsating, vibrating, hurling itself through time.

Missing a piece.

June 13, 2016

From: J.Leverett@deepxmail.com
To: GarrettShuttlesworth@physics.humboldtstate.edu

G, police inquiry was made. Museum staff reported that the Pollock work, *One: Number 31, 1950,* was cleaned and restored in 1998. Restorers definitely found pieces missing, other deterioration. Apparently the guy didn't really know what he was doing, and he splattered with the wrong kind of paint. It was never meant to stick around forever.

ABBY, JUNE 17, 2015

I drove slowly, creeping along Monsignor Murphy Street, an obscure rhomboid angling through the northeastern reach of the borough. Difficult, these days, in Brooklyn, to find a spot disreputable
enough for a meeting of antifa soldiers, but this neighborhood retained a whiff of bad old days, of undaunted rats and splintered
plywood and abandonment. House numbers were sparse. I parked,
then walked up and down the street. Really, there was just one
intact row house, listing slightly to one side, missing some of its
asphalt siding. Beneath the stoop, on the door to what one might
have called the garden apartment, if one could imagine a garden
here, I saw a red spray-painted slogan: NO PASARÁN.

Stood there for a while. Thinking of my Pete, whom I had just
dropped at an endodonist in Ridgewood. He was having a root
canal, poor love. Another parental failing: we'd burdened him with
weak enamel.

Watched ants charge in and out of tiny hills in the sidewalk
cracks. Far down the block, a trio of girls jumped rope, and I could
just pick up snippets of their chants—nickel, pickle, kicks, tricks—
and the smacking of the rope on cement.

Finally, I gathered my nerve. I knocked, waited, then pounded.
Tap, tap. Kicks, tricks. Then the door cracked. "Yeah?"

"I'm looking for Dmitri," I ventured. What was I so nervous
about? These were children. I could hear pubescent tremoring in
this voice from behind the battered door as it said, "Are you his
mom or what?" It opened just a sliver more. I could see a squinting
eye, a zitty forehead. "Anyway you can't come in here."

"Do I look like a fascist?" I demanded.

The eye scanned me. "You def don't look like a soldier," he said.
"This is a battalion muster."

But then I heard words behind him, the door opened wide, and out popped Dmitri. As he stepped from the dark arch of the cellar entry, I was struck again by his elfin qualities, how he looked like a sprite springing from the heart of hollowed oak in a fairy wood, an impression furthered by his black wool stocking cap, cuffed across his brow and tapering into a point with a fat red pom-pom at its tip.

"Abby!" he exclaimed. He grabbed my hand, pumped it, and urged me inside. "Come in, sorry about Babywipes—we call him that because, well, he is fundamentally opposed to public water systems—he's just doing his job." The boy scowled at both of us and slammed the door behind us. At first what hit me was the smell, truly overpowering, not just the smell of Babywipes, but also the funk of damp earth, the loamy Brooklyn underlayer I knew from my own basement at home, mixed with the aroma of human closeness. There must have been twenty-five people crammed into the low-ceilinged space. They collectively frowned at me. Except for the three large pit-bullish mutts, sleek urban swines accessorized with jaunty neck bandannas—they grinned at me, with malevolent enthusiasm.

"She's an ally," Dmitri announced. "Pete's mother."

"I can vouch for her." This from Twiz. She was wearing a tank top that bared tropical flowers and revolutionary slogans inking up her arms.

"The second I saw her standing at the door, I realized—she can contribute," said Dmitri. "She's an artist."

Fucking bourgeoisie, someone yelped from the back.

"Hold up," said a massive man whose bald pate was covered with tattooed tiger stripes. "We live in a visual culture, right? And have you seen our flyers? No offense"—here he turned to a kid with a halo of curly red hair—"but she could give us a better look."

"Yeah, yeah, Vincent," said Twiz. She started talking about flyers, posters, stickers, and temporary tattoos for her after-school kids, banners, and I stood there, listening. I had come here to tell Dmitri to stay away from my family. To threaten to alert the crew if they didn't steer clear of Pete. But I didn't say any of that. I listened. When she stopped, they all looked expectantly at me. "I'm just worried about my kid," I said, my voice choked. "I'm not here for any other reason than that. Now, Dmitri, please show me the way out of here."

Back at the endodontist's office, I sat by the burbling turtle tank, blindly paging through a magazine called *FamilyFun*. That crowded cellar is where Pete wanted to be. Acting on hooligan-like, misguided impulses, certainly, running with people who espouse violence, or at the very least thuggishness. But acting, committing, diving in. And since this new direction of his had come to light, Dennis and I had made our objections clear, in many talks and arguments, pleading and thundering. But we hadn't listened much. And now I wondered if our boy, through his stubborn silent actions, was pleading with us—drowned in our daily duties and our private dilemmas—to fucking pay attention to the bigger picture.

ABBY, JUNE 19, 2015

Dennis clearly found some sense of order and solace in packing lunches. Four days before the school year ended, in the kitchen in our all-beige room in the all-suites hotel, he slapped cold cuts onto white bread, and packed the sandwiches into bags along with sacks of cheese curls and bright pink wafer cookies. Dennis was a junk-food devotee, and the boys followed in his footsteps. I thought all of them ate horribly, but this was another battle I no longer chose to fight. Especially not at the moment, in the all-beige all-suites hotel.

But after they'd cleared out and I was dressing for work, I saw that Dennis had left behind the lunch he'd packed for himself. I had no early meetings, so I decided to detour through Bushwick to deliver it.

I hadn't yet made it to the studio. In the tough slog since the house burned, the plates of our marriage had shifted again. Grief had risen up like magma, pushing us further apart. And, thinking of his studio, I also felt scouring envy, that he had found himself a place to make his work and was busily prepping for Vienna, while I was still spending my days in my skyscraper cubicle, and my easel still stood forlorn in the corner of our water-damaged bedroom, in the house where all my paintings had been destroyed.

His studio was on the second floor, above a construction company's storage area, where pallets of bricks and concrete blocks lay scattered around, and old discarded doors and windows leaned against the walls. At the back of the space, a dark passageway ended at a staircase, at the top a rusting toilet and a blank black door. Dennis's name was written on a bit of painter's tape. I could hear the crackling of the arc welder and see its flare, in a strip of quivering brilliance under the door.

I knocked. Then a thought: Didn't I fear that I might find some other person there, if I came this way, unannounced?

He opened it with his hands still in bulky gloves, lifting the battered visor of his welding helmet to reveal his face shining with perspiration. He broke into a smile when he saw me there with his lunch bag.

"I know you aren't happy if you skip a meal," I said. He led me into the space, about the size of a two-car garage, with a glass ceiling, half tarred over. A dozen pieces ranged around the space, tall swerving forms. They were new, aligned with his previous works but grislier, somehow. Writhing shapes with torn edges and burned spots. At the room's center, rising up like a breaching whale, stood the largest sculpture, bristling with dozens of fins like knife blades, a contorted maw at its top, gaping open just beneath the skylights, as if it yearned to shatter them in its jaws.

"That's a bit terrifying," I said.

"Intended effect," he nodded.

"What does Mariah think of it?" I asked him.

He frowned, pulled off his welding paws, then picked up a toothed steel disc—a blade for his circular saw—and a pair of pliers. He began to bend its points. He had always manipulated his tools this way, to avoid straight cuts, to make every edge jagged and irregular.

"You have not been yourself all year," he said.

"I just want to know."

He grimaced over his work, the powerful tendons of his forearms moving under his sun-browned skin, the beginnings of his summer tan, he'd been riding the waves without a wet suit since Mother's Day. His eyelashes turned down, blond turning white.

"I don't know how we got here," he said.

"We capitulated."

"Maybe."

I ran a finger along a razor-like fin of the central monster, sharp enough to slice skin with gentle pressure. "Do you even see me anymore?" I turned to him. "Maybe I'm becoming invisible." My voice cracked.

"Abby," he said, reaching for my hand. I pulled it away.

"Can you remember who I used to be? The experience junkie?"

He shook his head. "You may have been a junkie, but some of those experiences you had, they fucked you up. And there are many you didn't tell me about too. I'm certain. You were like a shipwreck survivor, when we first met. Like you'd washed ashore without knowing from where."

"But I knew where I was headed. I was ambitious. Wasn't I?"

"Yeah, you were," he said. "And so fucking good. Better than anyone." He rubbed his jaw for a moment, staring at the floor. "So maybe yes, we capitulated." He inserted the blade into the yellow handsaw. "I remember how we wanted to make something new. Instead we just made the same thing everyone else does. House, kids."

"Our kids are good, though," I said.

"Our kids are great." He rummaged around in a box, extracted a pair of goggles. He turned to me, gently brushed my hair back and slipped them over my head. "I'm going to cut." His eyes were inches from mine. Lit up leaves pierced by sunlight. "Are you going to leave me?" he said.

"I guess I've been seeing someone too," I said. "A bit."

He backed away, pulled his goggles down, the plastic scratched and blasted. His eyes disappeared behind whiteness.

"Who," he said.

"Someone who came along."

He picked up his saw. Walked over to the breaching whale. Paused before it, looking up toward the skylights for a long moment. Then he pulled the switch to set the thing spinning, whining, and reached up and cut his creation in half, straight across its narrow middle, in one fluid motion. He hardly even looked at it as the top half twisted, pivoting on its last attachment point, then, just missing him, crashed to the floor.

Dr. Tristane Kazemy, JUNE 30, 2016

Le midi. The precise middle of the day, and on this day, the precise middle of the year. She marked this moment with a lunchtime run through the middle of Parque Mont Royal, her customary place, but rather than following the circuitous path to the pinnacle, she raced up a steep stairway through the woods, climbing skyward like the hands of a clock at the precise moment of *le midi*. Near the summit overlook, she flopped, winded, sweat-soaked, on a patch of lush summer grass. She stretched herself out flat, allowing the always-present breezes of this high place to cool her skin.

She had a notion. The anomaly could have appeared on the site of a previous head injury—the late effect of an earlier insult. Perhaps that damaged tissue had morphed over time in unusual ways. She would have to ask the New York detective if he could unearth any additional medical records, from earlier than 2015.

At the very least, the records might explain Mrs. Willard's fog. Dissociative amnesia, a common aftereffect of trauma. And certainly, it was clear from her journals, trauma was part of her story.

At the Club Sportif, near campus, she showered and changed back into her work clothes. By 13:00 she was again in her cramped office. Instantly she saw: someone had been there. A file had been opened. The scan—the essential scan of the essential slice of Abigail Willard's brain—had been left exposed on the screen.

She jumped up and peered down the hallway. Not a person in sight. But she knew. Returning to her desk, she could smell it. Suspended in odorant molecules in the airless cubbyhole: gin and unpleasantly musky cologne. The odor of the odious lab director. Eau du Laurin.

7/7/7/7

ABBY, JULY 1, 2015

Layer cakes of T-shirts. It is a leitmotif, I thought, as I watched them fill their suitcases.

My sons smashed the neat cakes. They crammed the folded tees into their bags, wedging them around their anti-boredom weaponry, plastic players of music and games and snarls of cords—plus assigned summer reading, Salinger stories for Benjamin, *Beloved* for Pete, and the jars of multivitamins I'd insisted they take along, since I knew very well what Dennis's mother would be serving. Canned fruit cocktail, frozen fish sticks, and powdered lemonade. The thrifty convenience foods Marlene Willard had discovered as a young wife at the long-gone base PX. She'd raised five robust boys on the stuff and stuck with what worked.

At the hotel the week before, Dennis pulled me out into the hallway. "We all need a breather," he said. He wanted to take Pete and Benjamin to Tustin for a while. The tickets were booked. I was hardly in a position to disagree. Still, I felt like he'd just opened my chest and hurled acid over my heart. Yes, Dennis and I needed time away from each other, but I didn't want the family torn apart. I hated the idea of being away from my boys, the sensory cyclone of them, their footfalls and barking laughs, the warmth of their hurried hugs. These utterly real beings. Without them, I'd be left with the ghosts.

Dennis was still talking, softly, sadly. "Ben can go to surf lessons, and Pete, well . . . Maybe he'll surf too."

"Pete won't surf," I said.

"I need to get my head straight," he said. "You do too."

A straight head. This had been repeatedly proposed. Did such a thing even exist? Was this a sensible aspiration?

He and I embraced. Because what else was there to do.

"I wish I understood what's going on," he said.

"It's like we woke up from a long sleep," I said, pulling back to meet his overcast gaze. "And I've realized I'm strapped down, restrained. I woke up fighting and I'm still fighting. I want to stop, but I can't seem to." The words were spilling fast from my mouth now. "And I've been seeing myself."

He nodded. "I've been giving myself a hard look too. And I'm determined, we're going to get past this," he said. He placed his hands on my head, their weight like a heavy crown. He slid them slowly down, smoothing my hair.

"No, I've been seeing myself, really."

He nodded, serious, sympathetic. "Time," he said. "Just give yourself some time."

"Yes," I sighed. "Time."

"And medical marijuana, maybe," he said, releasing me with a last, reluctant, soft brush of his fingers at the base of my neck. "Since I'm going to be in Cali."

"I'll stick with reality TV," I said. "This room gets so many channels."

So the three of them packed up and fled, as if in advance of a storm or contagion. Benjamin did look as if he were evacuating from his Brooklyn teenhood, with his Mets and Nets baseball caps tethered outside his bulging backpack, two pairs of headphones around his neck, and his Coney Island hoodie pulled up over his head.

After they'd gone, I sat in the silent ransacked room, again looking out over the endless static of the borough, bricks of light and dark that made no sense to my eye. Only one thing in this universe I cared to do. I drove to the burned house, to the master bedroom, where it all stood, a bit dirtied by the flames and the deluge, but ready for me. My easel. My tubes of paint, my brushes. I stood in the ruins and got to work.

ABBY, JULY 2, 2015

I painted for hours, fell asleep on the sooty sofa downstairs, and awoke remembering that I had a job. It now seemed like a holdover from a distant time. Without the ballast of my marriage, our home, what was I still doing, I wondered, fiddling with the outlines of an esophagus for the packaging of sore-throat spray? It didn't make much sense, but the bills continued to arrive through the mail slot, landing in the littered entry. Viennarte or not, Dennis wasn't earning right now. Someone had to pay.

So, Abby. Wear your yoke and be grateful for its sustaining weight. Without it, you might blow away.

Through a cool summer morning, I returned to the hotel, showered off the soot, swept up in a hopeful spirit—just keep moving, Abby, answers will come! It was still early. I decided to walk to work across the great arc of the bridge.

Bands of fog rose from the river and rested atop the towers like the bushy eyebrows of an old man. They reminded me of Bremer, my teacher, and, as I walked, I thought about him standing in front of my work in class, his belly drooping over his cracked leather belt, hands stuffed in the front pockets of a pair of voluminous brown tweed trousers. I recalled how his unlit cigarette bobbed in his mouth as he nodded at me and said, Best in show, Mrs. Willard. Very promising indeed.

The memory made me smile. I felt another surge of optimism. Maybe it was all going to be okay. The boys would soak up some Western sea and sun. Pete might shake loose this dark urgency that had overtaken him. Dennis and I could start a new phase, after our adventuring. A second marriage, of sorts. We'd all come back together later in the summer, rested and ready to rebuild.

Passing directly under the bridge's old-man brows, I stopped short.

An arm's length away, leaning against the guardrail.

Have you seen him? she asks. She stands on her tiptoes, scans the walkway behind me. I've been waiting a long time.

I follow her gaze, glancing over my shoulder, but all I see is the bridge arcing away, toward a Brooklyn obscured by fog. Then I remember. He would run, and I liked to meet him here on the bridge, and tag along for the last mile, the downhill stretch.

She has gathered her hair in a thick bunch on one side, an urban milkmaid. She reaches out and takes my hand. Her grip is cool and tight, and I feel the fine little bones, I know each one.

Prussian blue, she says, with a little smile, chasing the rime of paint at the edges of my fingernails.

I was up at it, almost all night.

She nods happily. Good to hear. She drops my hand. I have been trying to get a portfolio together, but . . . I've let it slide a bit.

She is thinner, I notice, her chin less soft, bones at the base of her throat more pronounced, her bright exhausted eyes.

You're getting lost in his trouble.

His trouble is my trouble, she says.

I remember now tagging along on his photo shoots deep in the city's bowels, in the ragged colonies of desperadoes who live in the caverns of the trains. Helping him cajole his way into drug dens in abandoned buildings in Inwood and Mott Haven.

She looks past me and her face suddenly blooms like a flower in time lapse. There he is, she says. I turn to see a figure coming toward us. Dressed in running shorts. He's still quite far away, the path is dotted with other walkers and runners, and he hasn't seen her, or us.

But one thing is very clear: he is not running. He's stumbling, one hand on the handrail.

I turn to her. He doesn't seem right.

No, she frowns. He doesn't. She starts to run. Moving quickly away from me, toward him, weaving in and out of the approaching pedestrians.

As I watch her go, her ponytail bouncing, the bottoms of her sneakers flashing, there's a sense of slipping again. Woozy. I turn to the railing. My gaze lands on the black water far, so far below. For an instant, I feel myself catapulting, plunging toward it. Then I steady myself and when I look for them again, I see no sign of them in either direction. Only the morning mist, which has thickened even further now, all around me, it's all I can see, draping over the bridge and down to the river, a heavy gray blanket dragging its hem in the flow.

ABBY, JULY 4, 2015

Forest Versteeg was as good as his word. He'd asked Dennis and me up to the country cottage he owned with his gallerist husband,

Matthew Legge-Lewis. But Dennis had departed, and so early
on this holiday morning, I drove far upstate alone, on increasingly
empty roads. The sky churned with storms, rumbling like God's
own upset stomach. Their bungalow sat in a half-abandoned ham-
let straggling up a mountain, facing north. I'd imagined subdued
charm and stunning art, but the place smelled of chimney ash and
dog hair and was full of broken-down secondhand chairs. I felt at
home.

Forest spent the hour before dinner hitting a tennis ball against
the concrete wall of a tractor shed across the driveway, while his
husband and I watched from a warped side porch, drinking powerful watermelon daiquiris, whipped up batch after batch in a little
blender plugged into an extension cord that trailed out a window.
"I have vowed not to apologize for our shortcomings, here," said
Matthew, a small plump man with a dark carpet of hair encircling
a perfect brown dome of baldness, and round spectacles perched
on his nose. Rain threatened. Their two mutts lolled and slobbered
across our feet. "We like to say that here we have a respite from all
fabulousness. It's just sloth and slovenliness here, and I love it." He
chortled loudly and happily, and the dogs thumped their tails in
response.

"Sloth is definitely in my wheelhouse," I said, holding out my
glass for another refill.

The ball smacked against the cement, and Matthew asked me
about my long-ago falling out with Jillian Broder.

"Not a falling out, really," I said. "My work didn't sell, and she
simply lost interest."

"Well, I'm interested," said Matthew. "I'd love to see your
work."

"I would have so happily shown you everything," I said. "But it's
all gone. The fire."

Forest suddenly stopped, the ball winging past him and into the yard. He swiped at his face, pinkened with exertion and slick with sweat and the raindrops that were just starting to fall. "I didn't realize that. I'm so sorry, Abby. I will always remember that work. It was absolutely unforgettable."

The downpour began. Forest ran for the porch, already soaked by the time he got there. The pups refused to budge, and we all stepped over them and retreated into the house.

"Do you realize," I said as we finished our drinks in the dim living room, listening to the rain ping on the flue in the cold fireplace, "if I'd sold all those paintings at that show, they'd be gone anyhow. So it kind of shakes out the same."

"You can mourn them, you know," said Forest, swirling his glass to get the last lumps of rum-soaked melon.

"But Dennis's work came through it?" said Matthew.

"He only had one small piece there in the house. According to him, it gained patina in the fire." I laughed. "And he's been able to get back into the studio. Since he lost his job. His new work is brilliant," I said.

"Yes, yes, so I heard, from Mariah Glücksburg. We bumped into her at some dive bar out on the island. She sang his praises, that husband of yours," said Matthew with a chuckle. "Viennarte. Not too shabby."

I said nothing.

"Then she said you were the real genius of the family," Forest added, quietly.

The rain let up as dusk fell. We headed for a fireworks display in a bigger town closer to the Hudson. I shuffled along behind Matthew and Forest in the dark, across a high school football field thronged with Americans in a holiday mood. Matthew spread a blanket for us. The fireworks began flinging out their shimmering tentacles. Once, during a silver moment, I glanced over and noticed that the two of them had snuggled close to each other and were holding hands. I felt a pang. After all, how many times had Dennis and I done the same on this same date? On sandy beaches in the years we'd taken our boys to the Jersey shore, two little orangutan tots clinging to us as they squealed at the noise and color. Or up in Massachusetts, early on, when I'd taken my new and clearly serious boyfriend back to Hartsfield to cuddle in the cool grass in City Park. I could still recall the kisses lit in flashes, under the lame yet heartfelt pyrotechnics of my hometown. Twenty years of Julys, next year. If we made it to next July.

The blossoms opened and collapsed into smoke. Booms echoed off the dark mountains. When the last ember faded, I rubbed my eyes, to clear the tears before anyone could see.

ABBY, JULY 8, 2015

I made him a pot of tea in our ruined kitchen, using a propane camp stove from the basement. We fucked in the ruined master bedroom, on the scorched wooden bed, in sheets feathered with soot. Afterward his back was covered in flakes of char, and my body was speckled by his smudged charcoal fingerprints.

Again I'd texted the detective. Against all good judgment and the many promises I'd made to myself. I waited for him at the house, where I also awaited a delivery of floor tiles. He appeared at the door, a bag from an Italian deli in his hand, dimpled smile on his face.

He kissed me, long, dropped the bag on the floor. It was very hot in the house, and I could feel his shirt chilled by his car's air-conditioning. His skin felt slightly rough like an almond's skin. We climbed the stairs to the bedroom and when he undressed, everything about him looked brand-new and festive. It felt like that to me, when I was fucking him—it was like crashing a party, where all was new and strange, you were treated to delicious sights and tastes, and you didn't know the people or the point, and you were very sure you didn't belong there. But that was the lure of it.

Afterward, he fetched the deli bag and unwrapped an eggplant parmesan sub, split into two halves, spreading the paper out on the bed. "DiFiori's. Best in Brooklyn," he said. "They grow their own herbs for the sauce." He said herbs with a hard *H*. He wolfed his half, lay down again, stared up at the ceiling, and let out a long sigh. "Fucking crazy day," he said. "When I get that promotion, I'll be setting my own hours. Which will be a relief. I'm wiped." He turned and smiled. "But in a good way, now."

"You really think you'll get promoted?" I was eating slowly, savoring. The sauce, tangy and sweet and thick, truly, the best in Brooklyn, he might be right.

"The chief gig?" He shrugged. "Yeah. Now I've decided I want it, I'll do what it takes," he said. "And let's face it, Pizziali is a dipshit. I don't mind the guy but he's a sneaky little dipshit. I just need to nail this one big thing I'm after, and I'm in." He turned on his side and watched me with a smile as I ate hungrily. "You like it," he observed.

"No. I hate it. I'm hating every minute of this." I licked the last of the sauce off my fingers.

"How's Pete?" he said.

"Pete's at his grandma's house."

"Great. No bad influences at Grandma's house."

"No. Just bad Technicolor food."

He looked baffled. "What?"

"You know, like pink coconut snowballs."

"Oh yeah, I love those," he nodded. Then he grinned. "Now you're making me hungry for dessert." We fucked again.

After the detective left, the construction crew arrived. I texted Dennis that I missed him and I pledged to myself that this would be my last transgression. I stood before my easel again. I raised my brush. But then, I lowered it, tapped it in my dish of water, walked to the window, where flakes of charred ash lingered in the corner of the panes. I ran the wet brush across them, to gather them, then walked back to the canvas and worked them into a field of whitened cobalt blue.

The work wasn't coming easily. Sometimes I stood there for hours, a dumb creature staring frozen, sniffing for a scent in an imperceptible breeze, trying to draw some meaning out of the air, only to find nothing. Sometimes I wished I could paint like someone else. Someone so much smarter and better than me. But the work was in front of me, just me, and only I could do it. So I persisted, a smallish creature, still standing there, open, hoping. Working in the ruins, with the trust that somehow meaning would drift in and settle around me.

July 17, 2016

From: GarrettShuttlesworth@physics.humboldtstate.edu
To: J.Leverett@deepxmail.com

I'd like to run some calculations on the Cori supercomputer at Berkeley. I know your need for discretion on this case though, Jameson. Willing to risk it?

ABBY, JULY 25, 2015

My boys sounded entirely too happy in California. Dennis was teaching both of them to ride the waves, driving every day to Huntington Beach Pier from his parents' parched acre in Tustin, the concrete backyard and the spiny plants that scraped you if you came too close.

Benjamin loved it so much, he didn't want to come back. Not even Gianna could compete. He asked if he could live with his grandparents and go to Tustin High. "California is bullshit," said Pete, on the other hand. "It's a failed system. The air is totally fucked up, the beach is full of plastic garbage. Also Granny and Gramps do not have Wi-Fi, I mean, they have a cable modem, Ma. With a cord that you have to plug in."

"But enjoy the weather at least, sweetheart," I said. "It's so muggy here."

I missed my boys terribly.

Mariah called, inviting me to the dwindling end of Long Island to meet her man. "It's well past the middle of the summer," she said. "Have you even seen the goddamn ocean, with all the excitement in your life? I think every artist needs to see the ocean at least once a quarter." I could not think of a reason to say no.

I was asleep on the train when I heard my name being called. "Excuse me, hi, Abby."

Dmitri Petamezas threw himself into the seat across the aisle from me and kicked his feet up on the armrest one row up. Acid green sneakers, bright orange laces. I complimented him on this bold footwear choice.

"I collect them, I have forty-seven releases, I think." He told me he was headed to his dad's house in Bridgehampton, which was boring beyond reason, he said, though lately there were some cooler bars opening up.

"You're not old enough for bars though, are you?"

He shrugged. "According to the Kentucky Motor Vehicle Commission, I am." He grinned at me, charming as a chipmunk with his dark eyes and plump cheeks. "I've been chatting with Pete," he said. "So they left you here, huh? California sounds good."

"I have to work."

"Wage slavery," he said, shaking his head.

I recalled him slurping cereal in our kitchen the morning of the fire. The smell of chlorine in the house. I frowned at him. "So how do your parents pay the rent, Dmitri?"

"They're entrepreneurs," he said with a smile. "I've tried to tell them that they're also in the path of the tsunami. They laugh." His irises shone like black oil. "But this movement is unstoppable, by any of us, parents, kids, it doesn't matter who is for or against it. It's the coming moment. The current conditions are not sustainable. We must do what must be done."

"You may very well be right," I said. I didn't want to agree, I didn't want to condescend. "Do those shoes glow in the dark?" I asked. The conductor rolled by us, yodeling about the Bridgehampton stop. He stood up and slipped his backpack straps over his shoulders. "Abby, think about this." He braced himself against the seatback and looked down on me, still smiling. Beneath our feet, jolts and vibrations, the island sliding past us as we hurtled east. "What do you truly want for your sons. Envision another way. They don't have to end up as rats trapped in a rigged maze. Like you. Like your husband Dennis Willard. Like both of you." He flipped his bangs away and fixed me with those eyes, ancient and newborn at once. "Be bold, Abby. I saw you out there on Flatbush.

You have rage in you. You can fight." The train slowed, pulling into Bridgehampton station.

He gave me a searching look. "Have you thought any more about us?" he said. "The Brigade?"

"I have," I said.

"And?"

"I guess I'm more with you than against."

He nodded, then raised a fist. He kept it high all the way down the aisle and off the train. Then I saw him standing on the platform, tapping into his phone, as the train continued along the island's forked tongue.

ABBY, JULY 26, 2015

Hyde is the name of Mariah's man. "I am a student of human anatomy, and your patellas are misaligned," he told me, as I walked into the room in my bathing suit, sun-blasted from the long beach day. He'd completed most of a kinesiology degree. His long bare feet were brown, his hair in a disorderly braid. He was chopping mint and cucumber for the smoothie he swore was about to change my life.

Mariah lay on a hammock hung just outside the open sliding doors, watching us with a beatific smile. "Every physical being is a book of runes for this man," she said.

Hyde looked up from his cucumber, perplexed.

"*R-U-N-E-S*," said Mariah. "Not ruins."

"Runes," he said, nodding.

"It's a system of symbols," she said. She looked blissfully happy, Mariah did, in cut-off jeans shorts and a bikini top, arms pillowing her head, there in the shade of her covered porch. She was curvy and soft-bellied and commanding as an odalisque.

I stretched out on a sofa beneath one of Mariah's paintings. A faint soft-edged slash, in a madder-lake red blended into ivory. "So how about Dennis," I said. "Dennis in Vienna. At this stage of the game. Remarkable, right?"

"Utterly," she said. She lay on her side, facing me, a silhouette from this angle, a set of curved shapes against the blue swimming pool.

"Were you behind that?" I asked.

She sighed loudly. "Abby, his work speaks for itself. Always has. It was only a matter of time." She disappeared into the soft crevasse of the striped hammock, voice floating to me. "But as for Viennarte, I may have put in the first word."

Hyde glided across the room holding a small tray aloft, balancing two spindle-stemmed wineglasses, brimming with green slush. He delivered one to each of us, a courtier paying tribute to a pair of queens.

"You gave up on yourselves too easily," Mariah's voice drifted over to me. "Giant talents like you two, taking office jobs."

"We were broke," I said. "We had children."

She laughed. "You needed more patience and maybe better advocacy."

"So now Dennis has you as his . . . advocate?"

"Hell yes," she says. "And you do too."

"Yes, but only one of us just got invited to Viennarte. The one who is fucking you."

She laughed even more. "Abby, come on."

"What did she just say?" Hyde piped up.

"She's joking, doll." Mariah sat up again and blinked at me, her face serious now. "What would I need to go and do that for? Look at this gorgeous specimen I've got here."

He smiled. "Thanks, babe."

I was sweating, my pulse pounding in my ears. "Tell me the truth," I said. "Maybe I'm just envious of him. Or you. Or both. Tell me what I'm feeling is artistic envy, or if there's something else going on."

She blinked those luminous eyes at me again, for a long moment. "Abigail," she said at last. "Your day will come, I know it will. You are just beginning to rise."

I lifted my smoothie to my lips, now feeling deeply ashamed and ravenously thirsty. My face was burning, from the day of sun, from my embarrassment and anger, my shins felt abraded by sand, my heart sore.

Who was she to assure me that my day will come?

Who was I to hurl accusations about out-of-bounds fucking?

I chugged the rest of the admittedly delicious smoothie then lay flat on the sofa and stared at the ceiling. I was surely the most confused person on the planet. Mariah passed by and kissed me on the top of my head as she padded off to shower.

Later that night, Hyde insisted we should all go out for a nightcap at the Marlin. "Shit, is that place still there?" I said. We were already drunk, and we rode bicycles the five blocks to the town center, me teetering on a too-tall model, gears a bit rusty. Mariah and Hyde rolled ahead on matching Italian trail bikes. She tootled a bulbed horn, waking half the sleeping town, I'm sure. She must have drunk half a fifth of vodka in the past few hours, and this was a petite woman. Still she held her own, Mariah. She had practice, drinking with the men of the arts for decades now.

A nearly full moon trembled above, eye of a dark swimmer in

a darker sea. The weekend was humid, tropical almost, with an unsettled whiff of hurricane season.

The Marlin was the town's eternal midnight heartbeat, an old fisherman's bar, with walls covered in pine paneling and many taxidermied ocean dwellers, dented and dusty, staring down in glassy outrage. The air was redolent of clams and beer and the scented body wash of the house sharers, the air mattress sleepers, the young office workers hunting the coast for sexual opportunity and perhaps even love. Tan skin, gelled hair, even a popped collar here and there.

Mariah gave the bouncer a kiss and swept regally to a small table, set up as on a promontory, front and center, and canopied in fishing nets. Hyde bellied up to the bar, his man bun bobbing over the heads of the youngsters.

Mariah scooped up my hand, held it to her hot cheek, closed her eyes beatifically. "Abby, you are in flux," she said. "I envy you." She leaned toward my ear and whispered, "You are rocketing toward your future." Despite the din all around us, I heard her as if she'd said these words to me in a silent vacuum-sealed enclosure, a space capsule or a quarantine chamber. They echoed in my ear, dizziness surged through me, the vertigo that was somehow becoming familiar, the tilting and sloshing, the nausea. I squeezed my eyelids shut. You will not vomit, you will not.

Hyde slammed down a drink in front of me, my eyes snapped open, and the smell of it—brown, cherry, something thick and medicinal—made me certain I would be sick. I pushed back from the table, gasped something about needing a breath of air. Stumbled away without a glance at them, my eyes fixed on the bar's exit.

Reeling now, the night air hit me like a dank lukewarm sponge, but at least it was quiet. I staggered to the dark perimeter of the parking lot, rested against the cool and unyielding butt of a pickup.

Straight ahead was the beach, a faint paleness sloping down to the very edge of the world. The void.

The void that beckoned me now, with a steady rhythmic murmur and fluttering fingers of ragged foam.

I can't find him again, she says. But here I find you.

And then she emerges from the darkness with a bottle in her hand, a pair of sandals dangling in the other, just barely perceptible as red in the light filtering from the bleared moon. She shimmers, it must be the sand coating her arms and legs, but each grain seems distinct, a particle of her matter, a body barely coalesced.

Did you see him, did you see him walk by, she says. He was here with me, until then he wasn't.

I haven't seen a soul, I say.

How has she come to be here? But then I recall, don't I, the weekends in a huddled one-room summer shack, left to Eli and his mother when his father consigned himself to an Oregon rehab retreat? A shack of pine-green shingles rotted at the edges, surrounded by hydrangea blooms as if adrift in a cloud bank. Inside, mildewed quilts on a big bed bowed in the middle like a rowboat.

I'm worried about him.

And she tells me about the vials rolling out of his pockets as he stripped by the bed. About how he swore he wasn't smoking it himself. This is how I bribe them, he said. I barter so they let me photograph them.

It becomes a catastrophe, I say. Get away.

She stands not six inches away from me now. I am frightened, but in my sick swoony state, I don't dare move from the support of the car at my back. I know I will fall.

Her breath barely brushes my face, and it is cold, oddly cold, and smells like the ocean. My legs are starting to shake.

You have to leave him, I say.

And who are you, to tell me what to do.

Her eyes are so black, and then something flares in them.

A reflection of flame. She turns, I turn, and there he is, down in the blackness closer to the water. We both see him at once. Briefly brushed by firelight, his face. Eli, lighting a cigarette, a crack pipe, I can't see what it is. Only a glimpse of his face in gold light and the memory of him on the balcony, with a flaring match and his deep-set eyes in shadow. Holding something precious of mine in his hand.

I feel a hole opening up beneath my feet. A destroyer, I say.

She lays her cold hand on me. You're on fire, she says.

At her chill touch, my balance begins to crumble, my strength draining away. My hands search for purchase, something on the car to cling to, a handle, a bumper. But they slide across the steel.

I'm falling, I say.

Yes, she says.

Then soft cold sand against my skin and darkness.

SESSION NOTES

A voice mail from A. In crisis, by the sound of it. Would like to resume consultations. She says she will pay what she owes.

But I am off for my Wellfleet month. I will see her in September.

Dr. Tristane Kazemy, JULY 30, 2016

Two could play at this game. This she had discovered, and so much else, while Laurin was summering in his family's ancestral *mas provençal*. She had discovered that his lab assistant, the graceful undergrad Molly Jiang, was more than willing to unlock the office of the man she called "*le monsieur professeur porc.*"

Slipping into his plushly carpeted sanctum on this day, Tristane discovered that Laurin had purloined the essential Willard scan. And, with his vaunted eye, he had spotted the irregularity that she had been contemplating for weeks. She saw his notes:

There is one abnormality, congenital perhaps. Likely not significant. No impact on brain function. Kazemy's notes theorize about hallucinations and dissociative amnesia, but these must be considered purely psychosomatic.

A note addressed to Buccardi: Dr. K squandering lab resources on an entirely unremarkable brain, without permission, to null result. Disciplinary measures apropos?

8/8/8/8

ABBY, AUGUST 3, 2015

Then I saw Eleanor Boyle in a cloud. Her voice message arrived late at night. "Abby, I know we haven't seen each other since forever," she said. "But fuck, something weird just happened, pertaining to you. I'm in Midtown, and I think you still are too? Come see me."

She worked for a casting agency on the sixty-eighth floor of a brand-new white-glass building on a silent far-western block. Her window looked out on a bank of cotton batting. She crossed an acre of carpeting with a nervous lipsticked smile, her body tilting toward me in a tight purple sheath dress. Such a vast office—I realized Eleanor must be the boss. She hugged me a bit breathlessly. I felt nervous to see her too. Reuniting after years of no contact usually feels awkward, though I'm not sure why that should be. Maybe it serves up the passage of time right there on a plate, naked and unavoidable?

Eleanor must've been thinking along the same lines, because she said, "Look at us. *Femmes d'un certain âge.* I'm fifty in three fucking years," said Eleanor. "And you in four!"

"Believe it or not," I said.

"I haven't managed to skydive yet. Have you?" She settled back into her white leather desk chair.

"Is that mandatory?" I said.

"Well, life can get a bit monotonous if you don't take a god-damn risk now and then," she said. She was still Eleanor, bony and leggy and profanity-inclined, her hair still in the red flapper's bob, sleek around her head like an old-fashioned pilot's cap.

"Well, it is possible that I may be drawn to other types of risk," I said. I felt propelled toward recklessness by her, just like in the old days.

Her brows jerked up, two slender leaves caught in a sudden gust, and she gave a delighted grin. "Oh, Abigail. You wicked vixen." She gave a little shrug. "I fuck mostly women now, and that helps." She waved her hand toward a cork-covered wall. Headshots pinned in a grid: rows and columns of rapt eye contact, scintillating teeth. "I meet a lot of lookers. Hazard of the job."

"I heard that somewhere, that you'd come out."

"I had an insane party at that hookah club to celebrate it. I tried to find you, to invite you, I think, but you were . . . gone, it was the most bizarre thing."

I nodded. "Yes, I know. I still feel guilty about losing touch, dropping off the map that way . . . You were so important to me."

"Aw, that's sweet." She swiveled a bit in her rolling chair, then leaned forward, resting her elbows on the desk. The front hanks of her bob pointed toward her brightly painted mouth. "Abby, I'm thinking you're in some kind of trouble?"

"Um, possibly," I ventured.

"A cop came to see me." She leaned forward even more and low-ered her voice a bit. "Handsome as fuck. At first I thought he was snooping around about an incident we had here, one of my partners developed a hard-on for a chorus kid and took things a little too far, left us very liable, the cretin." Her eyes glittered. "So at first this lawman was just asking about the agency, our business, then he said he'd read my bio on our website, and saw I had a degree from Western New England. And then he said, really casually, I know someone you might know."

The clouds roiled outside the window, making it seem like we were moving, as if we were in a ship in the sky. "Me," I said.

"Were we good friends, he wanted to know. Whether you'd used drugs. Your political leanings, of all things. Fuck if I know, I said. We were party girls, we liked to dance, I told him. And then I told him you met a guy, got very into him, and we kind of lost touch."

"True," I said.

"He wanted to know who the guy was, and at that moment, I thought, she's either banging this hot cop or she's in some kind of deep trouble."

I could feel heat rising in my cheeks. I thought back to when he'd asked me about myself, and I'd talked about Eleanor, my oldest friend in New York. He must've assumed we were in contact, and closer than we actually were. But why would he be poking around in my deep history like this? Making inquiries about me?

"I told him that I didn't remember your boyfriend's name. I said, all I know is that the guy's long gone. Dead."

This last word landed like a punch in my chest, and the punch unleashed a torrent. I began blurting everything—the night in the cab, the glimpses in the library and the paint store. Rock Center and the bridge and the beach. I told her about Mariah and Dennis, the fire, the detective.

As she listened, Eleanor rested her chin in one long white hand

and peered at me with a puzzled expression. When I finally stopped, she said, slowly, "You really think she burned down your house?"

"I've changed my thinking about what's in the realm of the possible," I said. "But tell me, have you ever experienced such a thing?" She sat back in her chair and stretched her arms overhead, revealing a pale tuft of rose-white fuzz in each armpit. I searched her face for reassurance. "I mean, I've sometimes wondered if maybe this sort of stuff happens often to women our age, but nobody talks about it. Like night sweats, loss of skin tone, and visions of self?"

Eleanor cocked her head to one side and regarded me silently for a long moment. Finally, folding her hands in her lap, she said, "How did he actually die, Abby? The boyfriend. I heard rumors. Suicide. Or fell off a fire escape when he was high on something. Or there was a structural collapse of some kind . . ."

My throat seemed to close up. I shook my head. "Not a fire escape. A balcony," I said. "I can't remember much else. How it happened."

"Well damn, Abby, it's all a strange story, isn't it."

She peered at me, assessing.

"I know." I let loose a long, shaky sigh. "You think I'm losing my mind."

"You know what I think, Abby? When we were in college, Dougie Corwin gave me pot cookies on the sly," she said. "I got so stoned, the world got strange, and I didn't understand why."

"I always hated Dougie Corwin," I said.

"Yeah." She nodded. "Any chance your teenagers are spiking your cookies?"

"I don't think that's it," I said.

She leaned forward. "This girl could be anyone. So she looks a bit like you. So her boyfriend looks a little like him. We all have our doubles, our slightly altered versions. Every other day someone says to me, oh my god, you look exactly like my fucking sister Sheila. Doesn't that happen to you?"

"But she lives in my old apartment," I said, my voice oddly pleading.

"You saw a sliver of a woman's face through a dark doorway. And the woman immediately slammed the door on you. Was it actually her?"

I stared at the floor. Frigid January morning, the climb up the stairs, the glimpse of her. Was it her?

"And you believe you were her—but what does she have to say about it?" Skepticism in her voice. "Does she believe she's going to be you?"

I turned over each encounter in my mind. Finally, I said, "No. She says she'll never be me."

A gentle knocking, then someone beyond the door said, "The two p.m. call is getting restless out here, and we're running out of chairs."

"In a minute!" Eleanor turned to me, gave me a sad little smile. "Abby, has she ever even told you her name?"

"A, is all she says." I shook my head. "I guess she thinks I'm a stalker or a lunatic or . . ." my voice lapsed.

"You need a therapist?"

"I've been seeing one." I didn't tell her it was Dr. Merle the Miracle Worker.

She rose with an expression of relief, straightened her dress, strode around the desk. "I better get out there. We're casting a genderqueer *Oklahoma!*," she said. "Tattooed ranch hands of all persuasions. Might get interesting."

We hugged at the door, holding each other a little more firmly and comfortably this time. "Thanks for calling me, Eleanor. For letting me know. I know this seems crazy, I'm sorry—"

"No apologies," she cut me off. "You just take care. Stay in touch. And Abby. If you see the younger me," she said, "tell that gorgeous little fucker I said hello."

ABBY, AUGUST 10, 2015

The detective texted, but I wouldn't answer. A stormy torrent of messages scrolled down my phone's screen, beginning with, "Let's meet again, just say when and where, I'll bring the DiFiori's," until the last, two nights ago: "Ghosting me?"

And this morning I woke to realize I'd been five weeks alone. Light leaked into the hotel room in two blinding stripes, over and under the black-out curtains. I was working hard to ready the house, hoping we'd move in again by the end of the summer, get it spiffy and shining for my boys. I rose to pee and brush my teeth. But I didn't make it to the bathroom. The floor went all atilt.

I barely made it back to sit on the end of the bed. I crawled across the rumpled sheets to my phone.

But who to call? Dennis would be fast asleep on the West Coast.

The detective? No. Clearly, no longer trustworthy. If he ever had been.

I tried Mariah.

She arrived at the hotel in her hulking SUV, careening up under the portico where I sat slumped on a bench, a jacket over my nightgown, a pair of polka-dotted rubber boots slipped over my bare feet, and a few belongings in a plastic grocery sack.

She rolled down the window and said, "You look like what they used to call a bag lady. What have they done to you?"

"Who?"

"Whoever is responsible for this evil twin of my beautiful friend. Seriously, you look awful. I'm taking you in hand."

The SUV gobbled the FDR Drive, assorted pylons and towers gyrating past, whirling like dervishes. I was aware of Mariah chattering about this year's art fair in Miami and a South African collector trying to court her with blood diamonds. "And I have no truck with blood diamonds, Abby, but wow they were sparkly."

The garage door to her carriage house rose with a flourish, and in we rolled. What a wonder, what an ultimate luxury in this city, an always-available place to park. And the storage space: cleaning tools arrayed neatly on hooks, shelves of surplus paint and thinners for her studio, cases of sparkling water and wine. I was ready to simply sleep in that organized sanctum, sunk into the comfy leather car seat, but then Mariah was easing me out, with my arm over her shoulder and her curls brushing my face, spicy and herby smelling, like rosemary.

And then it was morning and Hyde was bent over my bed with a purple smoothie on a tray. "Extra protein and vitamins D through F," he said.

"I think that only leaves E?" I drank it down, feeling sure I would vomit it up within the half hour. Which I did.

I called Dr. Singh to consult on this latest downturn. "Your CT scan appeared clean, but if your symptoms are still troubling you, I will order a detailed MRI. But Abigail, your house, your situation, this is also psychological trauma."

"Yes, yes, I'm seeing a shrink," I said.

In fact, I hadn't seen Dr. Merle since the single visit in May. I realized I'd never received her bill. Strange. I'd have to check in on that. In any case, after I hung up with Singh, I called her office and booked a date.

Later, sluicing water across my body in Mariah's pharaonic

marble shower, I realized it had been a while since I'd glimpsed the girl. Had she finally quit me? Had the city reabsorbed her, like in that vanished twin syndrome I'd read about—when an ill-fated fetus is reabsorbed, boosting the odds that its counterpart will survive?

Next, I called Dennis, who was incredulous that I'd landed at Mariah's place. I know it made him uncomfortable. And I admit, I enjoyed that. Benjamin was loving his surf lessons, updating me almost hourly with selfies, boy with surfboard, boy on surfboard, boy with cute girl in bikini on surfboard. He resembled an adorable sleek otter in these pics, in his obsidian wet suit and his hair slicked down wet and his big laughing eyes.

But Pete. He wanted to come home. "Grammy is mean to me; she's always after me to weed the driveway or run to the store for Miracle Whip. I want to come home. I have work to do."

"But home isn't quite functional," I said, flinching it a bit—because the degree to which this was true shocked me, how the summer had brought us to ruin. Still, he begged me and Dennis. At last we relented and we booked him a red-eye.

ABBY, AUGUST 13, 2015

My frail boy, he seemed to be backsliding, his voice more hesitant than it had been a few months before, the slight stutter, the muttering quality had returned. I gathered him from LaGuardia early in the morning.

"Did my Ministry vinyl ever turn up?" he said. "That was an original vinyl, I think it might have been worth something."

"No, I don't believe it did," I said brightly, turning around with a smile. "But remember your trumpet from sixth-grade band? That came through totally unscathed!"

He looked wan. I knew he must be weary from the overnight flight. I suggested he take a rest when we got to Mariah's.

When he went to unload his bag from the back seat, he noticed a tote bag holding posters. I'd printed them on the high-res machine at work that we used to test packaging designs. The color saturation was sumptuous. He stared down at the announcement for a Labor Day rally and march. "Those who do not move, do not notice their chains," he read out loud. He looked up at me. "Now you're quoting Rosa Luxemburg?"

"Murdered by fascists in 1919, Berlin," I said. "I've been reading."

He frowned at me. "Are you antifa, Mom?"

"No," I said, shyly. "Maybe a fellow traveler, a bit. Do you mind?"

He stared at the poster again. "I'm not sure." Then he said, "I'm starving."

At a diner around the corner from Mariah's we ate cheeseburgers and talked about what he'd need for the new school year, with the first day just two weeks out. New jeans, new notebooks, a new pair of sneakers.

I pointed to his grubby old shoes. "I guess you'll be saying so long to Dax?"

I'd read up too on the young Milanese man who had been knifed by a family of fascists—two sons and a dad, with a dog named Rommel—and was honored every April with a wreath laying in Milan. Pete set down his burger and said, "I knew you were up to something, Mom. Dmitri told me you'd contacted him. I think it's very weird. I thought you hated him. I mean . . ." He gave me a searching look. "Really, are you antifa, Ma?"

I blushed. "You know what I like about it? Its clarity. 'No tolerance for intolerance.' I realized that it appeals to me, the clarity, at this point in my life." I shrugged. "So I decided to help out, just a little bit."

He nodded, measuring my words. I opened my tote, rummaged around, and pulled out a pack of small square decals bound by a rubber band. Double flags, the stylized fist. In big block font, classic black on red: WE WILL NOT AGREE TO DISAGREE. I slid one out from the rubber band and handed it to him. "For your new shoes?"

He studied the decal, flipping it over and over, then looked up at me. "There's going to be an action at the end of this month. Not that I think you should go," he added. "Not that I think you would."

He asked me if I was going to finish my fries. I pushed their grease-spattered cardboard boat in his direction. We finished our meal, and not ten minutes after we'd returned to the carriage house, Dmitri turned up. He was coming, he said, from his new girlfriend's apartment just a few blocks away. "She is a certified flamethrower, this woman," he told me earnestly. "She's a French exchange student at Stuyvesant, but she's like pure French resistance." He turned to Pete. "She has a tattoo that says 'Killah P.'"

Pete looked impressed. Dmitri turned to me, with an air of patient explanation. "A Greek rapper, murdered by Golden Dawn faschos a few years back. Google him."

Pete toured him around the carriage house. He seemed, adorably, just a bit proprietary, proud to be staying in such a place, with its vaulted ceilings, the luxe living spaces, the studio with its appealing mess of works in progress. Dmitri took it all in, smiling and nodding politely. He laughed when he saw the portrait of Mariah's grandfather. "Damn, check out the medals on that guy."

And then he turned to me. "You should come to the Labor Day action, Abby. We need numbers, all we can get."

"She can't," Pete said.

"I can't," I nodded. "That's the last weekend to deal with the house, before Dennis and Ben fly home and we move back in."

Peter showed Dmitri into the tiny elevator, which Mariah had

lined with cream-colored linen and framed sketches—mostly portraits of her old loves, hung there like trophies. I'd looked for Dennis in this gallery, and didn't find him, but every time I took the
slow and jolting ascent to my room on the third floor, I'd stare at
one of the several empty spots, the naked linen, and I'd wonder.
Mariah had assigned Pete a tiny room up under the old carriage
house eaves, where she stored ball gowns from the 1950s, things
her mother and grandmothers wore to weddings of deposed royals,
the princes and princesses of Greece and Romania, who were now
dressage riders in the English countryside or worked at investment
houses in Zurich. Tulle and lace and satin, so thick and rich it hung
in slabs like meat, hung high on a pole that extended from wall to
wall. Dmitri reached up and ran his hand over the massed skirts.
"Oh shit, you can still smell the perfume," he said.

"Bye, Mom," said Pete, gently pushing me out and closing the
door. A bit later, I knocked with a tray of snacks and sodas. Dmitri
was gone, and my son had fallen fast asleep on a narrow twin bed
below their skirts, a boy in a bower.

ABBY, AUGUST 14, 2015

In Brooklyn, the spacklers were spackling, a toilet sat in the entryway ready to be set atop the wax circle around the frightening hole
in the floor of the bathroom. New ceramic tiles, square and white
as movie-star teeth, grinned at me from a carton. Finally. We had
talked for years of renovating that raggedy overworked single bath.
Dennis and I could never pull the trigger, but the fire had pulled
the trigger for us.

Pete's room held a pile of melted and waterlogged video game
gear and he kicked dejectedly at it. "Well, I've outgrown this crap

anyhow," he said. Once upon a time I had despaired about those games and the hours they consumed, but now I just felt a pang. Was it only eight weeks ago he and Ben had been excitedly designing a colony in space?

Downstairs, the whine of the saws paused, then the contractor on the job called up to me. "Someone to see you, Abigail."

In a linen jacket and blue gingham shirt, the detective stood next to the toilet in the entryway, one foot up on the seat, presenting a bouquet of pink roses wrapped in cellophane. "For you," he said, smiling brightly.

Then his smile vanished and he straightened. The bouquet fell, dangled by his side. My son had come down the stairs ten seconds behind me.

"How's it going, Pete," he said.

I turned to see a measure of comprehension cross my boy's face, the shadow of a moving thought.

"You remember the officer," I said, brightly.

Pete had halted a few steps above me. "Uh huh."

"A little goodwill offering," the detective said, putting the bouquet atop the toilet tank. "I hope all is OK with you, kid," he added.

Pete shrugged, his eyes revealing nothing. I noticed then that he had a package tucked under his arm. Oblong, wrapped in dirty brown paper.

I was reaching for it when the detective spoke from behind us. "I'm off then, just wanted to check in . . ."

"No, you stay, I'm leaving," said Pete. Evading my grasp he shoved past us, clutching this square to his chest like a shield, then dashed out the door and onto the sidewalk, the sound of his sneakered feet snapping like raps on a skull, away across the pavement and out of sight and hearing.

I looked at the man. Eleanor was right. He was handsome as

fuck. The powerful planes of his face, softened by thick eyelashes, lush brows, those bronze eyes, that flickered with intelligence and calculation. I felt them taking my measure.

"I know you've been snooping around about me," I said.

He nodded. "I thought that might be what you were pissed about. Just trying to help you out, and Pete."

"No, I don't think so. I don't know what you're up to."

"Yeah," he said. The slow-dimple grin. "I'm always up to something, so it's good for you to realize that. But you've gotten to me, Abigail. I mean it."

"Don't even try," I said. "I'm not falling for it."

As I said this, aggravating liquid started welling in my lower lids, eyeballs pressed from behind, painful knot yanked tight in my throat. He saw and moved toward me, put his arms around me. Even as I stiffened away from him and the tears spilled, in another part of my brain—oh, my poor, strange brain—I was absorbing the feeling of his bones again, tensile, strong, the clever architecture of him. But I gathered myself and said, in what I hoped was a cold and ruthless tone, "Delete me from your phone."

Driving home, in a woeful state, I steered, almost without thinking, to Rocco's on Bleecker Street. Sprinkle-covered Italian cookies and a cold Coke with plenty of ice. This has always been my go-to treat in times of confusion and despair. And always from Rocco's. So how could I be surprised to see her there?

I feel her first. A cool gust down the back of my neck, in the heat of the old café. I turn to see who is invading my personal space. I nearly jump out of my skin.

You don't look good, she says. Your eyes are like red planets.

I thought you were gone.

Not yet. But soon. He made some real money. We're going away, soon.

Yes. The turning point for him. Eli had been prowling the heat-addled neighborhoods of central Brooklyn on his bike. To photograph, to score, I'm not sure which. August 1991. On Utica Avenue, where West Indians and Hasids lived uneasily crammed together, a small boy and girl, children of Guyanese immigrants, were mowed down by a blue Grand Marquis station wagon in a motorcade carrying a revered rabbi. In the heat of the summer, as the day burned on, tensions boiled over, car windows were smashed, stores torched, and finally, a young Orthodox student was stabbed to death.

Eli, prowling the streets, heard the wild rumors, more death, another famed rabbi connected to it. Crown Heights was burning. He turned up at West Twelfth Street at dawn the next morning with bruises purpling on his back, cuts on his face. I rummaged for rubbing alcohol and cotton, but all I had was vodka and a balled-up T-shirt. I swabbed him while he told me, breathless with exhilaration, how he'd been photographing boys tearing the metal grille off a clothing store, "They turned on me, and I huddled on the ground over my camera and just let them kick the shit out of me, but no way were they getting my film," he said. He'd gone straight to the *Post*, who bought it all.

We got drunk, our boozy sweat blurring the copies of the *Post*; he ran out at dawn and bought more and left them lying all over the bed. We woke up at noon inky.

The memory makes me smile and she stares at me.

Sit and have a sprinkle cookie, I say. I open the little striped bag to show her.

Oh, she says, delighted. My favorite!

And so we sit there at a marbled Formica table dusted with the powdered sugar of earlier snackers. Severe summer sunlight bounces around the mirrored space. It is companionable, perching there together. We sit in silence, and I watch as she delicately presses a finger into each sprinkle that falls to the tissue-like napkin she's spread on the table—as I have—and licks it off the tip. Then I do the same.

He's full of hope. It's so good to see. I like our chances.

No, I say. I pull my phone from my pocket, power the launch screen. This is your future.

I slide the phone across the table. I know this is a dangerous impulse. She won't touch it. She just stares at the image there, dumbly. Her eyes go obsidian black. Her hair is piled atop her head in the heat, wet wisps are pasted to her neck.

She delicately lifts the phone, peers at the photo for a fleeting instant, then hurls it away as if she suddenly realizes it's searing her fingers. It bounces on the old table's marble rim, tumbles to the floor with a startling crack. She stands, a scream-like scraping of her chair. I see her turning away and moving fast toward the door, and I bend to retrieve the dark and fractured device, and as I double over, I know darkness is coming for me again too.

August 15, 2016

From: J.Leverett@deepxmail.com
To: GarrettShuttlesworth@physics.humboldtstate.edu

You've seen the data off the dead phone. All of it—texts, location tracking—support the story as she tells it. Some of the texts make me look like hell, I'll admit. I'm not proud of it, G. But as probably you recall, I've always been a bit of a shitheel.

Sending you and the neuroscientist, Kazemy, possible dates for a classified meeting here to present findings. You'll have your theories worked out, more or less?

ABBY, AUGUST 16, 2015

I woke to find myself in Mariah's bed. A velvety altar, decked all in the plushest fabrics in shades of white and chocolate and ivory. I rolled there groggily as I woke, felt myself adrift in a melting hot fudge sundae. A remarkable and pleasant sensation—but then I sat up with a jolt.

Pete. Where was my boy. He had run away.

Mariah wavered into focus, seated in an enormous armchair, wearing spattered painter's overalls and a bra, her hair spread in a dark corona around her head. So pink and clean were the soles of her bare feet, propped on a white ottoman, like treats on display in a posh pastry shop.

I realized after a moment that she was working a smallish clump of white modeling clay in her hands. She turned it and pressed it. Finally her eyes met mine but her expression didn't change. She didn't acknowledge my awakening, my stirring, didn't shift at all. She kept working the clay.

"Please tell me Pete is here," I said, propping myself up on my elbows, struggling to keep her in focus.

"Pete is here."

"Seriously. Is he?"

"He is downstairs, very happily sampling my music collection. The Breeders, I think. Listen."

And I did hear it, the shuddering baseline, just audible pumping up like blood through the heart of the house.

"Did I drive here?"

"God no. The waitress at Rocco's called you a cab, I think your car got towed."

"Shit. Thank you though."

"And some asshole stole your phone, apparently. Not in your purse, not on your person," she said.

"Shit," I said again.

"But on the upside, Pete told me you have a lover."

I checked her face for a mocking smile. She was impassive, still, apparently, sculpting. I dropped to the bed and closed my eyes. "Shit," I whispered.

"Abby, don't sweat it. It is high time for you to get yours."

Her hand moved so lightly. Unseen forces sent it this way and that. I watched, enthralled.

"And Dennis," I said. "Is it high time for him to get his?"

Her movements didn't stop, didn't even pause. "Ultimately, we're each and every one of us walking alone," she said. "Him, me, you. Paths will diverge and converge."

"So you are a divergence for him," I said.

"Your married love is so deep and so long, your paths will bend toward one another again, if you allow it to go that way."

"Or what we're doing now might destroy everything we've worked so hard to build."

"Or it might just destroy the constraints," she said. "The atrophied bits, that lock you in place. It might bring you both, Dennis and you, just the right degree of freedom."

"I don't know . . ."

"You think I'm just making a self-serving argument, I'm sure," she added with a smile. "But I love both of you, truly. I want what's good for you."

I sat up now, swung my legs over the edge of the bed, steadying myself by gripping a sleek dark-wood bedpost. Maybe I was close to attaining the right degree of freedom. I felt freer now than when I was her, in my twenties, with Eli, or than I'd been at any other point in my life. I stood, my feet shaking, but holding me. "I think I'm a bit angry."

"Yes," said Mariah. "You are."

She set the little sculpture on the ottoman. The head, face, hair was mine. The body too. And she had found so much beauty in me. "My dear angry Abby." She watched me take it in. "Rage is the great engine of our work. And of our future," she said.

ABBY, AUGUST 30, 2015

And so it was that this very morning, a luminous late-summer Sunday, a time chosen because the city was mostly empty and even the police force was understaffed, that the Brigade decided to strike at the heart of fasco-capitalism. Pete left early in the morning with Dmitri. I didn't intend to march. I headed for Brooklyn to check on the paint job in the living room and rehang some kitchen shelves, Dennis's big battered toolbox in the back seat.

But driving downtown, I saw them mustering, south of the old fish market buildings. I couldn't just drive past. I found a parking spot easily. From a bucket of cleaning supplies in the back of the car, I grabbed an old blackened rag—a scrap of one of those old T-shirts—and tied it around my neck, bandanna style. I slipped into the back of the pack, covering my face as the others did. Pete wouldn't see me. He was in the front line, with Dmitri.

Who handed me the hammer? I think it was Vincent, who moved through the pack, pulling bullhorns, bats, and other battle gear from an enormous sports-gear duffel slung over his shoulder. Just props, I thought. How did it begin, then? The destruction.

A splattering of eggs on an idling stretch limo. Some logos from a large real estate developer, torn down from a construction fence. A feeling of escalating wildness as the throng headed farther downtown, funneled into ever-narrower streets. But truly the only vivid recollection, finally, I have is that sound. And how it shocked my body, the juice of it, the energy mainlined as with a syringe, and this just through the sound, the sonic boom of the hammer on the thick plate glass, bouncing through the slot canyons, off the skyscrapers wedged so greedily into those skinny old streets way downtown. I still feel the waves of it vibrating through me as I write this, cleaning me out, purifying me in some fashion, scouring every artery and even those lacy passages that run through the center of my bones.

It was a Bank of America branch and its window finally succumbed after my seventh blow, cracking into great shark fins of glass. The fins fell inward, cracking into a thousand spears that scattered across nubby oatmeal carpet and a single rolling chair so similar to my rolling chair at work, and I thought of my window at work, my so-called artwork that I had consoled myself with lo these many years—how many? Thirteen? Thirteen years in the rolling plastic-wheeled chair yearning for color out the big window—and now watching these spears slice through the air of that bank lobby, I felt not an ounce of yearning. I felt power.

How life slows down at such moments.

"No hate! No fear! Fascists are not welcome here!" I could hear the kids screaming behind me, frenzied, a joyous, alarming hysteria.

I turned to see my son. Thrilled? Aghast? His eyes glimmered and in them I saw a face reflected—half covered, mouth, nose, and chin wrapped in a black rag. Was this pirate, this rabble-rouser, this transgressor—was that me? I couldn't read Pete's expression. He seemed to be attempting to chant along with the other bellowing onlookers, but when he opened his mouth to shout, no sound emerged.

Then, across the street, a young woman, not cloaked, not shouting or waving her fist. Just watching, intently.

Dr. Tristane Kazemy, AUGUST 31, 2016

Abigail Willard would not leave her. She had not opened the file in a month, since her incursion into Laurin's office. She could not risk termination. She tried to refocus on her duties in the lab, and in the evenings, on Samir, who had gradually coalesced into a boyfriend of sorts.

Then, an email: Could she present her findings in New York by year's end? Compare notes with the quantum physicist?

Pursuing a physics investigation into Abigail Willard's affliction was beyond the pale. She'd thought this all along.

Though she'd had to set the case aside, the woman had been haunting her dreams nearly every night. No Freud necessary to explain this, of course. Mme. Willard had been sent her way as a signifier of ambitions that refused to be thwarted.

She replied to the email. Yes, she would make the trip to New York, to present her evidence and her theories. Laurin and his lab be damned. Let him terminate her, if he must. She mused again about how her narrative seemed to flow as if directed by certain unseen forces. As if, for her life, there seemed to be greater designs.

9/9/9/9

ABBY, SEPTEMBER 1, 2015

I undertook a penitential journey to a block-long silvery cube in far uptown Manhattan, a megastore devoted to tools for creating household order. I rose early, leaving plenty of time so I could be there, a lone supplicant, waiting, when the turbaned security guard unlocked its gates and admitted me with a solemn bow. I bought myself a brand-new broom, hefty, janitorial, aluminum with black bristles, suitable for cleaning a warship or a crematorium. With my new broom, I returned to Brooklyn and began to sweep the floors. The planks that bore my boys' first toddles. Despite the new finish, the invisible tiny footprints serpentined all over the wood, down the hall, into the kitchen, and train tracks and bright plastic rings and blocks were still scattered across the grain.

The men from Pinsky's Moving and Storage arrived midmorning, hand trucks loaded high. It was strange, how much I'd missed our things. The jumbled box of flashlights and extension cords, the blue plastic laundry basket filled with pots and pans. They held meaning and memory and comfort, these bland ingredients of family life.

I cleaned the stairs, working my way up, step by step, pausing now and then to steady myself, leaning hard on my heavy-duty sweeper.

All I'd wanted to do was to create, to unfurl that will and honor that gift, and lately all I'd done was destroy, and destroy, and destroy.

Twiz saved me. She'd grabbed the sledgehammer right out of my hands, told me to run. She dodged the police, when they'd finally caught up to the Brigade's rampage on Wall Street, but a few others spent two nights in jail and were now facing charges. I gave Pete a fat envelope, money from the insurance, that Dennis and I had earmarked for new furniture. He gave it to Dmitri, who had set up the group's legal defense fund, with help from his mysterious parents.

The detective might have been able to ease the jailed members' way, if he'd been trustworthy. Apparently he was not. Still, with awful persistence, he lingered inside my head. I tried to drown the memory of his touch with lists of chores and items to buy. When his face appeared before my dreaming eyes, I swiped it away.

Dennis and I would have to reconstitute our marriage. Or would we decide to disband the entire venture?

I reached the top step of the steep and narrow flight, cradling the filled dustpan. Searched for a trash bin in which to empty it.

I shouldn't have been surprised, then, to find her there, in the scorched bedstead in my sullied master bedroom. Asleep. Sunlight sifting through her hair to find the gold bits, catching the sheen on the dirty mattress. I'd ordered a new queen-sized the day after my tryst there, and it leaned against a wall downstairs, plastic-wrapped, a new set of sheets in a bag beside it.

The drawer of the bedside table was open. Had she gotten into my sleeping pills? Please, no.

I grabbed the bottle, and it rattled, still mostly full. No, then. She simply needed rest.

Her legs were bare, tan from summer, her heels calloused. The tenderness I felt, standing over her. This wayward being. It was like seeing a wild bird trapped in my room. How had she gained entry? Maybe she'd slipped in during all those comings and goings, electricians and carpenters, the doors flung open wide to let floor varnish air and dry.

I listen to her breathe. Could I hear her breathe? Or is that me.

She opens her eyes then. Tears leak out of the corners.

We are in a bad place, she says. Her voice sounds scratchy, an old recording.

I know.

I didn't sleep for two whole nights, she says. Finally I ran. I ended up here.

She raises herself on her elbows, looks around at the modest room—the small fireplace defunct since the days of coal, the closet yawning open, emptied of our smoke-stinking clothes. My easel. Her eyes stop on my latest work, viridian with ash worked into the oils. She stares at it a long moment, appraising. I hold my breath.

I wish I could paint like that, she finally whispers.

I feel relief, a coolness washing through me.

She turns to me. Her face so round and vaguely there, a moon in daylight.

You will, I say.

No. This thing is going to kill me. He is going to kill me. You should see what we've been up to.

I did see.

She smiles, sadly. So you say.

He dies at your hands.

And as these strange, stiff syllables leave my mouth, I want only to take them back. The shock of them. The shock in my body, and in her eyes.

Why did my lips and tongue offer up those words?

The blast wave of this idea, the stricken look on her face, push me backward. I am stumbling, backward, away from her, out the bedroom door, but there really isn't room to back away, in that slot-like vertiginous house. And me already unsteady as it goes.

The floor disappears under my feet and my brain registers that I have stepped into the open air at the head of the staircase, I am hurtling, windmilling, backward and down.

As I fly, a thought: I already know how this feels.

How long did I lie at the bottom, in a pile? It was Dennis who found me, fresh from the airport. With Benjamin in tow.

The summer had come to its end.

SESSION NOTES

A back in treatment. Abusing substances. In terrible struggles with the young man in her life.

But more than that. She says she has split into two somehow. Acute schizophrenia? A difficult diagnosis but one I perhaps need to consider.

She seems so unstable, I fear I might not see her here again, though she assured me I most definitely would.

ABBY, SEPTEMBER 4, 2015

"It's called 'Stallion,' Ma. This is the color." Benjamin held aloft a swatch. His room would be the final painting job, and he wanted it black. At the hardware store, Dennis and I argued against it, but in the end, we acquiesced. School was about to begin. Benjamin would be in the tenth grade and, stunningly, Pete in twelfth. There was so much to attend to. Let the boy paint his room black.

Gianna was with us, just two days back from her summer job in Los Angeles, where she served coffee to many movie stars while interning at a wellness center. As we waited for the paint to emerge from the jiggling mixing machine, she ran through a long list of celebrities major and minor, who got the hot stones, who got reiki, and who had bad toenails. I hung on her every word.

After Dennis found me in a heap at the bottom of the stairs, he told Benjamin to call 911, but, in a state of semi-awareness, I urged him not to. I'm fine, I insisted. Thinking of course what emergency care might cost. In the meantime, the movers were still building a city of boxes. Dennis stood over me, pondering for a minute, running a hand through his hair, which was yellow again from the salt and sun of his homeland. Then he declared, "Screw Dr. Singh. We need an upgrade," and he maneuvered his phone out of his pocket. "Mariah will know someone."

"I have a shrink appointment tomorrow," I said, rubbing my temples, which seemed to be sinkholes, pressing inward.

"You think this is all in your head?" he said with the phone at his ear. "I don't."

He left a message asking Mariah to call him. Then I realized he was dragging his suitcase up the stairs, and I had a frightening thought—was she still up there?

But all he said was "Oh, shit, we need to replace this ruined mattress."

Yes, I ordered it, it's here. New sheets too. I tried to tell him but my vocal cords produced only a strangled whisper.

Later that night, with both of us settled atop the fresh bedding,

I reached toward the nightstand, looking for the relief of my insomnia meds. I felt an unfamiliar shape instead. It was a small silver matchbox. Printed with one word: Mobius. Yes. That was the name of the club, the nightclub of the collapsed umbrella, the running boy and the raspberry coat. The night I lost my taxi. Mobius offered little boxes of matches, in those long-ago days of cigarettes.

I slid it open. Inside, no matches. Instead, a chip of pinkish-beige paint.

ABBY, SEPTEMBER 9, 2015

Had Dr. Merle Unzicker wizened even more, summering? Her eyes seemed a bit more squinted and sunken, her nose more protuberant. I sat on the sagging sofa, across from her wheelchair. Dr. Merle regarded me from somewhere inside her wrinkles. Her head bobbed. I interpreted that as a signal to speak.

"I've taken some big steps." I chuckled, nervous. "Or mis-steps?"

"Yes?" Her voice was clipped, quiet.

"The first thing I did when I moved back into my house was fall down the stairs."

She emitted a small grunt. "Oh dear."

"And I've been getting into activism," I said.

"How so?"

"My son Pete led me to it. A political movement, in a way. I am finding it interesting," I said.

"An optimistic act," she said.

"I suppose so," I shrugged.

"And your work? Your art?"

"I've been painting in the ashes. With the ashes."

Dr. Merle cocked her white-fuzzed head to one side, just a few degrees, like an ancient, inquisitive poodle, her eyes in a squint, almost closed.

"But there's this other person, this girl . . . who is . . . troubling me."

She nodded. "Yes. I know." She faintly cleared her throat. I sensed she was about to spit out a pearl of wisdom. I sat up on the couch, hands on my knees, waiting.

Waiting.

And waiting.

Was she asleep?

I peered at her for a long time. It seemed like a long time anyhow. I could hear her gently rattling breath and the hum and thump of blow-dryers and disco music.

Dr. Merle had, seemingly, fallen asleep. Her feet folded in on themselves, like little fronds.

I stood up and began to tiptoe out of the room. "You have been given a gift," she said as I moved past her chair. "You must use it."

I froze. "Oh. Yes." I looked down, right down to the top of her head, the scalp more like membrane than skin. "My art, my painting? I should use that gift?" I stuttered.

She let out a strange impatient sigh. "No. No. Not that." Her head moved again, the mildest shake. "A much more vital gift." The veins on her skull throbbed slowly. "The chance to know yourself."

Blue rivulets on snow-white ground. Pulsating.

"To love yourself."

She dismissed me with a wave of her gnarled hand. "I will bill you," she said.

September 10, 2016

From: GarrettShuttlesworth@physics.humboldtstate.edu
To: J. Leverett@deepxmail.com

It's been 16 years since I was in NYC, since my divorce and departure from Columbia. I'll aim for a collegial atmosphere with the Canadian brain doc—just hope she'll come with an open mind and be ready to have it blown.

ABBY, SEPTEMBER 15, 2015

From Mariah's climate-controlled storage sanctum in the Bronx, a team of brawny balletic art handlers delivered nearly a hundred paintings to the carriage house. We watched as they carried them up to the studio and, when they ran out of room there, propped them downstairs in the living room, on the sofas and on the eighteen chairs that surrounded the dining table. She'd asked me to come help, to brainstorm with her on new frames and weigh in on curatorial choices for the inaugural show at the Jillian Broder Space, to open next spring in a Civil War–era warehouse overlooking the East River. It would be the biggest gallery the city had ever seen.

Mariah handed me a wine globe brimming with green-gold fizz. "Made with grapes from the family land on Crete," she said. "Kind of prickly and tarty and sweet. Like you," she laughed. We clinked glasses, then I wandered, contemplating the patterns and progressions, the incontrovertible evidence of her genius and energy, of her productivity and her aspirations and her ambition. Two decades of dauntless work. She wanted to reframe it all. It would cost a fortune.

sorryort

I lingered over the spiral series, carmines and crimsons and titanium whites, laid out on the floor under the sunny windows. Laid flat, with the bright rays glancing over them, the textured brushstrokes rippled and roiled like the surface of a pot just about to burst into full boil.

Mariah joined me there, gazing. "I have a favor to ask you," she said. "It's Jillian's sixtieth birthday at the end of the month, and I felt obliged to throw her a bash." She turned to me, and for the first time I could recall, she looked embarrassed. "Would you and Dennis be there as my dates? Poor Hyde, he's been texting me photos of his penis, as if that would lure me back." She showed me one. It made me very sad, this mottled pink offering, springing hopefully from a general hairy darkness. She told me she knew the end was near when he tried to prescribe a diet that would melt her belly fat. "I realized I was fonder of my belly fat than I was of him," she said.

She chuckled down at her phone, but when she met my gaze again, I saw vulnerability there. Though the notion of celebrating Jillian Broder—if I had a bête noire, she was it—made my belly fat clench, I would do this for Mariah.

We stood gazing at her spirals, and we talked a bit more about her show, and about Matthew Legge-Lewis, and his overtures to me. "I can't wait to go to your vernissage," she said. "Soon enough you'll be outgunning me." She reminded me of the time in school when she and I showed work together in a critique session, and the class clearly preferred mine over hers. After that, she said, "I made sure never to be in the same class with you again. I would go to the registrar and sneak a peek at your course load, just to be sure we didn't end up together." She shook her head at the memory. "Bremer actually told me I should study your brush technique."

Envy is twinned with admiration, and admiration is often suffused with love. As the two of us shuffled her work around the room, millions of dollars' worth of pigment and fabric, pairing this painting with that print, marking frames that would be replaced, I realized that love was now the strongest current that ran between us. I loved her, and this was the key reality. The other, the alternate Mariah reality—what was happening or had happened with Dennis—could play out beyond the wall of my perception. I would not try to establish its dimensions, trace its outlines. I would not delve.

I write this now and I realize how bizarre, how unnatural even, this position is or was. But not all things in love can be explained. In fact, most things in love cannot be explained.

I stared up at the portrait of her mustachioed progenitor. "I like the family wine," I said.

"He would've liked you," she said. "Eye for the ladies."

"I'm probably a bit to the left of his comfort zone, lately," I said.

"Yes, that reminds me." She opened a closet and pulled out a bag of placards. "You forgot this when you moved out." She lifted one. "No Pasaran." Smiled up at me. She handed me the bag. "You just keep on fighting the good fight, babe. That is exactly what makes you who you are."

ABBY, SEPTEMBER 26, 2015

"Missus, nice to see you."

"Abby," I said. "Just call me Abby."

"And how are you, friend." Milo Petimezas peered into the car at Pete.

"Hmm. OK," Pete stammered. The guy made him nervous and I did not blame him one bit.

"Dmitri will be out," he said. "He is probably fixing his hair."

He grinned at me through his beard, stiff hair gleaming in the steady rain. "You going bowling, then?" I guess this is what his brother had told him.

I smiled and nodded. "Yes. Keeps them off the streets, right?"

He shrugged. "Streets can teach you a lot, Mrs. Willard."

The Petimezas house was a bulky gray box of brick, framed by statues of lightly draped Grecian women. When we'd stopped in front, we saw Milo in the open garage, leaning against his hot yellow Mustang, looking a bit indistinct through the scrim of the downpour, as if seen on an old TV. He nodded to me as our car pulled into the driveway, flicked his smoke away, strolled out into the storm, not seeming to notice it at all.

Dmitri appeared and climbed into the back seat. Milo gave the hood a couple of blows with his hand. "Have fun, bowl good," he said.

The house on Monsignor Murphy Street seemed to have listed a few degrees farther west, and the curb in front was strewn with soaked garbage, diaper boxes, broken bikes, a gawping old washing machine. We all sat there for a minute, watching a plastic bucket roll back and forth in the wet wind. "Looks like one of the neighbors has been cleaning house," said Dmitri.

It was the day before Jillian Broder's birthday party. The glancing dregs of a hurricane had settled over the city, promising lousy weather for the event. The Brigade was gathering tonight for an emergency meeting. Pete said a message had come via the dark web, not that I knew what the dark web was, or where one might find it. Pete was supposed to be working on his college application essay—the topic was "How I Overcame My Speech Disability" as suggested by the nice lady with the spider plants in her office. (What was her name? She seemed a relic from another time.) But the essay would have to wait. He intended to be at this dark-webbed, rainswept emergency meeting. I'd agreed to drive him and Dmitri to these forsaken flats.

"Thanks for the ride, Abby," Dmitri said politely as he slid out of the car.

Pete turned to me. "You coming in?"

How much he looked like her at that moment, as he turned his head to me, the pointed chin, the dark-light eyes.

"You go." I took his hand and pressed it to my cheek. "And be careful, my darling." His pudgy little boy hand, his big, bony almost-man hand. Warm flesh of my flesh.

Dr. Tristane Kazemy, SEPTEMBER 26, 2016

Laurin cornered her by the microwave, as she stared in at a revolving dish of boeuf bourguignon, her mostly uneaten entrée from last night. She'd squabbled with Samir all through a candlelit dinner at Bistro Cinq. Then broke off with him via text.

You are on thin ice, said Laurin, coming up close behind her.

Yes? she replied. She remained fixed on the buzzing box. Her blood pounding suddenly, her lungs contracted.

I know you are pursuing that case again. Wasting my lab's time, he said. On an ordinary brain. On a pile of nothing, an American lady with a bad case of nerves. It is nothing!

The beep sounded. She opened the door and extracted the steaming plate. I carry the largest caseload of any fellow here, she said.

You do your duties. But I fear—

You must know your Latin, Doctor? She regarded him through the vapor. *Ex nihilo nihil fit.* From nothing comes nothing. She sidestepped him and headed for the door. Therefore, you have nothing to fear.

ABBY, SEPTEMBER 27, 2015

Dennis and I stood silently at the coat check set up in the front hall, listening to the roar from the riotous rooms beyond. I handed over my dripping raincoat but kept my silk scarf, wrapping it around my bare-shouldered dress, shivering a bit in the air-conditioning. In contrast to the rain-soaked streets, Mariah's carriage house seethed with humanity. Glittering, chattering, exclaiming in little bursts, craning this way and that to see who they could see, and to see who was seeing them. Women in tall black boots, like armor for their skinny little legs. Angular eyeglass frames. Carefully cultivated chin scruff. All of this backed by Mariah's artwork, eloquent, numinous, and, to the joy of everyone near it, stratospherically expensive.

At the center of the living room stood Jillian Broder in a gunmetal-gray silk suit, severe and thin as a scalpel. The shimmery long hair was gone—instead, she wore a snow-white buzz cut. Her long earrings swayed as she received greetings and searched the crowd for important faces.

I turned to Dennis. "Should we say hello?"

As we edged into her orbit, she spotted me. She was still nodding at someone else and talking. "Gruesome, just gruesome what some people will do," she said. "But look, it is the elusive Abigail Willard." She extended her hand to signal me closer. "One of New York's unheralded brilliances. One of the lost tribe." We air-kissed, and she rested a palm on my cheek for an instant. "You are still beautiful. Bereftly beautiful."

"I am not bereft," I said, trying to chuckle.

The corners of her mouth turned down and she gave a little sigh. "No, of course not. Except that, well, I would love to see what you're painting sometime." She dropped her voice and looked at me

204 I DEBRA JO IMMERGUT

with concern. Her eyes were arctic blue. "You are working, aren't you?"

"Yes," I answered with a tight smile.

She turned to a tall, big-bellied man with gray woolliness on his face and gray curls that wound down the back of his neck. "Charles, Abigail was one of my earliest finds, plucked right out of RISD back in the bad old days. And she is perhaps the most talented colorist I've ever known. Now she works in—what is it—the medical equipment industry?"

"Pharmaceuticals," I said.

"Pharmaceuticals," she said. "She designs boxes."

"Visual branding," I said.

"But I don't mean to denigrate, you know that, sweets." She gestured to the man. "This is Charles Moffat. Of Charles and Kay Moffat. The collectors."

"Of course," I said, reaching for his extended hand.

"So nice to see you," he said warmly.

"And this is my husband, Dennis"—I gestured—but he was no longer beside me. He'd melted away somewhere. "Well, Dennis Willard, he's a wonderful sculptor."

"Very muscular," said Jillian, and waggled her brows at me.

"I'd love to see your work sometime—and his." He put his arm around Jillian. "This lady has an unerring eye."

Jillian chuckled and laid her hand on his chest in a way that left no mistake. She'd fucked him.

"Do you have a card?" said this Charles Moffat, collector. "I'll have my assistant call you to set something up."

"I have work to show," I stammered, "but nowhere to show it. I don't have a studio at the moment."

He and Jillian looked at me. I could see a haze of doubt beginning to film their eyes. And then, suddenly, I blurted, "But Dennis does. We can show his work and my work there."

"Fine, email my assistant," said Jillian with a note of finality. "I'll play go-between." She took Moffat by the arm and started to lead him away.

I called after her: "Happy birthday, Jillian," but if she heard me, she didn't acknowledge.

Three cocktails later, I still hadn't found Mariah. Weren't we here for her sake, after all? I circumnavigated the room, sidling through the crowd. Scanned the white sofas (thronged, no Mariah), peered into the hallway leading to the bathroom (silent line of people checking phones, no Mariah), and the kitchen pantry (crates of wine and two sequined beauties in a glommy embrace, no Mariah).

And, come to think of it, where had Dennis disappeared to?

At the back of the kitchen, near the service entrance, stood the door to the elevator, and the narrow staircase rising alongside it. Did I dare check the upstairs bedrooms? The studio with its capacious chaise, where Mariah liked to stretch out for afternoon naps?

I wavered.

Then I noticed a compact man in a leather jacket and black leather sneakers standing on the landing of the staircase. He appeared to be studying one of our hostess's small, early collages. "Excuse me," I called. "Have you seen Mariah?"

The man shook his head. He never even turned around. Rude art-world monster.

Maybe look outside first? I could use the fresh air.

Then, Forest Versteeg near the coat check. Running a small brush over his beloved's back. He chuckled as I approached. "Our car is half canine. I never travel without an arsenal of lint removal devices."

"And this jacket is a fucking fur magnet," Matthew Legge-Lewis added, turning around and tugging at the hem of his velvet blazer. We exchanged embraces, and then I asked them if they'd seen Dennis. Perhaps he'd stepped out front to share someone's weed—hadn't he'd done that at the auction, after all?

"The only thing we saw out there was a pack of gnarly, angry, soggy people in black," Matthew said.

"Oh? Have they stopped letting guests in? It is overstuffed in here . . ."

"Those hooligans are not guests! Are you not aware of what's going on out there?" said Forest.

"Is anyone aware of what's going on out there?" said Matthew. He turned to his husband. "I need a drink," he said. "Before they shut this shitshow down."

JACARANDA PINK COILS, glistening with droplets of hurricane rain. This is what the colorist would see first. Pink locks quivering in gold-orange streetlamp light, shaking with every bellowed syllable. "Hey hey ho ho, fascist royals got to go." The fuchsia, the marigold.

But also, everywhere, the black.

Dmitri in black. Giant Vincent in his tiger-striped tattoos and black. Twiz in black. The entire crew, on the black asphalt, black face coverings pulled up high, right beneath their eyes. But I knew who they were.

The pack of protesters stretched clear across the street and halfway down the block. So many people in black. (Later Pete would tell me that extra bodies had been mysteriously mustered, unfamiliar men, from Jersey and as far away as Baltimore.)

A forest of signs scrawled with blood-red spray paint: ANARCHY NOT MONARCHY, NAZI BLOOD MONEY, and THE PAST IS PRESENT.

And there, in the center, my boy. Black hoodie, black bandanna. I stumbled down the front stoop—yes, I was definitely slightly soused—and grabbed Pete's arm. "This was the emergency action?"

"Go back inside," he hissed, shaking my hand from his arm.

Dmitri spotted me then. "This house stands on blood money, the bodies of Greek freedom fighters and the Jews of Europe," he cried, over the chanting. The dark energy in his eyes, once again. "The Greek royals were Nazi-loving fascists, Abby! Read your history!"

"Mariah is not a Nazi," I shouted. The words scraped my throat. The sidewalk was atilt. Or was it me.

Pete reached out to me then, perhaps he saw me teetering. He put his mouth close to my ear. "I tried to talk them out of this," he said. "But the truth is the truth, right, Ma?"

I shook my head weakly, the world spinning, I clutched his arm. The shouting of the crowd swirled into my ears, my brain. The sight of them stirring the thick air with their fists and signs made my mind fly to Eli. To A.

I was still that girl, really. I still wanted what she wanted.

Truth, freedom, passion?

Didn't I want these things?

The answer boiled up first in my abdomen, then bubbled up through veins, filling vesicles just beneath my skin. My skin practically steamed. Sweat prickled on my hairline.

My neck was on fire. My scarf suddenly felt too tight.

Loosened my scarf. Breathed for a moment. Deeply. Then I pulled the fabric up to cover my nose and mouth. I stood next to my son, taking my place. In rage, at the greed-fest inside, at Jillian, her acolytes, the billionaire collector, the swiveling, craning lot of them. Rage at the notion that any of this had anything to do with what mattered.

The others were raising their fists. Shouldn't I do it too—for Pete? For Benjamin. For Dennis. For Mariah even. She would understand. For the young woman I was, and the old one I would become. Didn't this feel like a good fight?

I made a fist and punched the black sky.

It ignited a shocking sound. A deep thrumming *thump.* Then a messy burst of crackling red sparkles, bouncing off the carriage house bricks, reflected off the wet sidewalk, in the glass windows of the house. A small puff of sulfuric smoke.

Pete and I exchanged astonished glances.

Someone had tossed a firecracker.

Dmitri appeared, the red sparks gleaming in his eyes. "Shock and awe," he shouted, nodding toward the back of the pack. "Firework mortars, harmless. The Jersey guys brought them."

The sound thundered in small echoes down the block, and now the chanting and the general mood upshifted, striking a more frenzied note. Up at the top of the stoop, the horrified faces of Matthew and Forest, among others, peered through the front windows.

Then a second incendiary popped. It was a soft bass *thunk,* almost a dud, but I saw another flash of red in front of Mariah's garage, and heard panes of glass breaking. A feeling drenched me, a burst water balloon of dread. Surely the cops would be called now, surely this was nowhere I wanted my son to be. I grabbed Pete's arm. I pulled the scarf off my face, and urged him farther back into the crowd, out into the street. "Wait a second, Mom, wait!" he said.

We turned to see many partygoers pouring out of the house now, some shouted insults flew back and forth. A shoving match almost erupted between towering Vincent and Jillian Broder. "Bring it!" she snarled. "I dare you." But he chose not to bring it. A ragged breathlessness and a sense of jangled nerves hung over the crowd, the antifa and the art world facing off, warily regarding each other.

A confused restraint seemed to prevail. Distant sirens could be heard.

I held fast to Pete's arm. I could feel myself still swaying.

Under each streetlamp, a cone of gilded mist.

Then. *BOOM*. Louder, by many multiples, than those firework pops.

A single horrendous blast.

All of us in the street felt it in gut, ears, bones. As one organism, the crowd flinched, recoiling from the blow.

Mariah's garage door lay smoking on the sidewalk, peeled off the house like a dead fingernail. A greasy cloud belched out of the opening. As it cleared, everyone seemed to gasp in unison.

Black dress, red blood. She lay on the floor. Standing over her, a stunned and soot-covered man.

PART 3

THE FIRE

10/10/10/10

ABBY, OCTOBER 1, 2015

On Avenue C, a new twenty-story condo tower has assumed command of a broken old corner, gray glass balconies rippling up its flanks like chain mail. It casts a heavy shadow even at night. Along this shadowed block, the building's residents walk little dogs buckled into plaid jackets, recount their workdays to their faraway parents in Phoenix or Shanghai.

I watch them. This is the tower that has replaced Eli's tenement. I search for A.

Maybe I'm simply unhinged in the aftermath. Dr. Unzicker might be able to tell me, but I haven't managed to see her either. The message on her answering machine says she's been unwell.

Join the club, Dr. Unzicker.

On the ground floor of this East Village condominium fortress is a blaring bright drugstore. For a while, I watch people purchasing hand lotions, greeting cards, allergy pills. Then I stare up again at the fifth floor. Is she somehow up there, even though the building is not the same one that smelled of cat and cumin? There are no junkies sleeping in the stairwell, and no cumbia music wafting up the fire escapes. There are no fire escapes.

I understand that I am needed at home. Dennis has been cata-
tonic; the boys are at loose ends. After all, schoolwork and dinner
and all those things still need to happen. And I am the breadwinner now. The only steady paycheck. I must keep my center, keep
my focus, keep my neck in the yoke and my eyes on the road ahead
of me.

And so I finally turn away from my vigil, walking back west,
away from the bewitched corner of Eli Hammond, toward the subway. Past the place where the heroin hole used to be, the sidewalks
of broken glass and discarded needles and lost shoes. Now clean.
Now lined with rows of bikes ready to be borrowed with the swipe
of a card.

And then I see an amber light in the darkness. An arched door.
The portal of destiny at the corner of Seventh and B.

A's head is on the bar. Her shoulders are shaking. I can barely
make out a bartender at the far end of the horseshoe, washing
beer mugs. The TV is switched off. Without its glow, the room's
gloom is very deep. And the place is deserted. But she is here and
so am I.

And she is crying, and I sit down next to her, and I too begin
to cry.

It's over. I think it has to be over, she says. She sobs steadily, then
cuts her eyes to me. I am slumping, barely holding my head up. The
vertigo has begun again, and the world is beginning to twirl. I put
my forehead against the battered wood bar.

I hear her say, But you? Why are you crying?

I can feel words forming in my voice box, words pressing on my
tongue.

I'm exhausted, carrying her fate.

But what choice do I have? None. If I know anything at all

anymore, I know that I am duty bound to say nothing. My life, my sons' lives, depend upon this moment of silence. Nothing can be changed. The excruciating parts of the story. The parts that remain in the haze. Nothing can be changed.

So I say nothing. But I let the tears fall. And so we both sit, heads bowed, tremoring, faces wet, moving slightly, undulating, in the manner of certain barely sentient things that live in the sea, anemones or sea cucumbers. Because sorrow is aquatic, somehow. It tastes salty, it submerges you, it makes you undulate at its will. Sadness can turn you into something drowned and dumb. As the world tilts, I'm scarcely aware that we're drawing together, she and I, as we rest our heads on this stalwart, scarred wood. Toward each other, until I think I can feel her skull, an opposing arc, meeting mine for a millimeter or two, just a point of pressure so close to my brain. And maybe the ghost of her hand on my arm. It feels like a frozen gas, like liquid nitrogen, spilling across my skin. Too light and fast to leave an icy burn, but painful just the same.

October 2, 2016

_____

From: GarrettShuttlesworth@physics.humboldtstate.edu
To: Tristane.Kazemy@montrealneuro.ca

Dr. Kazemy, I understand that we will be meeting soon in New York, and that we are somewhat at odds in our analysis of the Willard case. Quantum physicists are accustomed to having to win people over to our views—and given the evidence, I firmly believe that we are not simply dealing with the illusions of a broken brain. But for now, I humbly offer Susskind's admonition: those who ignore the implications of good evidence are simply averting their eyes from a vision they find overwhelming.

With regards,

Garrett P. Shuttlesworth, MS, PhD
Michael James Chair in Theoretical Physics,
Humboldt State University, Arcata, CA

ABBY, OCTOBER 3, 2015

I drove to the Petimezas house. Dark windows, a few rain-soaked newspapers littering the concrete steps at the feet of its half-clothed statues. I asked at school. Elizabeth Vong shook her head. His parents had pulled Dmitri out, she told me, apparently the family had moved back to Europe. "Some kind of job change," she said, "it was all very rushed." She lowered her voice. "The boy was bright but a bit of a handful."

I journeyed to the Brigade's meeting place in the far eastern reaches. Locked. I rattled the chain, pounded the door, but nothing stirred inside. A rustling in the trash pile made me flee.

Pete told me he didn't know where Dmitri had disappeared to. "Lately he was more your friend than mine," he said.

He'd plunged back into the screens, curled in the carapace of his room, which, a month after our return, still seemed a provisional place, his clothes piled in a corner, the walls bare. He refused all attempts at refurnishing it. He allowed only an air mattress, and he stationed himself upon it, back propped against the wall and sheets twisted at his feet, eyes fixed on his laptop.

So here again was silent Pete, reluctant and stymied. I studied his face for signs of an opening. There were no such signs. Just a stubble I hadn't noticed before. His beard was coming in.

Dennis emerged relatively unscathed—bodily. Abrasions on his hands and face, and lung inflammation from the superheated solvent fumes. The EMT said he'd have died too, if he hadn't been on the lucky side of Mariah's behemoth SUV at the key moment, and so shielded from the worst of the blast wave and the shrapnel. Still, the doctors told me to be alert for symptoms of concussion or ear damage. I tried to be alert. I could detect no symptoms. But he'd vanished into his studio in the days that followed. The Viennarte show was just over three months away, mid-January, and he'd need time to pack and ship his weighty pieces. He spent hours shearing, grinding, welding in a cloak of noise. I assumed. I didn't venture there. When home, he, like his son, was mostly silent. Raking at the wet rug of leaves in the backyard. Making toast for the boys' breakfast and burning it. I thought he might still be in shock. Or maybe he was just doing what I was. Trying to discover what to say, and how to comprehend.

For example, how was I to understand the fact that German Pizziali had appeared on the scene the night Mariah died?

First, a wavering aurora borealis of red and blue, as reflected in the dark wet street. Three police cars, then more, then a blocky train of fire engines and ambulances, zigzagging down the street. Farther back, a more diffuse white glaring light burst forth suddenly, bouncing off the mist, illuminating the scene for television cameras.

The antifa soldiers fled in the wake of the explosion, of course, scattered into the night before the air even cleared. Many of the party guests did too. Panicked and fearful that some larger violent act or cataclysm had been set in motion. Pete and I were left standing there, along with a handful of guests, who seemed stapled in place by horror. Transfixed by the shattering truth. Mariah Glücksberg was dead.

My friend Mariah. My foe? Foamy and pink tissue tangled in her blood-wet hair. Jillian Broder had been the first to rush to her, the fire was still burning, another explosion seemed likely. Jillian dove over Mariah, her silvery suit instantly slicked with crimson. She and Dennis dragged Mariah's body onto the sidewalk, away from the fuming, fulminating bottles and cans in the garage. Turpentine. Thinners and oil-paint solvents. The firemen had cleared everyone to the far side of the street and aimed their hoses at the smoking pile. Now the volatile fluids were dispersed, inert.

Mariah lay under a black vinyl shroud. More blood puddled on the sidewalk beside it, developing a patent-leather sheen. Many uniformed people milled around this small dark mound, in and out of the illuminated garage, up and down the stoop of the carriage house. The front doors were thrown wide open, spilling music, some endlessly looping playlist of Biggie Smalls, into the street.

Dennis, on a gurney, being bandaged by an EMT, regarded us in a daze. "Why was Pete at the party?" he kept asking.

A stout, round-shouldered man in a beige windbreaker ambled up, as if he'd just been out for a stroll in the damp night air. "What a terrible thing," he said, nodding at each of us. Then he directed his small, misaligned eyes at Pete. "Kids shouldn't play with matches, am I right?"

Pete looked down at his feet and said nothing.

"He was taking part in a peaceful protest," I said. "I think that's what most of the kids intended. I don't even understand how this happened."

"Fire chief says it looks like some of those cans of flammables were pretty rusted. So a piddly little firework breaks the window, a couple of sparks fly in, and then, ignition, blast-off."

Now the EMT began wheeling Dennis toward the ambulance. They would need to check him more thoroughly at the hospital. "Mariah was a friend, we both loved her," I said.

The cop nodded. "I think I get the picture, Mrs. Willard."

I glared at him. "And this was just young people trying to be heard. What happened was a tragic accident."

His imprecise gaze seemed to focus precisely now. On me. "Just excitable kiddies. Could be. With all the valuables inside, the homeowner had exterior cameras, of course. We'll review. See what we see." Then he turned to Pete. "You better keep your mind on your books, son," he said. "Your get-outta-jail-free passes are all used up."

ABBY, OCTOBER 8, 2015

In the morning, Benjamin was in tears. "Wowza is gone," he said. "He hasn't shown up for his breakfast and I can't find him anywhere."

Dennis looked up from his bowl of soggy untouched cornflakes. He wasn't eating much these days. His eyes were red-rimmed and dim.

"Let's go get him back," he said.

We split up, Dennis heading down the slope, Benjamin and I heading up. "Wowza. Wowza," we called, up and down the block. We searched behind the neighbor's trash cans and under cars. "Do you think he's gone forever?" Ben asked. His brows troubled, wrinkled. I pulled him to me, kissed his forehead. "I don't know if anything is ever gone forever."

At Fourth Avenue, he angled south and I turned north. Parents shepherded little ones toward the day care center. Bike commuters whizzed by. Schoolgirls in hijabs. Nowhere did I glimpse a cardboard-colored cat.

Up ahead by the curb, next to a construction dumpster, I noticed a grease-spattered old oven on the curb, its door hanging askew on busted hinges. If I were a cat, I'd hide in there, I thought. I pulled the door, causing the metal to yelp. I peered into the dark cavern of the stove, and then I felt a hand on my shoulder.

"Hey there, Abigail."

I straightened slowly and turned. "You're supposed to solve mysteries," I said, feigning cool. "Where's my son's cat?"

"That's not on my docket," he said. "But I'd try the fish store down the block." He folded his arms, in his fine camel-hair jacket, as he deployed that dimple. "Now maybe you can tell me where to find Milo Petimezas." He nodded toward a black sedan, clearly an unmarked police car, parked at the curb. "Just sit and have a chat with me, Abby, please. Just a chat."

In the car, he switched off the squawking scanner and turned to me. "Deep shit. I am doing what I can to keep Pete's name out of it," he said. "This group he was mixing with has all the wrong friends. The heaviest of connections. I'm hoping he didn't know. And you didn't."

"Heavy connections?"

"What did you know about the Petimezas family?"

"Not a thing," I said. "Their kid goes to my kids' school. That's it."

"Abby, have you joined the antifa, for chrissake?"

Something in his tone suddenly awakened my anger. "I was a guest at that party. And Pete hasn't broken any laws."

"I know," he said. "But how did this unfold? You're a woman with responsibilities."

"And you're a man who fucks around with such a woman, with nothing in mind but what he can grab for himself."

This landed. He sighed and cast his eyes down. "Not entirely false, not entirely true," he said. But then he hardened again. "Look. All I want to know is, where the fuck is Milo Petimezas, and how does a family that trades in drugs and weapons come to be stealing paintings from Mariah Glücksburg?"

Paintings? I couldn't really take this information in. "The whole family? Illegal arms dealers?"

"Dear old grandad did his first prison stint in 1964. I've arrested Milo three times myself, Abby."

Pete giving Dmitri a tour of the carriage house, his remarks on the old painting of the erstwhile prince of Greece.

The man on the stairs, the leather sneakers. Wasn't that Milo Petimezas?

"And you understand, how the paintings were lifted, that was not a job by some green kid. Pro tools and technique, fast work. Cut out of the frames. Five of her splatters—you're talking probably eight, ten million right there, correct? Plus old pictures, family portraits."

"They stole all that?"

"Your antifa commotion was great, noisy cover for a thief."

"But Dmitri seemed to be a true believer," I said.

"Yes, and apparently the Petimezas clan fought in the Greek resistance to the Nazis, and a few were strung up by the right-wingers during the war. But here, they're thugs. I'm thinking they involved their little one in the life, when it suited them."

"But Pete—he didn't know a thing. He really is a true believer." My voice was shaking. I didn't want to cry. "Anyhow, what the hell are you doing here? Are you following me?"

He shrugged. "I had business in the neighborhood. Listen, I'll do what I can for Pete. And you. I'm sick of slogging it out in the barnyard, Abby. This case is my ticket. I've just got to steer Pizziali the fuck away from it, and if I bring in Milo and his folks, that deputy commissioner slot is mine. You could help me bust these scumbags."

I heard Dennis's voice then, drifting into the open window. "Wowza!"

"This is why you fucked me."

"Abigail." He reached for my arm. I yanked it away.

"Do your job. But stop following me." I slid quickly out of the car and hurried toward the sound of my husband's voice. I looked over my shoulder once to see the sedan slowly moving away.

I spotted Dennis down the cross street, peering into shrubs and up into trees. Then I notice a girl walking up behind him. Pink coat. Messy hank of curls. In her arms, a brown bundle of fuzz, a tail draped over her arm, flicking this way and that.

She crosses the sidewalk toward Dennis.

I watch him reach out for the bundle. I see her smile at him. I see him smile at her and say a few words. She laughs and nods and relinquishes the cat and then he is moving toward me, he has seen me, and behind him, she glimmers away straight into the still-low morning sun.

"A lovely young woman saved the day," Dennis reported, as he handed the wanderer to Benjamin back at the house. "It gives you some hope, a thing like that," he said. He turned and put his hand on my face. "A thing like that," he said.

ABBY, OCTOBER 20, 2015

The human brain is 73 percent water, a saturated sponge sloshing around in a brimming bucket. "Such liquid makes it so nice to penetrate with the lovely radio waves of the MRI," said Dr. Alvarado, the fancy new neurologist who'd been sourced by Dennis via Mariah and her uptown connections. "So the waves will help us make a very fine map, and we will try to see then why you are feeling woozy and falling down." She spoke with the lilt of Chile or Argentina. Her lashes were thickly mascaraed, so they resembled many exclamation points, and her big eyes looked sad. She assured me all would be well. "No caffeine, no jewelry, no zippers on your clothes. Be very comfy because we will have you prone and still for quite a while."

The scan was scheduled for six days hence. Six days hence, they'll roll me into the tube of their great magnetized machine, and my every watery molecule will sway to its urgings, just as waves surrender to the pull of the moon.

ABBY, OCTOBER 26, 2015

In my arm, a shot of dye ("gadolinium, to give us a pretty contrast," said Dr. Alvarado). On my head, a snap-on plastic helmet ("It's called a coil, or, if you prefer, a robot hat"). Then a pair of headphones, burbling Bach cantatas, and a slow slide into the brilliant cylinder. Beyond the Bach, still I heard the muffled thumping, rattling, pounding, the percussive sound of the machine, doing its magic, mapping the saturated sponge. Mapping the clump of cells that adds up to Abigail.

I studied the patterns of veins in pink, the inside of my eyelids, which were blasted into translucence by the glare. I'd never seen this pattern in my whole life, even though my eyes and these lids were such intimate companions, I realized with druggy wonder.

They'd dosed me with some sedative, "a gentle relaxing will happen and this will keep you resting in peace," said Dr. Alvarado. Her English idioms could use a bit of tweaking.

I don't remember much, except that at one point, wandering crooked lines across pink landscape, I saw A. Strobing lights, hammering beats. Was she dancing? Her strange, sinuous movements. Was she in that club, the one I'd spotted her exiting, at the start of this unfathomable year?

A curious vision. The velvet coat, the silver shoes, gliding across the pink.

Am I dreaming? Tripping?

No. I am remembering.

Up the battered stairs on West Twelfth Street. Up into the apartment, the shoes kicked off, the coat flung over a chair. Eli Hammond outside on the balcony, in yellow glow. He is flicking his lighter.

He has taken the portfolio she is preparing to send off to RISD. Sketches, slides, written explanations, slowly and painfully composed.

Don't.

He has the fire in his hands, he is bent over the ash bucket. His hands are shaking. She sees the glass pipe, broken on the concrete.

Don't you dare, she says. She runs at him. Her hands reaching for it, the portfolio. The many color studies, the pencil and charcoal drawings done in cafés and bars, the atrium in Midtown, the diner on the corner over a breakfast of eggs and toast. The sketch of him, even, from the day they met in MoMA.

And one she has finished only this morning: a portrait in india ink, the head of a woman, not old and not young, wistfulness in her dark eyes, strength in the set of her mouth.

All of this. Tucked into a stamped and addressed manila envelope that he has singed with his desperate flame.

He pushes her away, hard, and then she falls hard. But she hauls herself up again, scrabbling for that portfolio, which now seems the only thing to live for. And she lunges for the envelope, and he lets it slip to the floor and grabs her instead, clutching her with terrible force. She looks up into his face in astonishment, meets his dark blue eyes rimmed with paler blue and she catches the very moment he chooses death over whatever would otherwise happen next. His body looms, he has her in a lock, clenches her tight, and the blues have gone flat and his beautiful hands, which she has sketched, which she has kissed, and had all over her and inside her—now they grip her upper arms like iron bands and he backs her against the railing, trying to lift her up and over it. She kicks at him. His bony body presses the length of her, he is thin with the poison he smokes and weaker than he should be but he is too heavy, and he tries to push her over the edge but she wraps her strong legs around him as she has so many times in love, fusing her body to his, and then a great cracking happens at her back as the old balcony railing gives way.

Falling from yellow light to black and silence.

The portfolio somehow lands in Providence. How?

And then Dr. Alvarado is there, and Dennis too. He is holding my hand and gazing into my face with concern. Each line and wrinkle, his ruffled wheat-silver hair falling over his deeply familiar gaze, his lashes lighter at their tips, the soft jawline and the feel of his hand, which I know as if it were a piece of my own body. All of these are guideposts back into the world of my world. Where I will and must and desire to live.

"I don't rule anything out, but I am pleased with what I see," said Dr. Alvarado. "We will read more closely and call with final results. But for now, Abigail, the scans look clean."

Clean.

The world where I desire to live. I just had to turn back to it. Later in bed, determined to relish this clean and happy result, I turned to Dennis. His fingers seemed to retain some heat from his work, from the fiery torch, as he slid them over me, forearms, small of my back, thighs. My mind retained a trippy residue that transformed his familiar touch into something otherworldly, made him into yet another visiting spirit. Yes, we do know each other's every curve and hollow but that doesn't mean we don't still surprise each other, and this night we did.

Dr. Tristane Kazemy, OCTOBER 31, 2016

Balcony railing collapse. Diffuse axonal head wound.

Written right there, in the additional records from New York. Old medical records showing that yes, she had been critically injured in a fall, and she had survived. Luck. And she'd healed well. Youth. No lingering effects noted. In fact, as Laurin would be glad to point out, the wound was almost invisible, just a void in the scans made last year.

But this void.

She needed to start writing her report for the New York meeting—still she sat here, hunched past midnight in her cubicle at the deserted lab, reading the woman's words instead.

For the better part of a year, she'd stared into the void, this interstitial space tucked beneath Abigail Willard's cerebellum, the black triangle in the red sulcus. She'd long diagnosed these hallucinations—these apparitions—as symptoms of whatever irregularity was hidden inside that triangle. But doubt had begun to creep in. The incidents—the library, the bistro, the night at the beach. She looked again at the photos of the broken phone. The scan of a torn page bearing the psychologist's scrawled name and number. The uncanny pen-and-ink likeness of Abigail Willard, unearthed via Leverett's policework, hidden deep in the files of the renowned art school.

She would fly to New York in a month and a day.

She needed to write the report. But increasingly she felt unsure about what it should say.

11/11/11/11

A color has many faces, Josef Albers says. Our eyes and our brains work in tandem to create a color, and this hue changes depending on the colors that surround it. Without these interactions, the professor teaches, a color is as lifeless as a single musical note. The art is in the in-between.

Dennis's eyes, for example. A conversation between green, blue, and gold. Green sea, cerulean sky, and ochre sand.

Color is personal. A point also made by Albers, a notion that, I now believe, has been a kind of controlling principle for my life. I return to this thought again and again, the idea that the infinitesimal body parts we use to see the world, our rods and cones, are as individual as our fingerprints. And these utterly singular seers send their impressions to our brains, which are even more singular, and there our universe is made. Therefore, it follows. No two people live in the same universe. My green is not your green.

There in Dennis's arms, on a long-gone afternoon by the bay outside of Providence, I perceived his eyes as the green of unknown waters, countless fathoms deep, yet infinitely infused with light.

I swam in them toward my future.

NEW YORK CITY IS, apparently, home to many minor royals, though some flew in from afar: Geneva, Turin, Garmisch-Partenkirchen. The extended family turned out in numbers, stolid and toothy. The men homely but impeccably groomed; the women, imposing in height despite stumpy low-heeled pumps, and done up in well-cut dresses and jackets pinned with fat jewels in whimsical settings: clusters of cabochon-emerald grapes, a daisy with a canary-diamond center big enough to choke a cat. There was a set of young princesses, mostly stuffed into short strapless frocks, and in them, I could see the boldness of Mariah, in their curves and silky curls and the knowing way they posed for the cameras, the cheeks prominent and pillowy, the odalisque smile. And yes, there were many cameras. Not surprisingly, given the violent and sensational nature of the death, it was a news event, MoMA opening its retrospective, assembled in the course of a hectic month, and accompanied by a luminary-packed memorial service, in tribute to the late and very lamented Mariah Glücksburg.

I wore black. A sleeveless sheath I'd had for so many years—bought when I was her, in fact, with money from that first job, working under the execrable Michael Hutcherson, and having learned from *Glamour* magazine that a city girl needed a classic black dress. I hadn't worn it since long before the new millennium—it had become too tight, reminded me of what I didn't love about my changing body, and it had been pushed farther and farther back along the pole that ran the length of my jammed closet until it was lost to me. But, searching for something to cover me in this unimaginable moment, I dug. And found it again. And it seemed fitting, the black. An echo of Mariah, in her final party garb, and appropriate of course for mourning her. I slipped it on and discovered that it hung with a degree of looseness. But wasn't it true that I couldn't quite recall the last time I'd really eaten a meal? Over the past year, my appetite had dwindled. Lately, it had vanished. Looking in the mirror, I wondered if I looked haggard or chic.

Dennis dressed in silence beside me. A sober charcoal suit, the bolo tie, and a pair of Vans, surfer shoes. Yes, absolutely. Let him show his personal flair. I no longer felt I had a right to an opinion about such things.

Our marriage seemed to have entered a different phase. Call it an afterlife. We had explored the outlines of our devotion to each other and our desire to be free. Neither of us cared to define the full extent of the other's adventures. We would let the edges remain indistinct, softened by a layer of cool quiet, like snow. In the end, here we still were. And so we dressed without talking, the un- thinking dance as we moved around the unmade bed, maneuvered together and apart in a space that had always been a little too small.

IT WAS THE ROYALS, I guess, that drew the crush outside of the museum, the sensational nature of her death, and yes, Mariah did count a few neon-bright names, hitmakers of music and movies, among her friends and collectors. Dennis and I were absorbed into the slow-moving crowd pressing toward the security checkpoint. Bomb threats had been called in. For weeks, speculation had been careening between two theories: that she'd been targeted by a ter- ror group, perhaps with a grudge over Greek nationalism; or that it was simply an art heist, carried out with indifference or carelessness re human life.

The detective hadn't been in touch. Neither had Pizziali. I won- dered about it, whether they were locked in some kind of battle over the case, or stalemate. Whether my name was attached, or Pete's, or whether the focus had shifted completely to the Peti- mezas clan.

Dennis must have had the same subject in mind. As we waited in the pack outside the doors, he scanned the street. "They wouldn't risk turning up here, would they?"

"No, they must be laying low," I said. The crowd pressed us forward, toward the revolving glass doors. We were launched into the bright interior, and it took my breath away, to see all of her work there, many of the pieces I had so recently touched, propping them on her chairs and sofas. Now they were suspended in these great stark halls, where the most blessed fragments of manipulated matter are allowed to linger after the hands that worked them cease to exist.

Dennis and I roamed together, for a while. Then we lost each other. I'm sure he felt as I did, faced at every turn with her creations, the blinding whites, the soul-scouring spirals. Overcome. Dazed. Grief stricken.

Toward the end of the exhibition, I found myself in a smaller room. Dedicated to her personal art collection.

A Matisse cutout. A collage by Josef Albers.

And next to those, a small still life. Two grapefruit, one tenderly rendered yellow orb, one halved to show raw glistening pink.

Painted in Professor Bremer's holy classroom. Hung that frosty, flurried night at Broder and Wilcox. Sold to an anonymous collector. Never seen again.

Till now.

And next to that: The green of the trees, the gold light on the bay. A flash of orange in the green.

The museum and the massed mourners vanished.

The whisper of the brush on the canvas. The outrushing tide of water. The feel of the grass and the sun and his skin on my skin.

I gaze at the painting, and the painting seems to gaze back.

Did that gaze hold some foreknowledge?

Crowds milling and murmuring behind me. And then Dennis, next to me.

I turn from the painting. To his eyes, green and blue and gold. Grass and ocean, sun and sky. Paint and flesh. The envisioned and the real. The past and the present.

I reached for him. Our arms knew where to fall, my cheek knew where to rest on his shoulder, our bodies like the plates of the continents, shaped by time to fit just where they needed to be.

Through the crowded rooms, up the escalator, I guided him to *One*.

I searched for the spot, to show him. The missing place. The void.

But it was gone—patched at some point over the last two decades by the museum's skillful restorers. Of course it had been. The act erased. The outcome changed.

Though not entirely. The silver box was in my evening bag. I carried it everywhere now. I opened it to show him.

He poked the flake of pigment with his finger. He turned to the painting, to the spot, then back to peer into my face, scrutinizing.

I inhaled, filled my lungs full of air, then said, "I have seen myself do so many things. I mean, I have this girl in my life, and she is me."

"A girl?"

"Me."

He put his hand to my forehead. "You're sweaty. You look very pale."

"Me, I mean, me." Behind him, I saw the Pollock dissolving, its tendrils of paint unraveling and drifting away into the air.

"I've got to get you out of here," he said.

I closed my fist around that little box.

ABBY, NOVEMBER 20, 2015

My three men rotated through my bedroom, to frown at me with befuddlement and offer a glass of water or a peanut butter sandwich. I passed hours in the room, somehow unable to rise. I wrestled the covers on and off and called in sick to work. "Bethanne can fill in, she will kick ass," Esther Muncie said, a bit cruelly, I thought. "I'll be in Monday," I said. Dennis held down the fort. I alternately slept and sketched the view out the window with a graphite stick, drawing over and over the trees with a few last brown leaves, the fire escapes and balconies on the five-story apartment buildings that lined the block behind our house.

Change the outcome. The phrase wouldn't leave me.

The final MRI results came in a call from Dr. Alvarado. "Clean," she said. "I showed it to four excellent pairs of eyes, and only one of them could see anything, just a blip, but I see nothing, so I say this is not something."

"Clean," said Dennis, sitting by me on the bed. "A good Thanksgiving gift. And no explanation for what's going on with you. But still, this is good news."

Thanksgiving, less than a week away. The holiday of Eli's end. The day after the feast day in 1991, the day after the first and only time I was able to show Eli where I'd begun my life, and to meet my parents. That was when we'd gone over the edge.

I could recall maples forming a bare brown net across on the cement sky. But that's just what anyone's memory would fill in, if they had ever spent a November afternoon in Hartsfield, Massachusetts. Winter seemed to arrive that very day, as we walked from the train station with our overnight bags, past the white wooden triple deckers and squat cape cottages, the steepled church and the brick municipal hall. At the foot of Prospect Street, we passed my parents' yarn-and-fabric shop, where they taught me to sort and shelve the skeins and bolts by complementary and analogous colors, and next to it, the little granite library where I'd paged through the first art books I'd ever seen, black-and-white reproductions mostly. So many afternoons, my parents busy trying to make ends meet with the sluggish business at their store, I came there to puzzle over the naked gods and goddesses, the confounding moderns. What I saw in those library books seemed to flow through my eyes directly into my hands, animating them in an almost disembodied way, moving me to push the books aside and spill out, on small squares of scratch paper I swiped from atop the card catalog, my own clumsy imitations.

The Thanksgiving dinner was modest, a mostly brown meal in the kitchen of the old Colonial on the outskirts of downtown. My parents were taken aback by Eli. "Is that safe?" my mother kept asking, as he talked about the photo work he'd been doing and all he hoped to do in Europe and Africa and the Middle East. She kept casting worried glances at me, while my father just set his lips tight, nodding grimly in an effort not to be rude, and appearing angrier and angrier as the meal dragged on.

As we settled into the seat on a city-bound train the next morning, Eli stared out the window for a while, then turned to me and said, Do you think they liked me? I planted a kiss on his lips and told him I didn't care. He opened the newspaper he'd bought in the station. Shit, the Balkans are really on the boil, he said. He spent the rest of the ride begging and cajoling me to go there with him, to leave right away.

I didn't know what to say or do. I did know that lately I'd found it very difficult to find the focus to finish my portfolio for the RISD application. The deadline was nearing. November 29.

ABBY, NOVEMBER 23, 2015

The evening of Dr. Alvarado's call, I decided to rise from bed. I stood on wobbly legs, made a halting descent of the stairs. The boys had already eaten dinner, but Dennis presented me with a bowl of what was left: the macaroni and cheese from the box, speckled with frozen peas. I ate thinking about the memories awakened in the tube, degraded images restored by the imaging machine.

I called Dr. Merle. "My brain seems healthy but my mind still does not," I said.

"I have been quite indisposed," she croaked. "But I will see you, Abigail. Because your case is singular."

"Should I be flattered?" I laughed.

"Yes, you are a once in a lifetime case. Or perhaps not." She emitted a sharp, long, dry cackle. "So, I will see you day after tomorrow. Three p.m. sharp."

But today when I arrived, the building was eerily quiet. Through the glass door of the hair salon, I saw an abandoned mop angled across the trash-strewn floor, a few hanging wires, crooked hooks where mirrors had been removed from the wall.

The hallway outside of Dr. Merle's office was even darker. I tried the knob but the door was locked. I peered through the little window alongside the door. Papers had been scattered, covering most of the rug. File drawers tilted open, spilling folders.

I stepped back, bewildered. Then: a bit of paper taped over the mailbox hung by the door frame. The scrawled notation. *Postal carrier: return mail to sender. Dr. Merle Unzicker deceased 11.22.15.*

ABBY, NOVEMBER 26, 2015

Pete set a lovely table. The old things we once used, those history-encrusted tidbits—crumbly paste-china plates passed down from my grandmother, the little handprint turkey place cards Ben had made in kindergarten—they'd disappeared in the fire. But we had a set of new white dishes and shiny new glasses and cutlery, paid for with insurance cash. For a centerpiece, Pete constructed a cornucopia out of aluminum foil, and filled it with weedy bits from the backyard, leaves and grass and a couple of apples from the fridge. This touched me deeply. My boys had never been crafty. Benjamin and Gianna proudly paraded back and forth to the table, bearing the turkey, sweet potatoes, cranberry sauce, and a gigantic salad dressed in sunflower oil and coconut vinegar.

Our children had reached sufficient age to understand that Mom and Dad were barely functioning. They stepped up. A most heartening turn, a true consolation, for a parent.

Wowza observed us from atop the chipped marble mantel, tail undulating slowly, a twist of smoke.

"I would like to propose a toast," said Pete. We all fell silent. It was very, very rare for him to call for an audience. "Here's to Mariah." He raised his glass toward Dennis and me.

Then he reached into his front pocket and tossed a fat roll of cash, size of a baseball, bundled in a rubber band, onto the table. It rolled around and settled right in front of me.

"That's yours, Ma," he said.

It was Dmitri who suggested that Pete might try to sneak a painting out of the chaos of our home's reconstruction. He'd heard that one of my pieces had sold for over two grand at a school auction. Dmitri had planted the seed of this idea, and said his brother could probably find a buyer, and Pete had acted on the suggestion the day the detective dropped by the house. But Pete, rattled by the bouquet-bearing police officer, guilt-ridden at having pinched his own mother's artwork, bumped into Mariah when he arrived back at the carriage house, the painting under his arm. She was stirring milk into her coffee in the kitchen. "What've you got there?" she asked.

He shrugged. "It's my mom's. She said sell it and give the money to a good cause."

"Isn't that just like your mom," she said. She licked her spoon thoughtfully. "So how much do you want for it?"

He asked for two grand. She gently admonished him for underselling his mother's work, and gave him twenty grand instead. Since it was for a good cause.

If not for Mariah, the green field by the bay would be hanging in some mobster's house in Athens. If not for her, the grapefruits would've burned up in the fire, like all my other work.

I contemplated the roll of cash resting by my plate. The outermost bill was a thousand-dollar note. My gaze seemed to penetrate the layers, to see them all at once and the deeper truth this layered bundle contained at its heart. All of life is like this. Love too. Comprised of layers. The layers are mutable, and the layers can be seen all at once, if regarded with open-enough eyes and mind.

Dennis raised his glass. His eyes were brimming and bleared. "To Mariah," he said. We all raised our glasses. "To Mariah," we said.

ABBY, NOVEMBER 29, 2015

Please let me record this last before I leave this earth. I'm fairly sure I'm already half gone.

They said the scans were clean, but for several days the headaches worsened again, the tightening and the throbbing, the wooziness. To Muncie's dismay, I called to extend my sick leave, but what could I do? I was definitely unwell. Through the afternoons and into early evenings I was lost in dreams, sometimes nightmares, sleeping away the hours. Dark was falling, inside and out.

This evening, after hours of half sleep, I saw a figure at the door to my bedroom, framed there as if projected on a screen, flickering in black and gray and white like a figure in a grainy old movie.

It was Eli. The restless attenuated silhouette, haloed in light from the hallway, one hand tracing the edge of the door's molded trim.

"I thought maybe you could fund your painting for a while," he said. "With that money."

Of course. This was my Pete, lingering there. None other. Of course. "Why didn't you give that cash to Dmitri?"

"I didn't trust him," he shrugged. He sat down on the edge of the bed. "But really. I want you to do what you were meant to do," he said. "Plus, you can use whatever savings you've been banking for my college tuition. No more school. I want to be out in the world."

I reached out and smoothed a lock of hair away from his eyes. "Don't rule anything out."

He rubbed his chin thoughtfully for a moment. He stood again. "Are you OK, Ma? Really? You're booking an awful lot of time in this bedroom."

This, from the boy who'd spent most of his teen years barricaded down the hall, made me smile. "I'm OK," I said. "I just need to gather my strength."

I must have drifted off again. I woke to an empty house. I remembered Dennis would be at his studio. The Vienna art handlers would arrive tomorrow morning to crate his creations. The glass panes of the ceiling would be removed and the crates lifted out by crane, trucked to a New Jersey cargo dock, fitted into containers, and, by ship, then train, arrive at a palace on the famed Ringstrasse where I imagined cherubs and angels hovering mutely on the gilded ceilings as Dennis's steel beasts reared up below. Now I recalled him saying that he wanted to recruit the boys, that he'd pay them a few bucks if they'd help with readying the studio for the packing crew and their crane.

I wandered the deserted rooms. Egg-encrusted dishes rose in teetering stacks in the sink. Socks were everywhere, shed and left behind like limp snake skins. A vague aroma of unemptied trash cans hung in the air. Or maybe it was me—I'd been wearing the same leggings and T-shirt for two days, and they were speckled with cracker crumbs and patches of spilled juice. Still, I couldn't be bothered to change. I found myself a pair of shoes and shrugged on a coat.

Under a malfunctioning streetlamp buzzing on and off at the corner I parked. Wind whispered down Monsignor Murphy Street, which was as empty as an inhospitable planet. But there in the cellar of the boarded-up row house, I could see a square of light. Twiz and Vincent were leading the regular Sunday-night muster. The door was unmanned, security was lax, the mood subdued, depressed, really, in the wake of Dmitri's betrayal and his abscondence with their bail fund. I inched around the crowd to a spot in a far dark corner of the room, getting my bearings. As my eyes adjusted, I picked out some familiar faces, and some unfamiliar faces too. Despite the setbacks, it seemed, the Brigade was still gaining recruits, a few people who'd raised their heads and heard this particular call. Twiz began to talk to the group about her Brigade-sponsored after-school tutoring center, which had finally opened its doors. Though

I tried to stay in the background, Vincent's hog-like pit bulls found me, snuffling my clothes furiously, as if I were a buffet of snacks. Then the redheaded boy stepped up to lead a brainstorming session about protests to greet the various fascist leaders who'd attend the next UN general assembly. I pulled Twiz aside. I pressed the wad of cash into her hand. "For the schoolkids," I said. She stared at the fat bundle with astonishment, then wrapped me in a fierce hug, her locks brushing my face with the aroma of cannabis and soap. Then she stepped back, tilted her head, and said, "You don't look so good."

But just as she said this—*BOOM*. With a single sharp crack, the door flapped open, the dead bolt tearing through the wood frame, one hinge giving way. Everyone in the cellar swiveled toward the noise. From my vantage point at the far corner of the room, I glimpsed only an inky shifting shape, shuddering and bellowing, pouring through the doorway. Then, like mercury beading, it coalesced into figures in police battle gear, bodies thick with padding and pockets and guns raised. One person hung a bit behind them, a rotund little man in an NYPD windbreaker, brush-cut hair stiff on his head. With his crossed black eyes, Pizziali scanned the room.

Pandemonium broke out, the padded figures barking and yelling "to your knees" and "hands behind your backs" and people falling to the ground, and a few screeched words of protest and general scrambling around. A small hand snapped tight around my forearm. Another hand shoved hard against my back, sending me stumbling through a doorway and into a little alcove, where I banged my knees against a set of steps. "Up," a voice hissed, and I knew it was Twiz, and she was right behind me, I felt her body pressed against mine as I climbed, a feather of her hair on my cheek, and her arms reaching around me and suddenly I felt a rush of night air and the coal hatch at the back of the house opened up to the dim desecrated yard, and we tripped through it into the next yard and the next and the next, thrashing at tossing nets of winter vines and chain link, and then I stumbled over a large plastic object and landed with my face hard up against a face, jolly smile and laughing eyes faded, but still Santa.

Twiz hauled me up again and we stood there for an instant, panting. She patted her pocket. "At least we have a bail fund now," she said, and, in the strange urban glow from an overcast sky, I could see her grinning. I nodded, breathless, and I thought of Mariah and I thought of my green painting even now hanging in that vast vaunted white mausoleum and I thought of how the marks we make upset repose, how they ripple away into the universe, how a creative act always contains consequences, and how these are always beyond our imaginings. Then I stopped thinking because behind us the curtain of tangled undergrowth began to rustle and Twiz's head whipped around and we both saw the same thing, a tall man, on the move, a lanky human form, crashing through the twigs. It hit me: they followed me here. The cops. I'd led them here. The thought made me want to wilt, bow at last to fate. I felt my knees buckling.

But Twiz. She grabbed me by both arms, hoisted me halfway up the sagging remains of a garden shed and practically threw me down the other side into an alley. Run, she said, and she darted away so fast I knew I would never keep up. My shins were banged and throbbing, my head swirling. Soon I lost her in the gloom and I thought I could hear her footfalls ahead of me, but then I realized they were coming from behind me, rapid crisp smacks on the broken tarmac and gravel. Then, dead ahead at the end of the alley, I saw a beacon pulsing in the darkness. It was the streetlight on the fritz and there underneath it glimmered my car and there in my pocket were my keys and I raced for it, punching my key chain to set off the car's loyal beep and flash and I clambered in and rammed the key into its slot, tires screeching and crunching and the car jumped forward and I drove blindly toward where I knew I had been heading all along.

THE COBBLESTONES RUMBLED under the wheels of my car as I glided slowly to a stop. Double-parked in front of number 268.

In my rib cage, my lungs struggled, like feral little things in a trap, a pair of panicking mongoose or fisher cats. Sweat slicked my face and neck.

A man in a bathrobe and plaid pajama pants appeared inside the glass door, in the brightly lit entry. He stood there for a moment, grinning down at his phone, his jowls shaking in amusement. At last he descended the front steps, dragging a log-like dog on a leash. I caught the door before it closed.

Up the endless flights of stairs. My mind racing, the dizziness tugging against the climb, my body fighting back. Fighting all the way to the top. Fifth floor.

I knock at the door.

You? she says. I can't deal with you now.

Beyond her, I see him on the balcony.

I see him out there, hunched on the bench with the portfolio, the lighter.

He's going to destroy your work, I say. And himself. And you, I say.

I push past her.

I feel her breath, ice cold, on my cheek. Wait, what did you say?

Then there I am, out on the balcony. The five stories yawning under my feet. I'm fighting the vertigo. He gapes at me, confused.

Please, I say, reaching for the envelope and meeting his gaze. Please come back inside.

Who are you, he says.

Recognition in his eyes. You? he whispers.

I grip the portfolio. The envelope is in my hands.

What happens can't happen, I say.

She stands just inside the balcony doorway, a shivery form against the light, edges blurred.

He wanted to destroy my work, she says.

He's lost, I say. I hold the envelope out to her. Take it.

Fury has turned her face into a mask. Her eyes are ignited, roiling dark to blazing to dark again.

I'm not sure what he meant to do, I say.

I look over my shoulder at him. Tears soaking his face.

It's good, this life, she says. A half-question in her voice.

Yes.

And the work. Hanging there in the museum.

So you saw.

It's good.

Yes?

Volition gathering, flashing across her face like heat lightning.

Worth everything, she says.

I feel the pure will, surging from the center of her being, toward me. I feel love surging from me, toward her, the same. I move closer, into the bright square where she wavers. I reach to take her in my arms and hold her forever. To keep her from the dark outside and below.

She eludes me. I grab for her, but I am weak, and she is strong, and she pushes me away, then I'm on the floor, she has actually pushed me down. I see her barreling toward the balcony, where he stands, a dark-on-darker shape, watching us.

She hurls herself at him, he is pedaling his feet backward and she clings to him and they collapse in a tight embrace onto the old railing and it buckles with an air-rending crack, I think I see her turn her head, her eyes meet mine, our gazes lock as the whole thing gives way and they are flying out into the night. They are gone. Both gone.

The mailbox there on the street corner. Deep blue and solid, the last solid landmark on earth. Just steps away.

A man, calling my name.

The sense of something shattered. The order of the universe.

That's what I can recall. The doctors are in the hall. Falling back into black now. I will forget it all.

12/12/12/12

ABBY, MAY 3, 2016

Turn the page so that the red circle is on the left.

If we stare for half a minute at the red circle, focusing continually on the marked center, and then focus on the white center, we do not see white. The color we see there is the afterimage of red.

Dr. Tristane Kazemy, DECEMBER 1, 2016

The Abigail Willard of her imagination, crafted from bits and pieces and clues from the file, was nothing like the flesh-and-blood being in front of her, haloed in the winter light that poured through great glass windows on the tenth floor of Mount Sinai Hospital.

Tristane had access to her for only a few minutes this first visit, and only with a team of her other doctors in the room. The woman was still in recovery, even, months later, a trip from Brooklyn to the Upper East Side was enough to tax her. Sitting amid the assembled physicians for just a short while, there in the sparkling examination room, amid the sunbeams, she appeared almost translucent. In fact, looking at her, Tristane thought, she is barely flesh and blood.

But perhaps, when one has had an earthquake at the center of one's existence, when one's every notion about life is shaken and tossed, one looks like this. Evanescent. Like a being who has come to exist in the spaces between cells, rather than in the cells themselves.

ABBY, JULY 24, 2016

Turn the page so that the bright pink rectangle is at the left.

It looks as if each of the outer colors are moving underneath the middle color and turning up at the other end—penetrating, or better, intersecting each other very softly.

PERSONAL WORK LOG: Garrett L. Shuttlesworth, December 2, 2016

New York City is full of ghosts. I get that. I felt it this morning, myself, in the taxi from my hotel on East Twenty-Eighth Street to the meeting uptown on Lexington. For anyone who's ever lived here, this place is a haunted battlefield. Your marriage died here, or your innocence, or your dreams. Maybe your great-grandfather died here, or maybe your youth did.

Spectral, is what the interesting Dr. Kazemy, the forensic neurologist from Montreal, said about Abigail Willard today. She said she looked a bit spectral. It was the first convening of Jameson's investigators, in a conference room at the Marriott East Side. Jameson's choice, an odd one, given what's in the woman's journals, but okay, the whole atmosphere was odd. So we sat around one end of a ludicrously long table, the three of us—Dr. Kazemy,

who yesterday examined our story's central player at
the hospital, and Jameson Leverett, the New York City
detective, my long-ago freshman roommate, who recruited
us for this inquiry and insisted on the black-box email and
the confidentiality docs, which were spread on the table for
signing when we arrived. Truly, odd.

What's driving all this? We know from the Willard
diaries about the sexual relationship. The entanglement.
Whether he cared for her, I can't say. He was using her,
that much seems certain, to bust a crime gang and earn his
stripes. Which isn't a shocker. Back in our Syracuse days,
he was a dog. An operator. But then later in life he seemed
to mellow. The wife and kids. So who the hell knows.

I hadn't seen him in years, and when he walked into the
conference room, I was surprised to see how he's aged. He
was always a good-looking guy, but the last year took a toll
on him, maybe. He has a kind of hollowness in his face.
He doesn't grin easily like he once did. I was expecting to
see him strutting around in the navy blue uniform, but of
course he's way too high-powered for that now. Chief of
Detectives.

Anyhow, I told Jameson and Dr. Kazemy that I'm not
going to let stand the notion that Abigail Willard imagined
it all. Hallucinations of a diseased brain, or an overtaxed
mind.

That's simply not a complete enough explanation. First,
because of the contradictory evidence, and second, and
much more crucially, because I think this case could be the
key to everything.

Then I tried to explain the theory of everything. I think
it went over their heads.

ABBY, SEPTEMBER 8, 2016

Eyes kind of tarnished bronze, tawny skin. A handsome face, but the mouth is too grim.

This police detective who comes around to question me. We've been over and over 2015. I just don't remember that much, from about January on. A few things. I tell him about how Benjamin dropped a basketball down the stairs and cracked a window, thinking it will make him laugh.

But he rarely laughs. His eyes have a deep, lovely color, but they look very distressed.

December 3, 2016

From: J.Leverett@deepxmail.com
To: Tristane.Kazemy@montrealneuro.ca,
GarrettShuttlesworth@physics.humboldtstate.edu

Thanks for meeting yesterday. In a case loaded with so much ambiguity, we will try to stay grounded in the known facts. To set a baseline for discussions this week:

1. Abigail Willard's behavior began to change in January 2015.
2. By August 2015, Mrs. Willard was participating in the violent protests of a Brooklyn-based antifascist group, a possible domestic terror cell.
3. In September 2015, this antifa group mounted a street protest outside the home of the artist Mariah Glücksburg. An incendiary device was thrown, triggering a chemical explosion that resulted in the death of Ms. Glücksburg.

Dennis Willard, spouse of Abigail, suffered minor injuries.
Abigail and Pete Willard took part in the protest, as
documented by security footage and eyewitness accounts.

4. Police continue to investigate the connections between
    the protest, the fatality, and the theft of valuable artworks
    from the residence. With the help of Interpol, Brooklyn
    Criminal Enterprise division succeeded in apprehending
    Milo Petimezas, his parents Nikolas and Ariana Petimezas,
    the juvenile Dmitri, all persons of interest, found in hiding
    on December 14, 2015, in the Peloponnesian region of
    southwestern Greece. They were in possession of the stolen
    artworks along with illegal assault weapons and other items
    of contraband.

5. On the night of November 29, 2015, Abigail Willard
    was delivered by an unnamed police detective to the
    emergency room at the NYU Bellevue hospital in downtown
    Manhattan. Medical records indicate that at the time of
    admission, Mrs. Willard was in a debilitated state, vomiting,
    apparently suffering shock and seizures. Mrs. Willard lost
    consciousness while in an examining room, after waiting 3
    hours to be seen.

6. Doctors determined she was in the midst of a traumatic brain
    event, possibly a bleed. They undertook emergency surgery
    to investigate and remove any hemorrhage. As the patient
    lapsed into critical condition, doctors excised a small area of
    her brain. A tumor or other abnormality was suspected but
    not, as of yet, definitively located in the removed brain tissue.

7. As a result of the trauma of the surgery, Mrs. Willard fell into a
    coma, which lasted 95 days.

8. The final entry of her 2015 journal concerns an accident at
    268 West 12th Street in Manhattan. A balcony collapse.

9. There is a record of a balcony collapse. It occurred at that location 24 years ago, on the night of November 29, 1991.

10. In Mrs. Willard's final journal entry, she describes seeing two victims fall that night: a young man, Eli Hammond; and a young woman, known to her as A.

11. City records contain note of the death of Eli Hammond, age 24, in the 1991 incident.

12. Abigail Wilhelm, age 22, holder of sublease on the apartment, escaped death but suffered internal injuries from the fall.

13. Police logged a call from the same apartment on the night of November 29, 2015. Tanya Novakovski, a 26-year-old digital marketing manager, reported that a female intruder, in a state of some agitation, had gained access to the apartment. Ms. Novakovski locked herself in her bedroom. She added that she believed the woman had appeared at apartment 5B one other time, ringing the buzzer very early one morning. By the time the police arrived, the suspect was gone.

Next meeting is tomorrow, 2 p.m. Same place.

Dr. Tristane Kazemy, DECEMBER 5, 2016

She at last met Abigail Willard one-on-one, again in an examination room in the Mount Sinai neurology department, but this one was cramped and windowless, tucked along a back hallway. The woman sat there alone, a blue gown tied loosely around her neck, her salt-white arms and legs goose-pimpled in the fluorescent light. She clutched a book in her lap. A bible perhaps? Christians were so prevalent and so observant in the USA, after all. But then she thought about the Willard journals, the episodes of infidelity and of course the radical activism. Not the actions of a Bible clutcher. Though of course one should never presume. When it was time for the examination to begin, she asked, May I set that down for you? She stole a peek at the cover: *Interaction of Color* by Josef Albers.

Squinting into eyes and ears through a scope, begrudgingly loaned to her by a sour-faced hospitalist, she asked about the book. It's from my school days, Abigail Willard said. I'm relearning.

Dissociative amnesia. A major case of memory loss, due to the axonal head injury and the psychic trauma from the fall, erasing so much of that year her boyfriend died.

And now, since her collapse last November, the brain bleed and coma that followed—the late effect of that original injury, an effect which started gradually then became acute—amnesia returned. But of course, a key piece of her brain was excised in emergency surgery. Thus much of 2015 had been wiped away. Clean.

The ever-changing brain can be a merciful master of forgetfulness and deceit.

The examining room interview yielded the woman's only remaining fragments of that year: mostly happy ones centering on her children. A school concert of love songs. Her son befriending a stray cat. A holiday feast made and served at home.

Obviously, her journal entries record other occurrences, much more momentous, more shocking, more triste. But, in support of the rehabilitation process, Chief Detective Leverett has suggested that she is not ready to read those journals. Maybe once my investigations are finished, he said. When she is stronger.

Did the husband know about the journals? If so, he would know that this police detective, Leverett, and his wife had . . .

And who was Leverett to make such decisions, and how had he accessed those journal files? She supposed police detectives had their ways. Especially a chief of police detectives.

Best to focus on the neurology.

Yes, dissociative amnesia, certainly it was part of the overall picture. But she was certain: Mrs. Willard's brain contained more complicated mysteries. They were to be found in that miniscule area of darkness. The part removed. The void.

She had four more days in New York to develop and present final conclusions. Tonight, she would dine with the California physicist, Dr. Shuttlesworth. A slight man with russet-brown skin and a rather prickly demeanor, and some very outré theories of his own. It should be an interesting night out.

She headed out from her hotel for a dusk run in Central Park, thinking of the woman, a devoted wife and mother and also, as her journals made clear, a furnace of ambition. Still burning, she suspected—look how Ms. Willard was determined to teach herself again, wielding that book of colors. Running through dark trees up a long sloping drive, certain synchronicities seemed increasingly clear. She wondered if the two of them—Abigail Willard and herself—weren't being twinned somehow, paired by some unseen hand. She is here in New York City trying to tease out the meaning of this woman's story, but who—what omniscience—was mapping her own?

PERSONAL WORK LOG: Garrett L. Shuttlesworth, December 5, 2016

Everything is happening all at once, I reminded them at today's meeting. The stack of photos, the layers of time. The math supports the theory, ever since Einstein.

But I know you two aren't big on math, I said.

My undergrad degree is in algebra and number theory, said Dr. Kazemy.

I stand corrected, I said. She smiled, with what seemed to me admirable good nature.

Anyhow, I said, let me read you this entry from her shrink's records.

(And, by the way, via what unorthodox means did her shrink's records get into these files? I asked. Jameson glowered, in a way that made it clear I should drop that line of inquiry.)

Then I read aloud to them Dr. Merle Unzicker's final notation on young Abigail, dated November 30, 1991.

SESSION NOTES

Treatment terminated due to a grievous accident.

I will see her again in 24 years. She mentioned this a few times, over the last several weeks.

I found it amusing, this pronouncement. Like something she got from a sidewalk psychic or a Chinese fortune cookie.

Now, I find it less amusing. This strange statement.

I have failed with A. This case will haunt me.

ABBY, DECEMBER 5, 2016

After all of today's medical business was finally done, I headed to the new studio.

Still getting used to it.

Just color studies. I started with reds. Terra rossa, carmine, Venetian. Square after square. The colors vibrate.

Dennis is in his place next door. The new soundproofing is doing its job. My space is large, quiet, clean, with daylight filtering in from the north, through two rows of high windows.

I paint here mostly early mornings and a few evenings, if I'm not too tired after work. Soon, I will scale up from part- to full-time at the new job. The pace at that office is breakneck, but designing for a global news outfit has turned out to be exciting. Dennis says we could do okay on what he's earning through sales, but I now understand that I need and truly value the satisfactions and steadiness and centering realities of a paycheck job. Plus my medical costs. Self-employed artists get screwed on health care, no matter how many big metal sculptures they sell.

When we returned to the house, Ben and Gianna had fixed dinner for us. Everyone takes such good care of me these days. Pete is in the dorm, but he calls almost every evening, to check in on me, he says. And Wowza the cat winds himself around my legs. He took a liking to me during the first months of my recuperation, when I snoozed most of the day and wandered a bit at night, like a cat.

I understand that I have lost something. I know this to be true. I wake up feeling absence. An ache I can't pinpoint or name. A void. With a faint gravitational pull, as if my inner light, which I hope to shine on the world, is instead looping backward and in. But, this feeling dissipates, usually, as I go about my routines. And as Dennis always says, the best thing for me now, the only way, is forward.

PERSONAL WORK LOG: Garrett L. Shuttlesworth, December 6, 2016

Last night, Dr. Kazemy and I met over astronomically priced rib eyes and Côtes du Rhône at a Midtown steakhouse. (Who set Humboldt State's per diem rate for research travel? They've clearly never set foot in New York City.) It started as a bit of a thorny debate, but it may result in a workable theory.

(She is formidable. Intense.)

"I've spent months staring at this space in the brain," she said. "Trauma-induced injury, damage from the fall. This damaged tissue resulted in amnesia, but as it changed with age and time, it also altered function near the amygdala. An abnormality in that area can cause hallucinations, for example."

"If it's just hallucinations," I said, "how do you explain the physical evidence?"

"The portrait in the application file, the paint chip in the matchbox. The location tracking on the phone." She sighed. "I'm not sure."

"All that," I said, "plus the house going down in flames. In my thinking, the party known as A torched the place. It represented a future she didn't want."

Dr. Kazemy scoffed. "Leverett thinks it was triggered by one of the sons, the miscreants, candles in bedroom, playing with chemicals."

"But in the journals, it was the girl who said, 'Burn it down.'"

"I've sometimes wondered if Abigail set the fire herself," she said. "One will see aggression, destructive impulses, when an abnormality impinges upon certain tissues. Look, the woman took a sledgehammer to the Bank of America."

(She chewed furiously. She is a petite person, this doctor, but I couldn't help noticing that she was wolfing down a gigantic piece of meat. I enjoyed observing an impassioned professional. Physicists can be so wooden.)

"Dr. Kazemy." I lifted my wine, sipped deeply. The tannins fortified me. "Will you indulge me, look up from your microscope and think macro, for a moment?"

She put down her fork and knife and nodded at me, solemn.

"I've played with some formulas and run the simulations hundreds of times this past year," I said. "It seems to me that there's something paradigm-shifting here. Quantum physics forces us to grapple with ideas our brains aren't able to process easily, but that doesn't mean these theories aren't viable."

"It is very outlandish, what you've been saying in that conference room," she said, frowning. She poured herself a second glass of wine. "She can see through layers of time?"

"It would explain some of the inexplicable elements of this story."

She swirled her wine, then sipped deeply. She stared at me for a long moment, in a way that made me a bit nervous. "There were things that troubled me," she finally said. "That didn't seem hallucinatory in nature, that seemed not logical but nevertheless true to life. I will admit."

At last—a bit of give. As my quantum prof at Berkeley said, we have to slow down from time to time and let the rest of the human race catch up.

"So you were a math major," I said, draining my glass, helping myself to more.

She nodded. "At the Sorbonne."

"Well, does the Sorbonne offer English lit classes, by chance?"

"I studied a lot of Shakespeare," she said, looking a bit baffled. "Why?"

"I took a lot of poetry classes."

She stabbed her last bit of meat and, chewing it, said, "Go on, then. Recite."

I swigged again from my goblet, looked down into that ruby pond, where I could see bits of myself refracted. I gathered it from my memory. "Time past and time future, what might have been and what has been, point to one end, which is always present."

Dr. Kazemy stared at me for a long moment. "Oh," she said. The table's candle reflected in her wide brown eyes, a rather distracting effect. She put her fork and knife down and waved for the check.

Dr. Tristane Kazemy, DECEMBER 7, 2016

Garrett Shuttlesworth had already arrived. In front of him sat a cardboard tray holding two coffees. She took her now-customary spot at the end of the ridiculously long table. "Thought we could both use this," he said, grinning and handing her a cup.

They had been texting all night.

When the chief detective walked in, she said, "We are ready to deliver our final conclusions."

Leverett looked from her to Garrett. "Together? OK then. Go ahead." He lowered himself into his spot between them, straightened his tie. He looked especially dyspeptic, she thought.

And then she began to speak.

Diffuse and mysterious. This is how neurology describes the aftereffects of axonal head wounds. They jostle the white matter of the brain. Such insults can wreak havoc on the impacted cells, rattle the connections between neurons, and alter functioning and perception in ways that are tricky to predict and difficult to treat.

Abigail Willard's head wound, incurred in her 1991 fall and then slowly healed in the months thereafter, is what planted the seed for her bizarre year of 2015. It is not uncommon for sufferers of head injuries early in life to develop brain-structure abnormalities in later years. A car crash at eighteen puts one at increased risk of aneurysm, hemorrhage, or a brain tumor in middle or old age.

So it is reasonable to conclude that the abnormality, or anomaly, from 1991, changing and shifting over time as all parts of the body do, began to dramatically alter her behaviors—and her perceptions—in 2015.

Since the area was removed following her brain bleed, the incidents have stopped. They will not recur.

But the girl she saw in 2015 did not live just in her mind.

The physicist nodded here, smiling broadly. Tristane felt encouraged.

Dr. Shuttlesworth has told us that although we experience time as unidimensional—as a unidirectional sequence of events—physicists have known this to be an illusion since Einstein.

And so working together, we have come to our conclusion. As T. S. Eliot wrote in his "Four Quartets," "Time the destroyer is time the preserver."

She exchanged a glance with him. He seemed trying not to beam.

The destructive injury, changing over time, nanometer by nanometer, created an opening. Through it, Abigail Willard saw life as it truly is. Moments preserved, always and forever, because those moments happen, always and forever.

A girl preserved, always and forever, because that girl lives, always and forever.

Mrs. Willard's brain anomaly, growing and morphing as her brain aged, cracked open a portal that allowed her to see what others cannot see.

What the rest of us can perceive only through a veil of shifting half-truths and guesses.

Even amid her anguish and confusion, she could see it with paradigm-shifting clarity.

The essential self. The timeless self.

ABBY, DECEMBER 10, 2016

Pete finished his finals and caught a late train home for the holiday break. So good to see him walking out of the station with his big bag over his shoulder, tossing us a slight wave, his dark hair falling across his dark eyes.

I miss him a lot, when he's off at school. I wonder if the transition has been a bit harder for me than for other moms from his class. One of them, Dennis said her name was Katharine Erdmann, had come by with a veggie lasagna, right after my release from the hospital last spring, and she said she couldn't wait for her daughter to get out of the house. "She's going to UCLA," she said, "and I asked her, wait, aren't there any good schools in Australia?" She laughed. And then she said, "I heard Pete is going upstate somewhere."

"Yes, I heard that too," I said. She'd looked at me very strangely. But I had been elsewhere when the applications went out, and, just a few days home, I was barely back to myself. The whole thing seemed more than I could manage, him going away. It added to the sense I had that I'd incurred some losses. I just couldn't quite say what the losses were.

But Pete was gone, and then he came back, and tonight, we sat up talking after dinner, he and I. The election, it had been clamoring all around me, but I have been focused on recovering.

"Inauguration Day," Pete said. "The Brigade. We're going to march on Washington."

My heart revved. "Yes," I said.

"You can't," called Dennis from the kitchen, where he was wrist-deep in dishes. "You'll be in Vienna."

Right. Viennarte. We'd been invited to speak on a panel about Mariah. Our romantic and political entanglements had been juicy fodder for the art-world gossips: "A tragic mess usually raises one's profile," said Jillian Broder when she'd dropped by the studio a few weeks ago. She demanded that we both show work in her Viennarte booth. "You were a star last time, dear heart, I demand you come for another round," she said to Dennis. Then she turned to me. "And Abigail. You continue to be the most astute colorist I know—in fact, this post-catastrophe work has a startling, unexpected, passionate freshness." She put her hand on my cheek. "My beauty. Never, never, no way, was I ever going to allow Matthew Legge-Lewis to poach my once and future discovery."

So, come January, we would be in Vienna.

And my darling Pete would take to the streets. But for now we sat together. I held his strong, warm hand in both of mine.

I wished I could be in two places at once. But no.

"I guess you'll have to march for both of us," I said.

December 15, 2016

From: J.Leverett@deepxmail.com

To: Tristane.Kazemy@montrealneuro.ca,
GarrettShuttlesworth@physics.humboldtstate.edu

To each of you, first, a word of thanks, for your expert analysis and your discretion up to this point.

I understand that you both see this case as "paradigm shifting." Ultimately, that's all above my pay grade. Not every question has been answered to my satisfaction, but there comes a time to move on.

Please destroy all files and records having to do with the Abigail Willard matter. And, with all due respect, don't cross me on that.

Dr. Tristane Kazemy, DECEMBER 23, 2016

Laurin has barely spoken to her since she returned. He has been as frosty as the merciless Quebec wind. Preparing his morning espresso, Buccardi whispers there is some kind of death watch—Laurin's assistant, young Molly Jiang, had filed a major harassment complaint. "The man didn't see the writing on the wall," he said. "But the dinosaur hunt has begun, and he has a target painted right on his derriere." Then he turned to her, stirring sugar into the tiny cup. "So, you say you won't seek publication on your findings from this New York case after all. I think that's a shame." But then he lowered his voice again. "No matter, Tristane. New staff appointments will be posted January 1, and let's just say your name has been bandied all about."

"January 1! I'll be on holiday," she said.

"Oh? Winter hiking, I suppose? Or skiing this time?"

"No. I'm going somewhere green. California."

"Ah!" Buccardi sighed. "I do love California."

January 1, 2017

From: J.Leverett@deepxmail.com
To: GarrettShuttlesworth@physics.humboldtstate.edu

Garrett, I always try to clean up a bit around New Year's. As part of that, I was getting ready to delete this email account. Consider it over and done. Forget about it.

But shit. G, I can't.

It's like you said. She's always here. All the time.

And it's not that I loved her. I suppose I did have feelings for her.

That's not what's bugging me. It's something else. Something I didn't tell you and Kazemy. For obvious reasons.

I'm the chief of detectives, and the breadwinner. I'll put one foot in front of the other, what else can I do. I don't get to understand this whole thing. I don't get to know what it means. I just feel empty. I don't know what any of it means. I only know it's shaken me so hard, I don't know if I will find solid ground again.

In Merle Unzicker's session notes, there was this line—the very first entry:

- A reports a night of wildness with a young man, whom she
  believes is named Jamie.

That was me. Jamie.

I did not remember the girl or the night until I read those stolen
shrink notes.

Then I remembered. She told me her name was A.

I'm just the punch line of a great cosmic joke. I can't shake this
idea. It haunts me.

I'm killing this mailbox.

See you in 2020, maybe? 25th reunion. Christ, we're old.

ABBY, JANUARY 21, 2017

The day after the inauguration was cold and clear. The crowds
thronged the Ringstrasse and the chants and drums echoed off the
old yellow palaces. Many marchers wore pink hats. I wore black.

Most of the women were young. Their faces, so open, so daz-
zling. So full of promise and passion and anger. I found myself
thrilled by them. Entranced. My pulse revved. There was one in
particular, I followed her for a while. I saw some familiar shading
in her, but then she turned my way, and no. A beautiful being,
bright and alive. Still I couldn't quite place her. I guess she just
looked like someone I used to know.

Acknowledgments

I cocreated this work with countless others, seen and unseen, people whom I now know only as part of my distant past, and people who live very vividly in my present. In profound gratitude, I must name at least a few. For fierceness and guidance of all kinds: Soumeya Bendimerad Roberts. For transforming my strange fleeting vision into a book: Megan Lynch, Helen Atsma, Miriam Parker, Sara Birmingham, Martin Wilson, Sonya Cheuse, Meghan Deans, and the talented staff at Ecco/HarperCollins. For essential writings that helped shape my imaginings: Josef Albers (whose seminal book *Interaction of Color* is quoted in these pages), Rudolf Arnheim, Anne Truitt, Mark Bray, and Brian Greene. For allowing me into their minds and studios: Franklin Evans, Elizabeth Meyersohn, Sebastiaan Bremer, Margot Glass, Susannah Auferoth. For support and solitude, the generous benefactors of the MacDowell Colony. For sparkling inspiration and endless encouragement: Ann Lewis and Edie Meidav. For early reading, kindness, faith, and love: Deborah Legge Lewis,

Kahane Corn Cooperman, Kandy Littrell, Miliann Kang, Mic Farquharson, James Hynes, Mimi Mayer, Alison Smith, Michael Ravitch, Nerissa Nields, Sandra Scofield, the Immergut and Marks families. For all of these things and more, always, John and Joe Marks.

About the Author

DEBRA JO IMMERGUT is the author of the Edgar-nominated novel *The Captives* and the story collection *Private Property*. She has been awarded a MacDowell fellowship and a Michener fellowship. Her literary work has been published in *American Short Fiction* and *Narrative*. As a journalist, she has been a frequent contributor to the *Wall Street Journal* and the *Boston Globe*. She has an MFA from the Iowa Writers' Workshop.